MW00940019

MYTHS OF IMMORTALITY

RAYE WAGNER

MYTHS OF IMMORTALITY

by Raye Wagner

Edited by Sara Meadows, Kelly Hashway, and Krystal Wade
Book Design by Jo Michaels
Cover Design by StudioOpolis

For Jacob, Seth, and Anna
A mother's love knows no bounds

THE SPHINX · BOOK THREE

MYTHS OF IMMORTALITY

ONE

ATHAN

HIS STOMACH DROPPED, and what little Athan had eaten turned to rock. He wasn't feeling well, far from it, but that was typical of being cut by a Skia blade. However, even though he was injured, it was the news from the demigod standing over him that made Athan's mind spin and his weakened body protest every single move he made. Athan clenched his teeth in frustration.

Hope had disappeared. Again. And Xan couldn't find her.

But Xan wasn't *psachno*. Not anymore. Years ago, they'd worked together to find demigods and bring them to safety. However, Xan had been punished and lost the right. But then he'd been mentoring Hope, so maybe he'd regained some of his privileges. Athan cursed under his breath, while he tried to convince himself that, despite what Xan said, he probably didn't know how to run a search anymore.

Xan's ice-blue glare contradicted Athan's feeble attempts at self-delusion. The demigod son of Ares clenched and un-clenched his fists before resting his elbows on the kitchen table and dropping his chin in his hands.

The darkness of night was fading, but it would be at least another hour before the sun was up. The shadows in the large kitchen had been banished when Xan turned on the light, but they seemed to be lying in wait to take back over, both in the hallway of the conservatory as well as the gloominess just out-side the windows. The clock on the wall ticked away the sec-onds, and Xan surveyed the picked-over fruit and cheese tray.

"I don't understand how she could disappear like that. Even that attorney doesn't know where they went." Xan grabbed a slice of cheese from the tray and took a bite.

As Xan spoke, Athan leaned across the table, drawn by the other demigod's words. But the edge dug uncomfortably into his ribs, so he sat back. "What attorney?"

He looked at Dion and then back to Xan. Xan continued chewing, staring back like he was measuring Athan, and he was coming up short. Athan simmered with frustration, and he re-peated his question.

Xan swallowed before answering. "The one Priska used to work for. He manages Hope's estate. Hope and Priska were there about a week ago. No contact since."

It wasn't easy to admit, but maybe Xan hadn't lost all his skills. Ten days was a long time to be out. Bits and pieces of the Skia attack and the drive back to the conservatory flitted through Athan's mind. "What happened?" He vaguely remembered arguing with Endy and . . . punching him? Had that happened? Athan looked at his hands, but his skin was unmarred. There had been lots of yelling, he was sure of that. What had Endy wanted with her? Had she gotten the information she needed to break the curse? Athan felt like there was a piece he was missing. A big piece. "Why did she run?"

Dion studiously drank wine as he rotated the bottle on the table. He didn't even look up from his glass as he mumbled, "Endy and his brothers attacked her."

At the same time, Xan said, "Endy and Obelia found her weapons."

Panic washed through Athan, and fear for Hope made his stomach churn. Apollo's sons were ruthless and cruel, and his mind raced through the horror that could mean. A driving need to find Hope and make sure she was okay made him want to leap up, but the nausea made his head spin, and he had to close his eyes to get the room to stop spinning. If he stood, there was a pretty good chance he'd pass out, and Athan refused to show weakness in front of Xan. Sitting back in the chair, Athan wished he hadn't gotten out of bed yet. No. That wasn't right at all. Guilt spread its tentacles of shame through his chest. He should've been up days ago. And if he hadn't been injured by the Skia's blade, he could've been awake for all of it. With a deep breath, he dismissed what could've been and focused on the moment. Gathering information would be first, which meant he needed help from the son of Ares. Athan fixed Xan with a hard stare. "What do you know?"

Xan clenched his jaw and balled his fists. He looked like he wanted to murder something. Or someone.

"Are you going to try to kill her?" Athan whispered. He was in no state to fight Xan if he said yes. So what would Athan do? What *could* he do?

Xan sat up, resting his arms on the back of the chair. "You shouldn't have kept that secret, Athan. She's a monster, and you knew it."

He sounded tired, but Athan gritted his teeth. He had no sympathy for the son of Ares. "I wasn't going to let you kill her."

Xan tilted his head to the side and studied Athan. He scratched his cheek, the scruffy growth making a chuffing sound with the friction. "Is that what you think?"

Xan used to boast of the monsters he'd killed. Athan had been there, more than once, when Xan had mercilessly killed a satyr or centaur. At one point, Athan even believed Xan's purported doctrine that monsters should be eradicated. Athan *knew* Xan killed monsters. "You want me to believe you wouldn't have killed her if you'd known what she was?"

Xan sighed and dropped his head to his hands. "I wouldn't have killed her." His blue eyes met Athan's green ones. "Not for anything."

Athan's heart stopped. He'd heard that tone before. He knew it even if Xan didn't say it. Rage, long suppressed, threatened to overwhelm Athan. He swallowed, pushing back the emotion. Later. He would deal with it later. After he found Hope.

Xan looked as lost as Athan felt. "But at this point, it doesn't really matter how I feel about Hope, does it?" Xan grimaced. "Apollo killed Endy and his brothers. Hope saw the whole thing, and Obelia . . ."

Apollo? Good gods! Apollo had been there . . . with Hope? Athan's stomach heaved, and he choked on the sour taste of vomit. The hits kept coming, and whatever he'd thought when he woke up seemed to border on the delusional. Athan closed his eyes and rested his chin on the table. It was time to face it head-on. Whatever *it* was. "Tell me everything."

Xan glared across the table. Whatever war seethed inside him seemed to center on Dionysus's son. Then, with unnatural speed, he reached out and grabbed the wineglass from Dion, who yelped his protest but relinquished the glass. Xan took a large gulp and then a second one, draining the glass. "I wasn't there," he said with a shudder. "When Apollo showed up. And Obelia was passed out for most of it. Apollo warned her, though, and made her witness as he killed his sons. He said he won't let anyone kill Hope. That she is his."

Dion scooted his chair back and stood. "I think I'll just be going to bed now. I say good night." He nodded at Xan and then at Athan. "It's good you are feeling better, friend." Dion's eyes were tight with worry, but he offered Athan a smile and grabbed the bottle of wine. "Good night."

Xan glowered at Dion. "Sit down, arseface."

Dion dropped back into his chair but remained away from the table. The demigod clutched the wine bottle close to his chest, and his gaze darted around the room as if he were looking for a way to escape.

"It's a bloody mess," Xan said, turning back to Athan. "Thenia demanded a full inquisition."

Worse than a quorum, an inquisition would involve one of the gods. Every single thing Xan said felt like a punch. A brutal punch. To Athan's rapidly dwindling hope. "What are you going to—?"

"Hope disappeared before Athena got here." Xan eyed Dion and pointed at the wine bottle. When Dion didn't immediately respond, the other demigod snapped his fingers.

Dion hesitated and then took a long drink right from the bottle before extending it to Xan.

Xan curled his lip but dropped his hand. With a prolonged exhale, he faced Athan. "I've got to find Hope first. Then we can figure out what to do." Xan unwound himself from the chair and pointed at Athan. "You better get some rest." Xan grabbed the bottle from Dion. "You should sober up."

Xan dropped the bottle in the sink on his way out of the kitchen.

Xan was an ass. But, regardless of his reasons, he'd been looking for Hope when Athan couldn't. A trickle of gratitude took residence in his heart . . . grudgingly. Athan rubbed his eyes then looked at Dion. The other demigod looked awful with red-shot eyes and rumpled clothes. At least Athan could count on Dion being cooperative. "How many did Apollo kill?"

Dion swallowed, and his hazy gaze looked for relief on the table before focusing on the sink where the empty bottle of wine now resided. His swarthy skin turned ashen, and he sunk into his chair. "All of them. Endy, Tre, Ty. Even Prax. All burned to ash. He made Obelia witness that no more demigods would try to harm Hope. Or Apollo will kill them. I think she is mad now." He grabbed the empty glass and held it upside down over his mouth. The last of the wine dripped on to his tongue, and he looked around the kitchen and sighed. "It's not right, Athan."

Athan wasn't going to worry about Apollo's sons. Even though they were demigods, the world would be a better place with four less bullies. But Xan's treatment of Dion made no sense. Dion was just being Dion, the same as always. "What's up with Xan?"

Dion shrugged. "They called for *apartia*. Endy and Obelia. Before . . . when they found Hope's knives. Xan was arguing for her to stay." He shook his head. "But with the inquisition . . . He almost seemed relieved she was gone. But I don't think he believed she would disappear. He was very upset."

Athan could imagine. Xan was used to getting his own way. Or making it. "What has he done?"

Dion shook his head again. "He went looking for her. Just got back last night. I stayed here. This makes him upset, no?"

7

Anyone opposing Xan would make Xan upset. So strange that he was actually fighting for Hope. More than anything, Athan hoped he was misinterpreting Xan's feelings. But, what else was in it for him?

"This is quite *chalia*, a mess, no? I'm sorry, Athan." Dion sat picking at the cheese tray. When Athan scooted his chair back, Dion stood. "I will help you." He motioned toward the stairs. "I know . . . I know I am not always a good friend, but . . ."

It was a mess, a cryptic puzzle, and Athan didn't even know the whole of it, let alone what and where the pieces were. "It's okay, Dion. If you help me to bed, I'll count you as my very best friend."

They both chuckled, but the gnawing fear in Athan's chest reminded him that there was nothing funny. Apollo was tracking Hope, and she'd disappeared. Athan needed to get better so he could find her.

Athan slept late. When his eyes pushed themselves into consciousness, his brain and body followed. His stiff muscles felt like he'd worked out too hard, but when he pushed to the edge of the bed and stood, his legs solidly held him up. He was *finally* better.

The hot water from the shower pounded the soreness from his muscles. After turning off the water, he grabbed a towel, wrapped it around his waist, and opened the bathroom door. The steam cleared, and Athan nearly dropped his towel. "*Skata!*"

Obelia sat cross-legged on his bed. She looked up at him with red-rimmed wide eyes. "Athan—"

"What in the name of Hades are you doing in here?" He didn't wait for an answer but crossed the room, pulled clothes from the dresser, and then went back to the bathroom, slamming the door behind him. He pulled his clothes on, his shirt sticking to his still-wet skin while he continued fuming. What was wrong with her?

He opened the door, and shook his head at her. Obelia needed to respect his boundaries. His nerves were raw with worry and unanswered questions about Hope, and he snapped. "Zeus and Poseidon, Obelia. Can't you wait downstairs like anyone else?"

Obelia's eyes filled with tears, and she looked up, blinking over and over again before she would meet his gaze. "I heard your shower running. I wanted to see—" Her voice dropped, and she coughed. "I didn't think you would mind. I thought . . . I . . . I thought . . ." She stood up, and the tears dripped from her cheeks onto her shirt. "I'm sorry. I didn't mean to upset you. I'm glad to see you up."

She didn't wait for a reply, and before he could think of what to say, she'd left the room.

"*Skata.*" She'd been there when Apollo killed his sons, and Dion's words came back in a rush. He'd told Athan that Obelia wasn't herself anymore. Maybe he'd been too harsh with her. But seriously, in his room? He went back to the bathroom and brushed his teeth. No sense making a big deal about it now. He'd do what he could to spare Obelia's feelings, but his concern was for Hope. He'd need to find out as much as he could before he went after her. As he walked down the hall, he braced himself in case he had to deal with Obelia again.

By the time he got to the bottom of the stairs, his knees were shaking. This fatigue was exasperating. His strength wasn't coming back fast enough. He braced his hand on the wall as he crossed into the kitchen. Relief washed over him when he saw the pantry door open and the curvy Kaia rummaging through the contents.

"Excuse me, Kaia?" he called out to her as he made his way to the table.

The raven-haired young woman stood straight. She turned slowly, her brown eyes, normally warm and friendly, hardened as she focused on Athan. "Yes?"

He sagged into a chair. He'd happily listen to whatever was bothering her after he ate. He waved at the contents of the pantry. "Would you please bring me something to eat?"

Demeter's daughter frowned as her gaze turned into a glower. "What?"

Athan's nerves twitched. He could feel the rising tension, but nothing about it made sense. "I don't particularly care, really, as long as I can eat it in the form you give me. I just need something: bread, crackers, cereal. Or there was a fruit and cheese tray last night—"

Kaia shook her head as if he'd asked her to cut off her own extremity and give it to him. "You think I'm going to help you?"

Athan stared at her. His mind strained as he tried to figure out what he'd done to offend her, but he was coming up blank. Kaia was always helpful. Patient. Sweet. *Nurturing.* He couldn't reconcile the sneer with the demigod before him. "Why wouldn't you help me?"

She barked a cruel laugh. "Because of you, the conservatory is all going to Hades. Because you decided to go out with a *monster.*" She spit the last word as if it were a curse.

Her words stung, and anger coursed through him. How dare she?

"Did you know?" She sneered. "Did you know you were courting a beast? That you were putting us all at risk? You're as selfish as a god." Kaia's voice was filled with incredulity and hurt.

He and Kaia had never been close, but they'd always gotten along fine. Her hostility was . . . disconcerting. It made no sense. At all. "Why do you care?"

"She's not a demigod. She's not even human, Athan." Kaia crossed her arms over her chest. "She's cursed, not fit to live."

He recognized Kaia's words as the twisted contempt for monsters that most demigods held. At some point, he'd probably said the same. But now the words felt like a tool to separate, to segregate. To *manipulate.* He crossed the kitchen and towered over her. "Who do you think you are to make that decision?"

"I didn't make the decision," she said as she puffed out her chest. "It was made long ago, by those smarter than you."

Years ago, he'd had no response. Now he saw her words for what they were: propaganda. And his experiences with Hope had given him perspective. "You're wrong. You think you're better. That as a demigod—"

"We *are* better!" Kaia screamed as tears filled her eyes. "We. Are. Better. And you ruined it." The tears spilled over, and her nose ran, but the daughter of Demeter wiped at the wetness with her sleeve. "And you're just a liar, anyway—"

She reached back, palm open, and Athan stared at her. As her hand swung forward, and his confusion turned to shock.

"Kaia! Stop!" Xan grabbed her wrist mid-swing.

Only then did Athan realize she'd intended to strike him. His jaw dropped as understanding dawned. Even after getting to know Hope, Kaia was still calling for her to be killed. That wasn't just hurt feelings. Was it a sense of betrayal? That made no sense. But what else was there? He had no idea, but the division among the demigods made it clear that not everyone agreed. And even with Hope gone, not everyone had resolved the emotional upheaval she'd left in her wake.

TWO

ATHAN

"**I SEE YOU'RE** spreading cheer already," Xan said, looking at Athan before turning back to Kaia. "Why don't you go find Obelia? See if you can get her . . . oriented to reality, eh?" Xan let go of Kaia's wrist but stood squarely between her and Athan.

"Fine," Kaia said as she glared past Xan to Athan. "I will." She stomped out, leaving the two young men in the kitchen.

"I hate passive aggressiveness." Xan's gaze stayed on Kaia until she disappeared down the hall then shifted to Athan. "Gods, you look awful. What are you doing out of bed?" Xan grabbed Athan's arm and led him to the table.

"I was feeling better earlier." He shrugged out of Xan's grasp, not wanting any help from the son of Ares.

Xan snorted, but released Athan's arm. "You made a boat-load of enemies when they found out you knew. Lucky for you, Apollo took care of the most violent ones." Xan crossed over to the fridge. "Do you need something to eat?"

"I can get it." Athan stood, but his legs wobbled, and he had to lean on the table for support.

"Ha. You'd probably pass out if you had to walk to the fridge right now. Don't be an arse. Sit down. You're not going to win an award for being stupid." Xan pulled a carton of eggs from the fridge and set them on the counter. "Tell me what you want; I'll get it for you."

He was not going to let Xan get him anything. He'd probably poison Athan if he got a chance. "No, I'll rest for a sec then get myself something when I'm ready."

Xan ran his hand through his dark hair. "Don't let your pride get in the way. I'm offering help—"

Clenching his teeth, Athan shot back, "Maybe I don't want your help."

Xan slammed both his palms on the granite counter. "Maybe that Skia blade addled your cognitive ability." As soon as the words were out, he sucked in a breath and pulled back. Shaking his head, he extended his arm and pointed at the empty kitchen. "Listen, I'm the only other person in the room right now. You need to eat, and you couldn't get yourself anything if you're life depended on it."

"I can do it," Athan ground out. But as he stepped forward, his knees buckled, forcing him to cling to the edge of the table to stay upright. His face burned, but he refused to be dependent on Xan.

Xan crossed the room, pushing into Athan's personal space until they were almost nose-to-nose. There was no hiding the sweat that trickled down the side of his temple.

"No." Xan put his hand on Athan's chest and applied the slightest pressure.

Athan's legs trembled as if resisting the force of a bulldozer, but he would not back down. He glared at Xan, hating him because of Athan's own weakness.

"You can't do anything right now." Xan pulled Athan away from the table and then deftly put his arm under Athan, preventing the inevitable fall. Dumping him back in his seat, Xan said, "Don't be an arse."

Athan took a deep breath. To acknowledge Xan was right was like drinking sour milk, and the words lodged in Athan's throat, refusing to come out.

Xan chuckled as he pulled things from the fridge. "You can thank me later."

Both were silent as Xan quickly assembled a scramble of eggs, ham, cheese, green peppers, mushrooms, and tomatoes. The smell made Athan's stomach growl.

Xan slid half onto a plate, set it in front of Athan and said, "*Bon appétit.*"

Athan's mouth salivated. Years had passed, but he still remembered Xan's breakfast hash. Athan grabbed the fork and hungrily stuck the first bite into his mouth, and then he shoveled in bite after bite. It was only after he'd eaten half of his food that he realized Xan was still standing next to the table.

"Pretty good?" Xan raised his brows.

"Yeah," Athan mumbled around his food. He swallowed the bite, and with it his pride. "Thanks."

"You're welcome." Xan walked back to the stove and dumped the remaining scramble on another plate. He grabbed the remains from the fruit and cheese plate and came back to the table. "You must be getting better. Your appetite is back."

"I'm awake—"

"Ahhh! Alive and kickin'!" Dion's gravelly voice preceded him into the kitchen. He stopped in his tracks when he saw Athan at the table. "*Filos mou*! It is so good to see you this morning!"

Xan stood, his posture rigid and tense. With his gaze fixed on Dion, he said, "Enjoy the rest of your meal."

Leaving his breakfast at the table, Xan brushed by Dion muttering profanities under his breath.

Athan looked from Dion to the now empty doorway. "What was that about?"

Dion shrugged, went to the fridge, and pulled out a bottle of wine. He grabbed a drinking glass and sat down in the vacated chair. "I think he is still, ah, how you say, anger with me?"

"Angry with you?" But Xan didn't get angry with people. He beat the crap out of them and moved on.

"Ah, yes, angry with me." Dion poured a glass of the chardonnay and took a long drink, as if the wine were water and he'd just finished a marathon.

At that rate, Dion wasn't going to be buzzed but full-on sloshed soon. "Why?"

Dion picked up Xan's fork and dragged it through the plateful of food. Steam rose from the still warm eggs, and he stuck a forkful in his mouth.

The tension in Athan's chest knotted tighter and tighter. "Dion?"

Dion looked up, but he shifted his eyes, refusing to meet Athan's. "*Oui?*"

"Why is Xan mad at you?"

Dion exhaled slowly. "I . . . I did not do what he wanted me to."

Athan snorted. "So he's mad because he couldn't push you around." Nothing surprising about that, but there had to be more. Xan wasn't one to avoid confrontation, so why had he left? Dion, on the other hand, hated confrontation, but he'd only tell what he wanted when he wanted. Had Dion really defied Xan?

Dion nodded, shifting his gaze back to the plate of food. "This is quite good. Did you make it?"

Maybe Dion was already a little drunk. "No, Xan did. Scoot it over. I want a little more."

The two of them quickly devoured the rest of the scramble and then sat picking at the fruit.

"What's on the agenda today?" Athan asked before biting into a large strawberry. The sweetness burst in his mouth, and he promised himself he would never take food for granted again.

Dion shrugged. "I do not know this. It's been pretty quiet, pretty boring, the last few days. Maybe you want we play some poker?" Dion's lips pulled up on the left side, his eyes bright at the prospect.

That would have to wait. "Maybe after I find out what's going on. Who else is here?"

Dion looked up at the ceiling, his face measured concentration. "You, me, and Xan. Obelia and Kaia." He was quiet a moment more. "Ah, Dahlia came in last night. Thenia is to be back soon."

"Do you know when?" Athan didn't relish the idea of going to Xan or Dahlia, and Kaia and Obelia weren't really an option.

"*Den xero*, I don't know."

Athan sighed. "I guess I'd better go find Xan."

"Or, you see Dahlia. She is very pretty; maybe she knows this." Dion tipped the wine bottle over his empty glass, and the wine sloshed up the sides.

Athan grimaced. "Maybe." He shook his head at the proffered wine and stood cautiously on his weak legs. Feeling stronger than he'd thought possible, he nodded to Dion and started down the hall.

THREE

ATHAN

A MUTED POUNDING reverberated through the walls, announcing exactly where Xan was. Athan walked into the matted room of the training arena in time to see Xan backfist a bag so hard the leather split. Clearly, he was still pissed.

Athan sat on a bench against the wall and watched while Xan moved to another bag hanging from the ceiling. There were two additional bags on the floor, one with a broken chain, the other torn along a seam. Athan looked up at the beam from which the bag was suspended and saw it had been reinforced. His attention returned to the demigod of war, and, after a series of strikes set the bag swinging, Athan wondered how many bags Xan would go through.

Xan struck rapid combinations of kicks and punches, and the bag rocked back and forth. The staccato rhythm of Xan's attack was no fewer than eight techniques. Athan thought of potential counter attacks only briefly. The timing would have to be perfect. And with the irregularity of Xan's count, and the rapidity of his techniques, he'd be a very difficult target. Xan's movements were a blur of punches, knife-hand, and ridge-hand strikes that were followed with jumping spin kicks that would easily crush a man's skull. The beating continued. Athan's eyes felt heavy, and he leaned his head back against the wall to wait for a pause.

A loud thud followed by silence awoke him. Athan opened his eyes to see Xan walking toward him; two more bags now lay on the floor. Xan's blue shirt was dark with sweat, and his face glistened. Despite the obvious signs of exertion, his breathing was still regular, and as he approached Athan, the corner of his mouth pulled up into a half-smile.

"Nice rest?"

Athan grunted. "I guess so. I didn't think I was that tired." He leaned his head side to side, stretching out his stiff neck muscles. "How long was I out?"

Xan shrugged. "Who cares?" He sat down and pulled a duffle bag out from under the bench. He wiped his face with a towel and pulled off his shirt. Bands of black tattoos covered his arms in Celtic patterns that climbed over his muscular back.

Athan knew the tattoos were a tribute to Xan's mother and her Irish heritage. But Athan had never understood the reason behind marring one's skin in memory of someone who'd never be forgotten anyway.

Rummaging through the bag, Xan pulled out a white T-shirt and put it on, the dark markings almost bleeding through the thin fabric. "Do you have an appointment to keep today?"

Athan couldn't help but notice the disparity between the two of them. Xan was built like a professional MMA fighter—broad shoulders, narrow waist, and thick thighs of pure cut muscle. Athan's frame was leaner, ropier muscle, like a marathon runner. It's who they both were. Except that right now, Athan looked like an emaciated refugee. How fitting. "No. No agenda. But I was hoping we could talk."

Xan sat down next to Athan, the bench reverberating with his weight. "What's up?"

It was a bitter pill to ask Xan for help, and even more bitter to actually need it. "Can you tell me what happened?"

Xan exhaled slowly, and his shoulders fell. "She left."

Athan gritted his teeth. "What do you mean she left? Voluntarily, or did you force her to go?"

Xan turned to face Athan and looked him squarely in the eye. "Come on, Athan. It was crazy here. Apollo came and killed his own sons then threatened to kill anyone that harmed her." Xan ran his hand through his hair. "Death inside the conservatory. Threats from a god. You know what that means. And the fact that she's a monster? The gods were bound to get involved."

Athan wasn't about to tell Xan the gods had been involved long before Hope came to the conservatory. Even Hermes was on the hunt for Hope. That was why Athan was originally hunting her. He should've contacted his father as soon as he'd found her the first time. Then none of this would have happened.

"It was the best I could think of, what with Obelia screaming for her death and Thenia demanding we contact the gods for a tribunal. A head start was the best I could offer." Xan grimaced. "I thought I'd find her by now."

Athan's blood boiled. As if Xan really cared. Athan knew, he *knew,* how brutal Xan was when it came to monsters, and now he cared about Hope? Whatever act he was playing, it needed to stop. "Zeus Almighty. Enough with . . . this. You don't really care, except what it means to you." Athan glared at the other demigod. "What does she mean to you?"

Xan clenched his hands then released them, and his jaw tightened. But his gaze stayed rooted on the ground as he whispered his response. "Don't assume to know me, Athan. You've been gone for years." He swallowed and then fixed Athan with a stare. "If I recall correctly, you've claimed to have changed a little, too."

There was no mistaking Xan's meaning. The dig was well aimed, and it stung mostly because of its truth. There had been a time when Athan manipulated female demigods into believing he liked them romantically so he could get them to the conservatory. He'd justified his actions as the end justifying the means and never even considered how it might make someone feel. It was only when he'd started dating Hope, and his feelings had changed . . . Athan dropped his head in his hands. "How much do you know?"

Xan sat back with a sigh. "Only what she told me." He explained how she'd come to the conservatory looking for information to break the curse. "But judging by the ash that's still in the corners of her room, and the fact that she's disappeared, she must not have found much."

"Do you know where she went?"

Xan shook his head. "No. She said no one had ever broken a curse. But she had that look she gets when she's determined. You know how her chin juts out?"

The fact that Xan knew her so well was like a punch to the gut. Athan merely nodded. Judging by how well she'd fought those Skia, she and Xan had spent a lot of time together. Maybe Xan really did care about her. The thought somehow made Athan feel worse.

Xan quirked a brow. "Did you know she had an aunt here in town?"

Athan shook his head. "It's not really her aunt. Her name is Priska—"

Xan swore. He threw one glove across the room and swore again as he threw the second one. "*Shite.*"

"You know her?" Clearly.

"It's the demigod she was staying with when I picked her up. She's definitely not her aunt." He swore again and kicked at his sparring bag. "She's not in *The Book.*"

The Book of Demigods, their recorded listings of demigods and their divine parents.

Athan frowned. Hope hadn't told him much about Priska when they were in Goldendale, only that she was like family and she'd gone missing. While at the conservatory, he'd overheard Ty and Tre bragging about beating the crap out of Priska, and because it was such an unusual name, he'd put two and two together. He didn't even know she'd come back, but it made sense why Hope came to Seattle when she ran from Goldendale.

But who was Priska? Demigods were all listed by their parentage somewhere. "You mean she's not in the one here?"

"She's not in any of them. I went through the entire Olympian database. There is no Priska. Are you sure that's her real name?"

The records went back hundreds of years. Maybe even thousands. Athan shrugged. "I've never met her, but that's the name Hope always used."

Xan let out a slow, controlled breath. "I don't know who she is, but someone matching her description has popped up in conservatories around the world in the last year. Athens, Greece, then a few weeks later in Nashville, Tennessee, and she was here the night Hope disappeared. Obelia slammed the door in her face."

Athan rolled his eyes, and his frustration with Obelia ballooned. Not that it would do any good. "But we know she's a demigod? Have you seen her mark?"

Xan shook his head. "I've never been that close. But she's a demigod all right. I've talked to her on the phone. She called the conservatory before we picked up Hope. She knows way too much to be anything else."

"Why is she helping Hope?" Athan couldn't think of a single reason a demigod would knowingly befriend a monster. "What does she have to gain?" It made no sense. A chill danced across his skin, and he shivered.

"No idea," Xan said with a shrug. He stood, grabbed his bag, and took two steps toward the door, then turned and came back to the bench, standing over Athan. "You're no good the way you are. Thenia is supposed to be back next week with her mum. I'm going to be gone. You need to be well afore then or I won't take you with me, right?"

Xan was going to search for Hope again. Of course he was. He was nothing if not tenacious. But Athan wasn't going along. He needed to find her first. Which meant a call to his father.

Athan nodded. "Right."

As soon as Xan left, Athan locked the door and pulled out his phone.

Hermes answered on the second ring. "*Yeia sou?*"

"Dad?"

Hermes laughed. "Athan! It's great to hear your voice. How are you?"

"Fine. Fine." Athan told his dad how he'd found Hope at the conservatory only to have her disappear again. "I just want to find her so I can help."

His father said nothing, and Athan wondered if they had been disconnected. Was that even possible on his father's phone? "Dad?"

"I'm surprised you would even consider that," Hermes said.

Athan flinched from the steel in his father's tone.

"What madness is this? We're talking about the monster that almost got you killed a couple of weeks ago. Olympus was in an uproar after Apollo killed his sons over her. And now you want to put yourself in more danger for her? Are you even recovered from the Skia's blade?"

"I . . . I'll be okay."

But his father continued in the same harsh tone, "She is selfish and dangerous, and you should leave her alone."

Athan reeled. "How . . . How can you say that?"

"Wait. You . . . think you love her? Is that what this is?" When Athan didn't respond, Hermes continued, "Mother Gaia! She is a monster."

Athan sat on the padded floor in shock. Since he'd woken up, he'd be surprised over and over again by the vitriol against Hope. But his father? This vehemence was so unlike his normally supportive attitude. And surely he understood that Hope's curse wasn't her fault. "We're talking about Hope."

Athan felt like his world was upside-down. He stared up at the exposed beams, wondering if he was going to wake up in bed in a few hours. No, if he were dreaming, he wouldn't feel so awful. His father was speaking again, and Athan tuned in hoping there would be a way to reason with him.

"Son, everyone around her dies. She is cursed and spreads that destruction everywhere she goes." Hermes sucked in a deep breath. "Stay away from her, Athan. Don't ask me to help you find her. The best I can say is that I hope she stays gone."

Athan opened his mouth, but nothing came out. Protest after protest ran through his mind. What his father was saying was preposterous. It was insanity. Athan tried to think of a way to tell Hermes what Hope meant. How unfair life had been for her. How much potential she had. How much good.

"One day you'll see I am right. Let her go. She's not worth your time." Hermes sighed. "She's not worth your life."

As if Hope would ever ask for any of that.

"I've got to go," Hermes said. "I'll come see you in a week or so. In which conservatory are you residing?"

"Seattle," Athan whispered; his world tilted and rolled, totally out of control. His father, his rock, hated Hope.

Athan disconnected the phone and looked around at the gym. He needed to be ready to go when Xan went back out looking for Hope.

Athan spent the next few days rotating his time between the kitchen, his bed, and the treadmill. By the fourth day, he was able to run five miles without stopping, and he could've done more. He was finally healing. On the fifth day, he ran twenty miles in under ninety minutes. Not anywhere close to his best time, but he was well enough to be on his way.

Now, if he only knew where he needed to go.

FOUR

HOPE

THE FLAT-LINE SIGNALED the end, confirmed by the sickly smell of death. The wide room held only the one bed, and its occupant was tied down by the wires and tubes that led from his body to the monitors that were now alarming. They were stacked, a conglomerate of four screens to the left of the bed, keeping track of his heart, vital signs, and intravenous fluid pumps.

The hospital was lit in the soft grays of early morning in the Pacific Northwest, and the sterile room smelled of chemical disinfectant and the poorly sponge-bathed body of its incapacitated occupant.

Hope glanced at Priska. In the next few seconds, the nurses would burst in and tell them to leave as they tried to resuscitate him.

The older woman flattened her lips. "He should be here at any time."

Hope didn't know who *he* was. Did Hermes escort all the dead? Or was there another god that did this? Or did they send minions? A lot of people died every minute all around the world, so there couldn't be just one, right? And whoever it was, at what point after death did he show up?

Hope and Priska had been to several hospitals to visit the dying in hopes of catching one as they crossed over into the Underworld. It was the only plan either could think of, a way to access the portal to the realm of the dead.

The *Books of the Fates* were bound in the Underworld, as were the gods of that realm. Hope needed to talk to her mom about the curse, and possibly the Moirai. She needed to know why Leto's story wasn't written in their *Book of the Fates*. And she needed to know how to break the curse. The Moirai had helped Phaidra shortly after the curse was placed. Surely Hope could get some answers if she could only get to the Underworld.

But so far, they'd only watched people die.

And it was getting depressing.

The alarm continued, indicating the patient's lack of heartbeat, and on the other side of the door the sounds of pounding feet and yelling drew closer.

"Mrs. Johnson!" A nurse in blue scrubs bustled in, pushing what Hope now knew was called a crash cart. "I'm so sorry, but I'm going to have to ask you and your daughter to leave. I'm sorry. I'm so sorry!"

Two more nurses came in yelling orders and pulling things from the cart.

One leaned over to turn up the oxygen, and someone else said, "I'll start chest compressions."

Hope pulled on Priska's sleeve and whispered, "Let's go."

Which was just as well, as the nurses herded them out the door.

Behind them a nurse yelled orders, and in the hall two more nurses were running to help the newly deceased. Hope backed out of the way, plastering herself to the opposite wall, and the nurses pushed Priska aside as they charged in.

"It didn't work," Hope said. What she didn't say, but really wanted to, was "again."

Four hospitals. Eleven—no, twelve deaths. And not a single portal to the Underworld.

Priska said nothing as they walked down the hall and through the double doors of the Intensive Care Unit.

Hope pushed the button for the elevator to take them back to the garage. "I think we need to try something different. There has to be a way to get me into the Underworld."

The elevator dinged, and the doors slid open.

"Let's go get something to eat," Priska said. Her voice was as flat as her expression. "Then we can go back to the hotel. I have another idea."

Hope slammed the bathroom door. The cheap motel's fan whistled and hummed, but Priska's voice carried through the thin barrier. They'd arrived back in Seattle earlier that day and checked into a hotel just south of downtown.

"We have talked about this before, Charlie. I'm not willing to not help. Not this time."

Hope was no longer under the pretense that Mr. Davenport, aka Charlie, was just Priska's boss. All of the phone calls Hope had been forced to listen to had blown up that little charade. But Priska never brought it up, and so Hope didn't either.

Love makes people do both selfish and unselfish things. Sometimes at the same time.

The argument continued, and Hope was forced to listen to the one side.

"She almost died." Priska's voice broke. "It would've been my fault, and I can't live with that. I won't live with that. Please don't make me choose."

Once Hope knew Priska wasn't really her aunt, she couldn't help but question the demigod's devotion to her family. What had made her so faithful to her grandmother, her mother, and now her? It was clear Priska loved Charlie, so why not be with him?

"We'll leave tonight. If . . . I love you. No matter what, remember I love you."

Hope sat on the closed toilet lid, put her head in her hands, and waited. Priska's tearful goodbye made Hope's heart ache,

31

and guilt gnawed deep in her soul. No one should have to give up their love. Not for someone else. And definitely not for her.

The conversation stopped, but Priska's muffled sobs kept Hope trapped in the bathroom, wrestling with her conscience. It wasn't like it was going to be easier if she waited. In fact, if the plan was to go to the Underworld tonight, there wasn't really time to wait.

Biting her lip, she squared her shoulders and opened the door.

Priska sat atop the patterned bedspread, a pillow on her crossed legs. Her dark hair was still long and hung halfway down her back in a waterfall of pitch. Her hazel eyes were bright with unshed tears.

"I know." Hope summed up all her knowledge of Priska and Charlie's relationship in those two words. Then, just so there was no room for confusion, Hope pointed at the phone sitting on the white pillow in Priska's lap.

Priska nodded, her gaze fixed in her lap. Her eyes were red and swollen from crying. "I never deliberately hid it from you." She picked up the phone and flipped it over in her hands. "Your mom knew, too."

"When did it happen?"

Priska's hands froze, the jeweled arrow on the back of her phone case glittering in the dimming light.

Being this close to the airport and downtown buildings filtered the sun's descent through the sky. Warm, sugary tones glistened through the open curtains, casting a hopeful glow across the two beds.

Priska grimaced. Then her face softened. "It was before you were even a blip on the radar. Charlie helped your grandfather with his estate when your mother was still a child. He was just out of school then."

My grandfather? "How old is Charlie?"

Priska laughed. "He's fifty-two. I've been working for him for twenty-seven years. On and off depending on your family's needs."

Twenty-seven years? "How long have you been together?"

"Almost thirty. He was in law school when I met him."

Hope felt like the rug had been pulled out from under her. Somehow she'd deluded herself that her aunt's relationship had just happened at work and was ready to offer a platitude of comfort. This was way beyond that.

"Why didn't you ever tell me?" Hope liked Charlie, and he could've been like an uncle, right?

"The fewer things the gods can hold over you, the better. You would do well to remember that."

The advice was painfully pertinent. "Is that why you kept it a secret?"

Priska offered a wan smile. "It was never a secret for us. We just didn't let our relationship dictate everything we did."

The statement was a slap upside the head, and Hope's initial reaction was to defend herself. This quest was not about being with Athan. It was about being free to choose whom she wanted to be with. "You don't understand."

Priska let out a slow, deep breath. "Then enlighten me."

"If Athan didn't even exist, I would still want to do this. I'm not so naïve as to believe he is the one."

Priska nodded. "Good."

Hope hurried to finish so there would be no misunderstanding. "But he could be." She held her hand out to stop whatever protest was forming. "Not that he's *the one,* but I just don't want to have to worry about a god killing whomever I'm with because of some misplaced belief that I'm destined to be with him."

She wanted Priska to understand. This wasn't about Athan. It was about possibility, and the freedom to choose. "What if you wanted to marry Charlie, but if you did, one of you would die?"

"One of us could die at any time, Hope."

"Yes. But that's not a guarantee. If I get married and have a baby, I will die. Guaranteed."

Priska rubbed the remaining tears from her eyes. "Then don't get married. Don't have kids. There are plenty of relationships that work without those conventions."

Was she talking about her and Charlie? "It isn't about the wedding, or even if I have kids. It's about being able to choose. For myself."

Priska nodded. "Then why exactly do you need to go to the Underworld?"

Hope had debated the options endlessly. None of the *Books of the Fates* she'd read had given any indication of a way to break a curse, only that they could be fulfilled. She'd also learned that the dead could not lie. For some reason, her mother's story wasn't recorded in their book. It was why Hope didn't know Apollo had Leto killed until Athan told her, and Priska confirmed it after being kidnapped by the god's sons. Even after that, Leto's story remained incomplete, and Hope knew she would need to talk to her mother to get the information. Because before she could do whatever came next, she needed more information.

The crease between Priska's eyes deepened as Hope explained why she needed to talk to her mom, and when she was finished, Priska shook her head. "Gods, those are some incredible risks for maybe."

Hope opened her mouth to defend herself, but Priska held up her hand. "I get it. I do."

"If I stay, there is only certainty."

The waning crescent hung in the night sky, the skirting clouds making the shadows wax and wane in their inky darkness. The cobblestone street was empty of patrons, and the market sat eerily quiet.

"You're sure this will work?" Hope asked, staring into the dark stalls. Memories flashed through her mind: Priska running to save Hope and her mom from Skia, fighting to save Obelia, and more recently with Athan.

Priska drew herself up to her full height. "It will work. When Hermes comes, tell him he must take you to your mother."

Something was off with how Priska was talking, and a nagging discomfort settled in the pit of Hope's stomach. "Or you could tell him."

"Or I can tell him," Priska conceded with a laugh. She pulled her long hair back and adjusted her fitted blouse.

"How are you going to call him?" Hope had never heard of a demigod being able to summon any other god besides their parent. Maybe Artemis had a thing for Hermes . . . or the other way around.

Hope stared into the night sky, dreaming of flying. The wind kissed her skin with its cold caress. Gods, she hoped this worked. She sent the silent plea up into the darkness above and closed her eyes. With a deep breath, she declared her intentions to any deity that might be listening.

Her thoughts swirled with doubts; her plan was reckless, foolish, and risky at best. She could die, or worse, get stuck in the Underworld forever. She might never find her mom. Might never see Athan. Or Xan. Or Dahlia. And for what?

Peace descended with the misty drizzle from above. Hope's worries washed away. If she died, it would be because she failed. Not because she didn't try.

And freedom was worth it, wasn't it? The question was entirely rhetorical because she already knew the answer. Determination and resolve pulsed through her. She could do this. She *would* do this.

The smell of garbage wafted from an empty dumpster nearby.

Hope opened her eyes and froze.

Three Skia surrounded Priska, their blades of pitch and death drawn and pointed at the demigod.

"No!" Hope yelled and reached for her immortal blades. Blades she no longer owned. Her hands trembled as they came up empty. Anger fueled the fire of her fear. The blades were not her only weapon.

She advanced on the demons of Hades. She knew how to fight, and while the odds weren't in her favor, with Priska's help, they could do this.

"You will not touch her!" Hope spit the words out as she clenched her fists.

But Priska stood there, not moving. Not fighting. Just giving in. Her eyes widened, even as she gave Hope a sad smile. "I love you, sweet girl. This was the only thing I could think of—"

Hope screamed as the black blade sunk deep into Priska's chest. Priska's petite body flinched. Another monster drove his blade into her side, and Priska fell to the ground.

Hope startled from her shock, and her resolve hardened. "No!" she yelled as she advanced on the Skia. They would not kill Priska. Hope would not let them, but the three stood to the side, even as Hope approached, and then held up their hands.

What?

Hope ignored the creatures from the Underworld and rushed to Priska. Tears clouded Hope's vision, and she knelt at her aunt's side.

"What are you thinking? You can't do this!" Hope looked at the blades still protruding from her aunt. Was there a way to help? Gods, oh gods. Priska had *meant* to do this.

Tears dripped from Hope's face onto Priska's, and Priska raised her hand to brush the tears away. "Don't . . . cry. He'll . . . come and . . . take . . . you."

Hope fumbled with Priska's body, her hands fluttering over her face and chest. She didn't want to hurt her, but she didn't know how to help. "Should I pull it out?"

Priska's panic-filled eyes widened. Her breath was heavy and wet and rattled in her chest. She grasped the hilt of the blade in her side and pulled futilely.

"Do you want me to pull it?" Hope asked between sobs.

Priska's eyes closed and then opened slowly. Her lips moved, but the only sound was her rattling breath.

Hope grabbed the hilt and pulled. The weapon slid out so easily Hope fell to her butt. She righted herself and pulled the other blade from Priska's chest. Priska seized, her body shaking and thrashing.

Helpless, Hope sobbed while she watched her aunt die. When Priska's shaking subsided to tremors, Hope pulled her aunt's head and shoulders into her lap. Wiping the tears and snot from her face with her sleeve, Hope gulped for air through the drowning waves of emotions.

Blackness seeped from the wound, spreading over Priska's chest like oozing honey. Her breaths came further and further apart, the wet wheezing making Hope cry harder. "Please, don't leave," she whispered, choking on the words. "Please don't die."

But the silence told her it was already too late.

A power pulsed beside her, and Hope's mouth went dry.

FIVE

ATHAN

ATHAN HEARD THE staccato beat of gloves against a heavy bag and followed the sound to the gym. He should've come here first. Of course, Xan was training. He was always training. That aspect of the son of Ares hadn't changed. But when Athan pulled open the door to the gym, he froze. Xan wasn't in the gym.

Dahlia's dark hair was pulled up into a high ponytail, and her warm russet skin glistened with sweat. She delivered a flurry of kicks and punches that were only a blur of activity, and the bag swung far away from the demigod's force. She paused a beat, and then spun and delivered a round kick that split the seam of the black bag. Dahlia wiped her brow with her hand and flung the moisture to the mats. She glanced up and frowned when she spotted Athan.

"You're up." She grabbed a towel off the bench and dried her face, neck, and chest then pulled a shirt over her black sports bra. "Are you well enough to come?"

"We're leaving tomorrow?" He did the math in his head. "Don't we have another day?"

Dahlia quirked a brow at him. "Where have you been? Didn't you hear Obelia at dinner tonight? Thenia's coming tomorrow." She flipped the top on her water bottle and started drinking.

And Athena, her mother, would be with her.

Trepidation beat through his chest. They needed to be gone before Athena got there or they would have to answer to her.

"What time?"

Silence hung between them while Dahlia finished the last of her drink. She closed the bottle and let out a long breath. "It isn't my show. I'm just going along for the ride."

It was times like this, when she was deliberately obtuse, that reminded Athan why he didn't like the demigod bombshell.

"But do you know what time we're leaving?" He pinched the bridge of his nose against the pressure building in his head.

She shrugged. "You should talk to Xan."

Dahlia picked up her gym bag and brushed by Athan, bumping him as she passed. It was just hard enough to let him know it wasn't an accident. Surprise.

Athan looked at the bag on the floor and remembered the brutal practices with Xan all those years ago. He'd been merciless as he drove Athan to improve his reaction time and accuracy.

Pushing back the memories, Athan resumed his search for his former friend.

The heavy wood muffled Athan's light rap on the door, so he followed up by pounding his fist on the dark wood. He'd searched the entire conservatory and was now back at the beginning, in front of Xan's room.

"Xan," he started as Dahlia came out of her room.

She wore fitted leather fighting gear with the hilts of her blades strapped to her thighs. Her dark curls were still pulled up in a high ponytail. She dropped a canvas duffle bag on the floor and turned back to lock her door.

"Hunting gear?" Athan asked.

She ignored him.

The click of a door opening made him glance down the hall. Obelia stepped out of her room, and internally he groaned.

Dressed in tight jeans and a bright magenta top, she looked ready for a night of clubbing. She squealed as she barreled toward him, "Athan!"

He took a step back and bumped into the wall. There wasn't enough space to avoid her.

Obelia jumped and wrapped herself around him. She whispered in his ear, her lips grazing his skin, "Are we going out tonight?"

He couldn't help the flinch that came with her intimate contact. He wanted to be gentle with her feelings, but he wanted her off even more.

"'Belia," he warned as he pried her off and set her on the ground.

The petite demigod pouted, her full lips pulling down into a frown. "You said—"

"More promises you don't intend to keep?" Dahlia sneered, curling her lip in disgust.

If he could go back and change one thing, this was it. He'd never meant for Obelia to fall in love with him when he found her five years ago. Well, that wasn't completely true. He'd just never thought her feelings would last this long.

"Why don't you two go out?" Dahlia pursed her lips as if suppressing a chuckle. She leaned toward Athan and in a low voice continued, "Really, you two deserve each other."

Obelia's frown morphed, and her eyes lit up as if Dahlia's words were a blessing.

Like she didn't know Athan didn't like the demigod daughter of Hestia. Not like that. "Don't you—?"

"What the bloody Hades is wrong with you, Dahl?"

Athan had been so absorbed in the other conversation he hadn't heard Xan join them.

"Are you trying to cause more problems?" Xan grabbed Dahlia's bag then threw it through his open doorway. The large duffle landed on the hardwood floor with a thud.

"Just calling it like I see it," she said as she sauntered past Athan into Xan's room.

Xan's black hair glistened, and when he ran his hand through it, small rivulets of water dripped onto his pale-blue T-shirt.

He stepped between Athan and Obelia, and towering over the young woman, he said, "He doesn't like you. He probably never did. So stop skulking around waiting for something that's never going to happen. It's time for you to . . . grow up." He nodded. "Right then. Go cry and eat some chocolate, or whatever it is you do."

Athan was dumbstruck by Xan's cruel words. Not that they weren't true, but—

"And you!" Xan turned around and poked Athan in the chest. "Quit being so nice to her. You're giving her false hope, and that's not right."

Xan moved, and Athan was able to see Obelia. Her skin was ashen, and her eyes glistened with tears.

"'Belia—"

She held up her hand, cutting him off.

"Is it true?" she asked, her voice cracking over the fragile question.

"I . . . I like you a lot." He sighed. Why were the lies easier than the truth? "But not . . . not like that."

Obelia's chin dropped, and her shoulders sagged. When she looked back up, tears streaked her cheeks and spilled onto her flowy top, turning the pink to a dark crimson.

Xan cleared his throat. "Right then. All done here?" He didn't wait for an answer but pulled on Athan's sleeve. "We need to go find Hope now."

Athan stumbled forward a step and then righted himself. He ached for Obelia. She'd always been so nice to him. So sweet. Guilt gnawed at his heart, and he racked his brain for a way to fix the pain he'd caused.

But at the mention of Hope's name, Obelia sucked in a deep breath. She glared at Xan and wiped the tears from her face, her pain seeming to disappear with the moisture from her cheeks. "Really?" Bitterness laced her question, and she turned her anger on Athan. "You're going after her? How can you even like her? She's a monster!"

The remorse he'd been feeling also evaporated. Something deep in his chest flared to life. A sense of possessiveness and protection. "She is not a monster. She's cursed." He stepped closer to Obelia. "You would do well to remember that I love her."

Obelia took a step back as if he'd slapped her. Her jaw dropped, and her gaze darted away from his face. With a ragged breath, she choked out a feeble, "No."

He nodded. "I do."

Obelia's wide eyes filled with fresh tears, but she turned and ran down the hall and then down the stairs. Seconds later, the front door slammed shut.

"You did that all arseways," Xan said, clapping Athan on the back. "You better go pack a bag so we can go. And tell Kaia to hunt Obelia down. She really shouldn't be out on her own."

With that, Xan went into his room where Dahlia sat on the bed.

"Do you want me to go get her?" Dahlia asked. "You know Kaia will never find her."

Xan shook his head. "We need to leave now." He turned back and stared Athan down. "If you're not back here in five minutes, we're leaving without you, pretty boy."

SIX

HOPE

HOPE KNEW WHO the power belonged to, which god it would be. Priska's direction made sense now.

"She's not there anymore." The male spoke with a musical lilt to his inflection. "She's standing right beside you."

Hope looked up at her side but saw nothing. She glared at the god. "That was unkind."

Hermes shrugged. His bronze hair was exactly the same shade as his son's. "Just because you can't see her doesn't mean she isn't there." He indicated the body on her lap. "The soul separates at death. Her body will stay here in the mortal realm, but as a demigod, I will take her soul to Hades for judgment."

"You will be her guide?"

He inclined his head. "It is her right." His gaze unfocused for a moment, as if he were looking at the air around her. "As it will be yours someday, Immortal."

Two thoughts coalesced in her mind. "Did you escort my mother?"

He raised his brows. "What type of monster are you?"

He couldn't tell? "I thought the gods were omniscient?"

Hermes chuckled. "Whatever gave you that idea?" He pointed at Priska's body. "Why did she sacrifice herself for you? She's a demigod . . . "

Fresh tears sprang to Hope's eyes, and she had to swallow the lump caught in her throat before she could choke out an answer. "So that you would come. I . . . I need a guide to the Underworld."

Hermes clenched his jaw, and his hazel eyes flashed fire. "I don't run a guide service. Now, what is your name, Monster? Who cursed you?"

"My name is Hope. I'm the Sphinx."

Hermes's jaw went slack, and he paled. "Where is my son?"

The fact that he hadn't escorted his son to the Underworld meant Athan wasn't dead. "I . . . I left him at the conservatory."

Had it only been a week ago that they'd been attacked? It felt like an eternity. Had he woken up from the Skia wound?

"What do you mean, you left him?" The god pulled back. "Is he all right?"

Hope stood. "We were attacked, not too far from here actually."

Way too late, Hope thought about how Priska had repeatedly said Pike Place Market was always swarming with Skia. Guilt settled deep in Hope's chest. She should've known what Priska was planning . . . Should've put it together . . . If Hope had only known . . .

Feeling completely disconnected from the reality around her, Hope faced Athan's father and said, "He's recovering in the conservatory."

The god of thieves and travellers narrowed his eyes. "There is more you're not telling me, Sphinx."

She could think of no reason to lie, so she told him. Everything. Ending with Priska's request that he take Hope with him. Searching for a way to make it right, Hope asked, "Do you think Hades will let Priska come back?"

The psychopomp god cocked an eyebrow at her, as if the question had taken him by surprise. Certainly, with all the travel back and forth between realms, he'd been asked this before.

"No," he answered. "She was killed by Skia, and she was quite old. Hades is all about balance and order." He studied her for a moment. "In the Underworld, you'd do well to remember that."

A small spark of possibility flickered in Hope's chest. "Wait. Are you saying—?"

"I will take you there." He grimaced as if the idea was distasteful. "It would give me immense pleasure to thwart the god of the sun."

The two Skia hiding in the shadows stepped back into the darkness and disappeared with Hermes's declaration.

Hope kissed her aunt's cheek, the body still warm despite her soul having left.

"I love you," she whispered, straightening Priska's clothes.

Hermes cleared his throat. "She's ready to go, so save your goodbye. We're all going to cross into the Underworld together."

Hope crossed over to him, her heart still aching for Priska's sacrifice. Maybe Hermes was wrong. Maybe she'd be able to get her back. "What do we need to do?"

"Follow me," he said as he stepped into a dark shadow, his leg disappearing. He waved for Hope to follow.

The darkness smelled of compost and overripe fruit. Hope followed Hermes through, but she couldn't help looking around for Priska as they crossed over into the realm of the dead.

Dusky, dark rock extended as far as Hope could see, the opaque inky stone of the Underworld just shy of black. Above her, in what Hope thought of as the sky, pale green dots, reminiscent of stars, glowed. The stench was overwhelming, and Hope covered her nose with her sleeve as her eyes watered.

"You're close to the Acheron, where Charon ferries the dead." Hermes directed her with a wave of his hand. "Hades's palace is on the other side of that river, through the barren barrier, over the river Lethe, through the Fields of Asphodel, and then you can go through or around Persephone's gardens. If you go through the gardens, you'll find Elysium, just to give you a heads-up. It's on the other side of that."

"You're not going to take me?" Her stomach clenched.

The god laughed, a mirthless chuckle. "Of course not. Your plan is hopeful at best, but more like naïve foolishness. I want no part of it, for me or my son."

"Then why would you bring me?"

"If you are here, Apollo cannot get you. It will drive him mad." He turned as if to go.

Hope glanced away from the god . . . and saw Priska. "Wait!"

Her aunt's mouth moved in silent speech, and Hope couldn't control the tears. She wanted to demand her aunt make this better. She wanted to yell at her about her sacrifice. But in that moment, Hope knew this was her one chance at goodbye.

She ran to the woman she'd known her entire life, the only family she had left, and wrapped her arms around . . . nothing.

"It is her soul only. She will not be corporeal here until after judgment." With that departing comment, Hermes grabbed Priska's wrist, and the two of them disappeared.

Hope collapsed, crumpling down on the uneven ground, and let the mists swirl and eddy over her. Burying her face in her hands, the dam burst and she sobbed. It could've been minutes or hours or even days that Hope spent releasing her grief. She screamed until her voice was hoarse, cried until her eyes were dry, and even then her heart mourned.

When her muscles ached and her eyes were no longer swollen, Hope decided she needed to move. She would not be a victim. She would not be a tool. She would not let Priska's sacrifice be for nothing.

Hope kicked at the ground, stirring up the dark mist, and muttered, "Stupid gods."

Someone behind her chuckled.

Hope turned and dropped into a defensive stance, her arms coming up to guard, as she readied for attack.

The man staring at her was pale, like he'd spent too much time indoors. His skin was a stark contrast to his inky-black hair, and his thin frame was clothed in soft grays. His eyes danced with amusement.

"Do you think you can take me?" His voice was like the rasp of snake scales rubbing over each other as they coiled. He cocked his head to the side and studied her.

Hope dropped her arms and stood straight. "Probably not."

She started walking toward the river Hermes had indicated she would need to cross.

The man appeared beside her and matched her stride. "Smart girl. Much more so than I would've thought."

His arrogance settled it.

"Who are you?" she asked.

He raised his brows but didn't answer.

"Which one?" she asked, then she counted them off on her fingers. "Hypnos, Thanatos, Hades, Charon?" Were there any more she'd forgotten? She shook her head, trying to clear it. "Look, whoever you are, I'm really not in the mood for—"

He held up his hand with another dark chuckle. "I'm Thanatos."

God of death. He'd killed her mother. *Ripped her soul from her body* was what Athan had said. Hope tripped and stumbled forward.

The god of death did the one thing she least expected. He cupped her elbow, steadying her, and asked, "Are you all right?"

"Are you going to kill me?" Death honestly didn't sound all that much worse than how things were going anyway. She let out a deep breath and coughed on the humid stench.

His skin was cool and dry, and as soon as she was upright, he pulled away and frowned. "You are the Sphinx."

Deep within, she knew she should be afraid. Terrified even. But her emotions had been tested to the limit, and every bit of her reserve had been drained. "Gods! I'm so sick of that. Do you even know what it's like? No one, and I mean no one, ever sees me for who I actually am, only"—she made air quotes—"the Sphinx."

A slow smile spread across the god's face. "Actually, my dear, I know exactly what you mean."

And then he disappeared.

Hope threw her hands up in the air and cursed into the void of the Underworld. As the sound of her own voice faded, she realized it wasn't silent. The sound of waves washing ashore was faint but distinct. With a whoop of triumph, she ran toward the sound.

The banks of the river Acheron were crowded with the dead. Souls paced near the water, and after only a few seconds Hope had the distinct impression that something was wrong. Not necessarily incorrect, but more amiss, unethical, *damaged*. These people were in various states of frustration, agitation, or anger. Many of them had their mouths open, their faces distorted with hostility, as they silently screamed at each other.

The stench of the air was marked with the weight of despair.

A small skiff broke through the mists of the river, a tall, cloaked figure standing at the back. With a long pole, he guided the ferry. As he maneuvered the wood shaft, a hand rose from the black water.

Hope watched in horror as the pale limb grasped the edge of the vessel, and then the head of a person—no, it couldn't be called a person. This thing was like out of a zombie movie. Oh gods, what was it? Stringy hair hung from its scalp down a pruney, pale back. Pieces of skin hung, torn away from the muscle underneath, and the eye socket she could see was empty, just a black hole surrounded by the bony prominence of what was once his or her . . . cheek.

The ferryman turned with a quick rap of the pole, and the creature screamed as it let go and sunk beneath the water.

Clearly, she couldn't swim across.

The boat docked, and the ferryman stood as if waiting.

Hope watched as souls clamored around the dock. But only a few actually stepped onto the weathered wood. As the souls stepped from the short pier to the skiff, they handed something to the cloaked figure. Charon. And he would be getting an obol as payment for transport.

She watched as the boat disappeared with its few passengers, leaving the majority still milling around on the shore.

The festering smell of decomposing meat was stronger the closer she got to shore. Hope opened her mouth to breathe in an attempt to lessen the intensity of the stench, but it almost felt like she was breathing it in that way, so she endured the odor.

The souls stepped out of her way after she passed through a couple of them. All she could think was it must be just as uncomfortable for them when they touched as it was for her. Maybe. Although if they were dead, could they even feel anything at all?

She pushed through, determined to find a way to get on the next pass over the river. As she drew closer to the dock, the crowd didn't thin, and it felt like she was walking through cold wet spiderwebs. She cringed. A fresh wave of rot hit her, and she bent over and threw up.

Her stomach wanted to continue to roil and heave, but she refused to let it. She wiped her mouth on her sleeve, adding another layer of grime, and straightened. Her eyes locked on a familiar dark gaze, and she froze.

Obelia's eyes narrowed. The demigod daughter of Hestia was dressed as if ready for a night on the town, in a bright magenta top and fitted jeans. She turned, and Hope saw the gaping holes in the back of her shirt.

Skia. Hope ground her teeth, and then she dropped her shoulders. Athan would be so upset if he knew. Maybe he did know . . . Maybe he'd been there.

Hope pushed through the crowd with a new sense of resolve. She had to know. She got to the dock just as Obelia handed Charon a coin.

"Wait!" Hope yelled.

Obelia turned, and with a raised eyebrow, she flipped Hope off.

As if Hope even cared.

"Is Athan okay?" she demanded.

Obelia curled her lip into a sneer. Turning her back on Hope, the daughter of Hestia pushed her way through the other passengers, crossing to the far end of the skiff.

Hope stepped onto the dock. She needed to get across, and she wanted to ask Obelia if Athan had recovered from the Skia attack. Hope ignored the fear bubbling up in her chest, the what-ifs, and the consequences of failure. She could do this. With a fortifying breath, Hope moved toward the boat.

A pale, bony hand extended out from the dark robe. When Hope tried to step onto the ferry, the hand firmly pushed her back.

"No," Hope protested, "I'm not dead."

Surely, the living wouldn't require payment. It wasn't like she was going to be staying.

"No fee, no service," the god intoned. His voice was rough, like he didn't use it enough, and the coppery smell of blood wafted from under his hood.

She gritted her teeth. "I just need to get across."

The god continued to bar her entrance.

"Fine. At least let me talk to my friend." Hope waved toward the front of the boat where Obelia stood.

"No payment, no entrance," he said. This time, he brought his pole out of the water and set it on the dock in front of her.

It was ridiculous. She understood the dead were required to make a payment, but she was *alive.* Why wouldn't the walking corpse get it through his head? She wanted to talk to Obelia to find out if Athan was okay, but Hope *needed* to get across the river.

She pushed the pole away and stepped forward.

Blinding pain cracked against her back. Hope stumbled, lost her footing, and fell forward. Instinctively, she extended her hands to brace for the impact. Sharp pain exploded from her extremities to her brain, as if she'd landed on shards of broken glass. Agony stole her breath, and Hope scrambled to stand, to get off of whatever was causing the blinding anguish. A vice gripped her wrist and pulled her forward, acid splashing on her face, burning her skin.

Oh, gods! She was in the river. She screamed and thrashed, refusing to let the water-demons take her. Bones crunched and snapped, the vice released her, and the pain briefly waned. She struggled to stand, and although it felt as though her feet were being bludgeoned, the lapping waves were only past her ankles.

She splashed through the water, the liquid searing her skin like flaming blades. It was only when she stepped onto the dry rock that she saw why she'd been able to get free.

Thanatos stood at the edge of the Acheron, his arms extended as if pushing away a foe. In fact, he was. The river and its demons were cleared from her path. He'd used his power to help her.

She wanted to thank him, but the emotional and physical turmoil had pushed her to her breaking point. As she opened her mouth, she collapsed.

SEVEN

ATHAN

BRIGHT LIGHT CUT through the darkness of the motel room. The space between the curtains glowed with the morning sun. Athan rolled over to get out of the blinding sliver and sunk into the middle of the bed. The white sheets smelled of bleach and fabric softener but couldn't quite hide the mustiness of the old room. Grunting his frustration with the accommodations, he forced himself to sit up.

"Sleeping Beauty! You finally decide to join us, eh?" Xan sat at a cheap table surrounded by Styrofoam plates filled with motel breakfast foods. He picked up a plastic knife and fork and cut into a waffle the size of the plate.

Waffles sounded good. Athan stood and took a deep breath. But the stale air let him know the food wasn't fresh. He frowned, but his stomach didn't register the same disappointment. He was starving.

Crossing the room, he grabbed a banana and peeled it. The starchiness was slightly bitter, and the green tinge of the peel was confirmation the fruit was not quite ripe. Not that it really mattered. He needed to eat. He pulled the foil lid from a yogurt and grabbed a white plastic spoon.

"What's the plan?" he asked between bites. "Any ideas where we need to be looking?"

Xan shook his head. "I saw the attorney yesterday. The one Priska used to work for."

Athan set the spoon down and stared at Xan. "Yeah?"

Xan had tracked Priska to an office on Mercer Island back before he'd brought Hope into the conservatory. Back when he thought she was a demigod.

"He doesn't know where they went. Said he hasn't seen Hope for months. And the last time he saw Priska was the same day Hope ran off." He ran his hand over his face and blew out a deep breath.

"So nothing?"

Xan grimaced. "Priska called him a couple of days ago. That's the last he's heard."

Athan gave a derisive snort. "You weren't kidding when you said you had nothing. Hades, Xan. What have you been doing, walking up and down the street with fliers? How could you have found nothing in a month?"

Xan's eyes turned to ice. "Do you think you could do better?"

"Well, I don't see how I could do worse. Where have you looked? Have you thought about calling for help?"

Xan clenched his jaw. "I scouted out the U-district, Madison Park, First Hill, Magnolia, West Seattle, Mercer Island, Bellevue, and the Eastside. I've driven up to Vancouver, BC, and down to Portland, as well as over to Yakima. No one seems to have seen or heard anything unusual, but I haven't called out the big guns. Think, Athan."

Xan didn't need to say it. Athan understood. If they started asking specific questions, there would be no way to keep Hope's identity a secret, and neither of them wanted a full-scale man, or rather *monster*, hunt.

"What's your plan?"

"At this point, I'd love to hear your thoughts." Xan sounded sincere. "This floundering thing has been pointless. I'm not sure if I should be worried sick or proud of her."

"Proud of her?"

"Yeah." Xan poured amber-colored syrup over the remains of the waffle. "She's so incredibly unique she should stand out like a sore thumb, and yet she's been able to blend seamlessly. How did you ever find her?"

Athan thought back to their time in Goldendale. "Actually, she kind of fell into my lap."

Xan raised his eyebrows.

Athan chuckled. "Not like that, although, that would have been nice. I was looking for her, the Sphinx, but didn't even know it was her. I spent countless hours in the mountains, searching for a monster." He chuckled and touched his cheek. "I even found a few. Did you know there's a Cyclopes in the Snoqualmie range?"

"You're kidding."

Athan tore the plastic wrap off a fruit pastry and took a bite. "Nope." He swallowed and set the Danish aside. "I saw a herd of centaurs, too. I actually thought Hope was a demigod. Even tried to get her to a conservatory." He still wondered what he could've done differently, both back in Goldendale and at the conservatory.

Xan snorted his disbelief.

"Skia attacked her in Oregon, and I happened to be driving by her house when I noticed her sitting in the car with the lights on. She was in shock. That was the turning point. She let me in after that. But I still didn't know."

"How did you find out?"

"The same Skia attacked us both. When she could see him, I knew she was a demigod. But we got in a fight, and she took off. I thought she'd come right back, that she needed to cool off. I saw a box with the name Leto on it, and I found a *Book of the Fates* inside. I was curious, and by morning, when she came back, I knew. It was fine. I didn't care. But she overheard me and my father talking at Myrine's house. Something he said must have freaked her out, and she took off. She's really good at hiding." Athan picked at the white frosting on the packaged Danish. He was still hungry, but the food was disgusting.

Xan sat up straight as if he'd been shocked. "Myrine."

Athan looked at the door, willing Dahlia to come in. Then maybe they could go get some real food. "Myrine was living in Goldendale. She's actually the one who alerted me to the Sphinx being in the area." Of course, Myrine could have told him Hope was the Sphinx. Could have told him a million times. Who knows why she hadn't? Oracles were so—

Xan leaned forward and smacked Athan upside the head. "Can you get ahold of Myrine? Can't she tell you where Hope's gone?"

Athan rubbed his temple. "Don't hit me."

Xan frowned. "Can you get in touch with Myrine?" He spoke each word as if talking to a child.

Athan hated to be patronized. "Maybe. But—"

Xan pulled his cell phone from his pocket and slid it across the table. "Call her then."

Athan pulled his own thin black device from his pocket. "Even if I get ahold of her . . . she may not have anything helpful to say."

A knock came at the door, and Xan stood to let Dahlia in.

The smell of bacon preceded the daughter of Eris into the room. Athan groaned as he tapped on the screen. He stood and reached for the bag Dahlia was carrying, but she refused to relinquish it.

"What is that?" she asked, pointing to the food still on the table. It was practically as full as when Athan had woken up.

Xan shrugged. "It was all they had in the lobby. I didn't want to leave Sleeping Beauty unattended."

Dahlia snorted. "You couldn't pay me to eat that rubbish."

Xan swept the plates of cold waffles, packaged pastries, and dry toast into the garbage. As soon as there was space on the table, Dahlia set the bag down.

Athan continued to tap on the screen. If anyone could locate Myrine, it was his father. As messenger to the gods, Hermes had access to some type of divine tracking that worked better than anything the mortals had ever invented. Hopefully, Hermes would be so busy he wouldn't question why Athan was asking. And if he did, a text was probably the safest way to lie.

The food smelled amazing, and Athan's stomach growled a demand for attention. But this was more important, and his father was responding.

"Got it," Athan announced a few minutes later. He looked up to see both Xan and Dahlia chewing. Two black plastic containers, shiny with grease, were all that remained on the table. "Come on!" They had eaten everything. Only the scent of bacon remained. "Seriously?"

Athan collapsed in the chair and glared at the two demi-gods.

Xan smirked, and Dahlia's lip curled.

"Don't get your knickers twisted." She reached into the bag on the floor and pulled out another plastic container, the clear lid revealing pancakes, bacon, and eggs all piled atop each other. "Here's the syrup."

She handed him a small plastic jar, as well as a knife and fork.

"Did you find her?" Xan asked.

Athan nodded but said nothing as he scarfed the food almost as fast as the other two demigods had. Only a few minutes later he sat back in his chair, still not full, but definitely feeling better.

"She's in Olympia."

Dahlia furrowed her brow. "Who's in Olympia? Hope?"

"Nah. Myrine is." Xan shifted in his seat, and the wood creaked with his bulk. "Hopefully, she can tell us where Hope is."

"How do you know that?"

Athan pointed at his phone. "My dad found her."

"Why not tell your dad to find Hope?"

If only it were that easy. "It only works on immortals that are registered."

And there was no way Hermes would help Athan with anything that had to do with Hope.

Dahlia nodded.

Monsters would never register. Why would they want immortals, gods or demigods, to know their location? Athan wasn't even sure Hope knew such a thing existed.

"Should I call her, or do you want to drive down for a visit?" It would only take a couple of hours from where they were on the northern side of the Olympic National Park. Of course, Xan and Athan had both agreed to drive close to Mount Olympus with the thought of hiding right under the noses of the gods. Not that the Mount Olympus in Washington State was *the* Mount Olympus, but there was a portal there to get to the residence of the gods.

"Let's go for a drive. I want to see the whites of her eyes so I know she's telling the truth."

Athan rolled his eyes. "Oracles can't lie."

"Right." Dahlia dragged the word out, laying it thick with sarcasm. She pursed her full lips as her face scrunched up in what could only be disgust. "They don't lie, but they can be convincingly misleading. Not to mention vague and ambiguous."

Athan wanted to defend Myrine, but Dahlia's vehemence had him debating if it was worth engaging.

Before Athan could say anything, Xan put an end to the discussion. Tossing Athan's empty container in the bag, the demigod son of Ares stood and said, "I want to make sure she's clear. Whatever it takes to get answers. We need to get Hope back before a Skia, or something worse, finds her."

Athan shuddered. There were far too many possibilities in that statement.

"**DO YOU REMEMBER** when we went to California?" Xan asked.

Athan shifted in the leather seat, pulling his gaze away from the window and the inadequate entertainment it provided. The sun was making a valiant effort to burn through the clouds, and as he stared at the back of Xan and Dahlia, the tall evergreens blurred in his peripheral vision.

Dahlia said nothing.

"Oh, right," Xan said with a chuckle. "You were too piss-drunk to remember anything."

There was a fair chance Xan was baiting him, or possibly Dahlia. But the last thirty minutes had dragged by mercilessly, so Athan bit. "You went to California? Was that recently?"

Xan raised his eyebrows as he glanced back in the rearview mirror at Athan. "Aye. Bit of a problem with the Mer. Again."

Poseidon was a bit lax on keeping his realm separate from the mortals. Not that it usually caused serious problems.

"Why'd you get drunk?" Athan asked Dahlia.

She turned around in her seat to glare at him but said nothing. After a few awkward seconds, she faced forward and stared out the window.

There was nothing new out there. Not for the next hour. Just the same trees and Olympic Mountains on the horizon.

"We had to go to Half Moon Bay," Xan answered.

Where Dahlia and Roan had been married. Ouch. Athan thought of all the times he'd wanted to escape reality after Isabel died. He'd avoided every single place they'd ever been, or at least as much as possible. It was what had eventually driven him to go to Africa.

"She was super fun," Xan continued, pushing on regardless of his cousin's discomfort. "Like that time you got drunk in Mexico."

Athan choked and then chuckled. Vague memories of him and Xan drinking something foul in a dingy bar flitted through his mind. Xan had convinced him to sing karaoke. As the son of Hermes, Athan was quite capable of singing. But then Xan had sung an Irish song about lasses and ladies, and wasn't there a ballad to Dionysus?

"You two were idiots," Dahlia muttered. "I thought you were going to get yourselves killed."

Not likely. The only occupants had been mortal, so they weren't in any real danger. But now that she mentioned it, Athan did remember a brawl.

"You were a terrible fighter then," Xan said with a low chuckle. "I had to pull that lumberjack off you."

Athan struggled to remember, but time, and probably the liquor, had made the memories hazy. "There was a lumberjack?"

"And that girl making calf-eyes at you. I think she snuck you drink after drink in hopes that you would take her with you."

He definitely didn't remember a girl. "What girl?"

"Not surprised you don't remember her. I don't think you ever really saw her." Xan smirked in the rearview mirror.

Dahlia's throaty chuckle was filled with dark mirth. "You have a habit of not seeing people. That's part of what gets you into trouble."

The comment stung. Mostly because Athan could see the truth in it.

"But then Xan sees the people and still doesn't care a whit, so there may be some hope for you."

"That's not true," Xan protested. "I care . . ." He stopped as if considering his next words. He cleared his throat, and without any defensiveness admitted, "No. You're right. I don't. But that's because people are idiots."

Dahlia raised her hand in a palm-up acknowledgment. "Like I said."

"Didn't you have to bail him out?" Athan asked Dahlia. "That night in Mexico . . . ?"

Had it been three years ago? No, it was more than four years now. Right after that, Athan had left for Nairobi.

Xan laughed. "And she lectured me the entire way back to the conservatory."

"Wanker," Dahlia said, but her smile reflected in the mirror.

"Aye. A real tosser. Can't be helped." Xan winked at his cousin.

Three hours later, Xan pulled up to a small white house with beige shutters. After turning the car off, he faced Athan. "You're sure this is it?"

Athan looked at the immaculate yard. Granted, it wasn't much bigger than a postage stamp, but the grass was thick, green, and freshly cut. The walkway to the door was lined with vibrant shrubs trimmed into a knee-high hedge. The door was painted a robin's-egg blue, and a rocking chair sat on the clean porch with a small end table in a matching dark stain.

Myrine wasn't known for keeping house. Or yard. Unless she was getting ready to move. "Let's hope she's still here."

Dahlia skirted around the boys and bounded up the steps. Without waiting for them to join her, she knocked on the door.

The recent rain made the air smell of dirt and pine. Athan stood next to Dahlia, and when he heard something scraping across the floor inside, he pushed her behind him.

"Don't be a bloody idiot," Dahlia said as she stepped around him. "I'm a way better fighter than you'll ever be." She pulled a silver dagger from its sheath, the fire opal in the hilt looking like the jeweled sea.

The lock clicked, and the door slid open an inch.

"Myrine?" Athan asked, peering into the darkness. His green eyes met her blue ones, and heavy fear settled in his chest.

"You should not be here." Her gaze went to each one of them on the porch and then came back to Athan. "You . . . You're still alive, right?"

"Can she see the dead?" Dahlia asked Athan.

Athan pointed at Myrine. "She's right there. Why don't you ask her?"

Dahlia narrowed her eyes and then sniffed. "Whatever. We're here. Ask her where to find Hope so we can get out of here."

Myrine yanked open the door.

"You should not be in such a hurry, Daughter of Eris. The discord you've sown still haunts you, yes?" Her white hair was pulled up into a bun, and gentle wisps framed Myrine's unlined face. But her blue eyes, normally bright and vibrant, were hooded. Guarded. She leaned against the doorframe.

Dahlia looked like she was ready to throttle the petite oracle.

"Is it time already?" Myrine asked. Stepping out of the doorway, she looked up at the gray skies still heavy with unshed moisture.

Xan shrugged and stepped to the side, out of the path of the oracle, as if she were a leper.

Of course he did. Myrine was acting weird, even for her.

"We want to find Hope," Athan said, drawing Myrine's attention away from the sky. "Do you know where she is?"

"Kitty, kitty, kitty, kitty." She shook her head as if trying to dislodge it from her neck.

Dahlia cleared her throat, and Athan shot her a warning look. They needed Myrine, and whatever she was doing might be part of getting into her spirit of prophecy.

"I'm going to sit in the bloody car," the daughter of Eris announced, and then she stormed off the porch muttering, "Stupid witch."

Athan glanced at Xan, who met his gaze with raised eyebrows.

Myrine sat in the rocking chair and started chanting to herself.

Athan strained to hear the words.

"Pussycat, where have you been? I've been to London to visit the—"

Xan crossed the porch in two strides and grabbed Myrine's arm. "Tell me where she is," he hissed. "Where can I find Hope?"

Her eyes rolled back into her head, and Myrine slumped in the chair, toppling forward.

Xan caught her before she fell to the ground. He scooped her up in his arms and looked at Athan. "Now what?"

Athan gritted his teeth. Xan certainly wasn't helping get Myrine to talk. "Let's take her inside."

Athan opened the bright-blue door and stepped into an immaculate cottage. The dark-stained hardwood floors were covered with braided area rugs, and a quaint table in the entryway held bright-yellow daffodils. He led Xan back into the living space, and Xan laid Myrine down on the plush beige couch.

"What happened to her?" Xan asked, running his hands through his hair. "Why'd she drop like that?"

"I don't—"

"She is not living," Myrine rasped as if she'd aged a hundred years. She sat up, her eyes glazed over as she stared at the wall. "Nor is she dead, but she sleeps soundly in a white clad bed. For you to find what your heart most desires will require strength you don't have, Son of the Liar. And not so fast, Son of Combat. You have no way to get to where she's at. Take those that are willing, those that will soothe, but remember this: To win you must lose." She dropped back onto the couch, and her eyes cleared. She met his eyes briefly and then turned away. "I'm so sorry, Athan. So, so sorry."

Her eyelids drooped, and she whimpered as she curled up in the fetal position. "Sorry, sorry, sorry."

Her body shivered and then relaxed into unconsciousness.

Athan stood rooted to the floor. His mouth gaped, and the panic that sped through his brain caused the words to crash into an incoherent mess.

"Is she for real?" Xan glared at the oracle and reached out as if to prod her.

"Stop." Athan choked on the word.

Xan's hand froze midair.

"She's for real." Athan's stomach clenched. Dread warred with frustration. Not alive, but not dead. There was only one place she could be. "I know where she is."

"Bloody Hades." Xan rocked back on his heels as he pointed to Myrine. "If that's true, then I know where she is, too."

The silence was interrupted by Myrine's soft snores. At some point, she'd told Athan that prophesying was exhausting. Something about the spiritual taxing the physical. Athan grabbed a blanket off the back of the couch and spread it over her small frame.

His mind reeled with the information. How could Hope have gotten to the Underworld alive? Only, somehow she wasn't alive? How could that be? What did it mean?

"Well?" Xan asked as he crossed his arms over his chest. "How are we going to get there? Can you open a portal?"

EIGHT

HOPE

THE STENCH OF earth, blood, and decomposition wasn't gone, and Hope knew she was still in the Underworld before she opened her eyes. However, the odor was less pungent, competing with the innocuous smells of lemon and rosemary. She was lying on something softer than the rocks at the banks of the river Acheron, and she sat up to see where she was.

Her vision swam and then settled on the god only a few feet away.

"You didn't have obols for passage?" Thanatos asked as he perched on the foot of the bed. "If you'd said something to me, I could've given you some."

"I didn't . . ." But she did know. She just hadn't thought about it. She ran her hand through her hair, and her fingers stuck in her tangled, golden locks. "Where am I?"

Thanatos stood. "My home."

Hope shuddered and then scooted to the edge. "I think I need to be going."

She stood. Her vision blurred, and she put her hand out to steady herself. "Please tell me I didn't drink any of that river."

Thanatos chuckled. "You did not. Although, I think it ironic that you know not to drink the water but you forgot payment for the ferryman."

Hope rolled her eyes. "I didn't think I would need to pay him."

"Why ever not?" he asked with raised brows.

She opened her mouth but thought better of her sarcastic reply. Instead, she mumbled a lame, "I don't know."

"Interesting." He stood and indicated a side door. "There is a bathroom there you may use. As well as bottled water from the mortal realm. I will have dinner brought up to you, if you'd like."

She waved him away. "I won't eat it."

He nodded. "Of course. Well then, I'll await you downstairs."

With that, the god of death left.

He was being awfully nice. But try as she might, she couldn't figure out why. And it didn't matter. He'd killed her mother. No matter how nice he was, she hated him.

It was amazing what a shower and clean clothes could do for a person. Hope smoothed the cotton T-shirt over her abdomen.

She dumped her dirty clothes in the garbage and left what she hoped was the guest bedroom behind.

Thanatos stood at the bottom of the stairs in a large foyer. The entire house was apparently the same rock as the rest of the Underworld, but the floor had been smoothed and polished until it looked like glass. The walls were marbled with a deep sapphire blue, and the chandelier dripped with cut crystals that scattered rainbows across the open space.

He was again dressed in a gray sweater and black jeans. Another figure stood next to him, and the two of them exchanged heated whispers. The god's dark hair fell over his eye, and he brushed it back in a youthful gesture. Thanatos met her gaze, and he dismissed the other person.

Thanatos smiled and pulled an orange crystal rose from behind his back.

Warning bells pealed in her head. Clasping her hands behind her, Hope warily returned the smile. "I don't normally accept gifts from the gods . . ." Like never.

He studied her as she descended. "You are angry at me?"

"You killed my mother." She cleared her throat of the emotion that came with the declaration. Just saying the words tore at her heart.

He pinched his lips and waited until she was at the foot of the stairs before responding. "If I did, I had no choice." He extended the flower toward her. "If you won't take a gift, consider it a loan."

It was such a ridiculous thing to say; she couldn't help the small smile that teased her lips. Even so, she refused to trust him. "I'm being rude, but I don't want to owe you anything."

"Yes. That's understandable. Your history with the gods, and what little you know of me, has been . . . unpleasant."

That was an understatement.

A tall figure rounded the corner, and Hope gasped. She dropped back into her standard defensive stance, wishing she had her knives. "Why are there *Skia* here?"

Thanatos straightened and waved the creature away. "You do realize you're in the Underworld?"

She watched the monster turn the corner and disappear the way he'd come. She took a deep breath of the stale air and grimaced. "But they're in your home. I thought they were minions of Hades."

"Ah. No. We each have our own, actually." He cleared his throat. "But you are my guest. No Skia will harm you here in my home. They all answer to me."

She contemplated her options for a moment. Leave or stay? Was he a liar or telling the truth? At this point she needed time to rest and regroup, and this might be her best option. Hope straightened. "All right then."

"Will you tell me your name?" Thanatos asked as he extended the flower to her; when she didn't take it, he shook it once. "A gift means that you won't owe me anything. I'm only trying to be a gracious host."

If he'd wanted her dead, he could've killed her already. Or had his Skia do it while she slept. As it was, he'd been only nice, and she didn't need to piss him off. She accepted the flower. "Hope. My name is Hope."

"A beautiful meaning, young lady. Shall we go into the library to talk?" He couldn't have chosen a more enticing invitation.

"Yes, but . . ." She didn't know how to set boundaries without being rude, but she didn't want him to get the wrong impression.

"You are my guest. That is all. No strings attached. You may leave when you want."

She wrinkled her brow in confusion. The gods were not this gracious.

"You are the first living . . . being to treat me as if . . . as if I were a person too. It is . . ." He pursed his lips as if weighing his words. "It is quite a pleasant change for me, my dear."

And he was the first god to make no demands, suggestions, or try to manipulate her in any fashion. At least not yet. She might pull this off after all. "I completely understand."

He extended his arm, an invitation for her to lead. "The study is the second door on the right. Are you sure I can't get you anything to eat?"

She shook her head. It didn't matter how nice he was. She would not eat or drink here. Even in the bathroom, she'd spit the water out when she brushed her teeth. "Thank you, though."

She opened the door, and her jaw dropped. The room was almost as tall as the Olympian library and possibly as deep. The shelves were cut from the same stone as everything in the Underworld, but again, it had been polished smooth. The books were shelved by color, ranging from deep red to vibrant purple. Two Skia were visible shelving several of the heavy tomes.

Hope forgot all about her host as she stepped into the room. A welling of emotion bubbled from her chest to her throat, and she reverently stroked the spines on the shelf. "They are the *Books of the Fates?"*

Thanatos came to her side. He pulled the nearest one from the shelf and opened the bright-orange tome. The parchment was so thin it was almost transparent, and Hope recognized the spindly scrawl. "This one always writes in a crisp and succinct manner. She doesn't use adjectives or adverbs. Sometimes she . . ."

The god of death was staring at her, his pitch-black eyes wide with wonder. "You've read the *Books of the Fates?"*

She may have revealed too much. "Our history."

He pulled several other books down, and while she was tempted to read them, sorely tempted, she refused to even glance at the three distinct scripts.

"Well, since I can't tempt you with *The Books,* why don't we sit down and you can tell me why you're here?" He shelved the green volume in his hand and indicated they return to the front of the room.

Thanatos pointed to two cigar chairs angled toward one another and waited for Hope to sit before taking the other.

"What brings you to the Underworld?" He reached over to the end table between them and proceeded to cut a cigar.

The last time hadn't gone so well. Hope bit the side of her mouth as she watched him and contemplated what to say.

"Do you mind if I smoke?" he asked.

She shook her head. It was his house. Who was she to protest?

"I'm guessing you're not trying to free your lover." He raised his brows.

She shook her head.

"And I doubt you're here on a dare, right?"

She couldn't help the forced exhale of incredulity. "People do that?"

He smirked. "Not so much anymore, but eons ago it wasn't so uncommon."

"That's insane," she said with a shake of her head.

He puffed on the cigar.

And she realized her own hypocrisy. "Right. I . . . I wanted to talk to my mom."

He exhaled, watching as the smoke floated into the vastness above them.

"I heard you can't lie in the Underworld. And that . . . well, truth will set you free. I want to know how to break the curse. Is it true? That you can't lie here?"

Thanatos sat up. With a flick of his wrist, a crystal ashtray appeared on the table, and he set the cigar down.

"The dead cannot lie; there is no reason for them to." He rested his elbows on his knees and leaned forward. "You are tired of being a pawn, yes?"

She nodded and whispered, "Yes."

"I am the agent of death, Hope. But I do not choose who will die. I'm sorry about your mother. But . . . I am a pawn, too." He stretched his legs out and leaned back in the chair. "Let's make sure it stops." He blew out a slow breath. "You are lucky *I* found you and not Hades. He's been trying to get you here to the Underworld for years."

"Why?"

Thanatos raised his eyebrows. "To be a pawn."

NINE

ATHAN

"Not by myself." He could contact his father. Hermes would be able to get them into the Underworld, but Athan just as quickly dismissed the idea. As much as he trusted his father, Hermes had made his feelings about Hope perfectly clear. And there was the risk that if Athan contacted him further, the other Olympians might find out. He definitely didn't trust the rest of the pantheon. "We'll need help getting through a portal, but once we're in we should be good."

At least he'd been in the Underworld enough to know his way around. Not that it would be easy. There were several areas they'd have to be especially careful of.

Xan scratched his chin and then grimaced. "Is that what she meant? One of us will have to die to get there? Is that how we're going to lose?"

Of course. That would be Athan's luck. But he pushed away the pessimistic musings. Myrine wouldn't send him to the Underworld only to be killed. But Xan had hit on something. "I doubt it. But that's a great idea."

"I'm not volunteering, just so you know."

Athan chuckled. The idea was solid. Death would lead them through a portal. "Let's go."

He pulled out his cell phone as they crossed the small house and let themselves out. Athan punched in one word and waited until several listings came up. "SOMC is only a few miles away."

Xan climbed into the driver seat, and Athan circled around to climb in the back.

"What happened with the witch?" Dahlia asked once the doors were closed.

Xan started the car and pulled out onto the quiet neighborhood street. "Which way are we going?"

Athan handed Xan his phone, and the app chirped directions at them.

"Where are we going?" When Xan didn't immediately respond, Dahlia poked his shoulder with a manicured fingernail. "Stop ignoring me."

Xan shot her a pointed look. "Hope's in the Underworld. We need to go watch someone die, so we can sneak in after them."

"Holy Mother Gaia!" Dahlia breathed. Her eyes dilated, and she shifted in her seat. "You're joking."

Xan shook his head.

Dahlia twisted around and faced Athan. "That's crazy. We're not going to try to sneak into the Underworld, are we?"

Hearing the words out loud did sound crazy. His thoughts went to Myrine's prophecy, and the slim likelihood of them all making it back alive. Even so, leaving Hope in the Underworld wasn't an option he could live with. "You don't have to come."

Xan snorted.

Dahlia's eyes hardened, and she pinched her lips together. "Are you saying I'm scared?"

If looks could kill, Athan would have a gaping hole in his chest while he bled out. It was quite possibly the worst thing he could've said to her.

"Nooo." He drew the word out for several seconds.

"Someone's going to die. Athan doesn't want to feel guilty." Xan met Athan's eyes in the rearview mirror.

"That's not . . ." Actually, that was exactly it. "It's just I know Hope doesn't mean as much to you—"

"Don't presume to know me well enough to tell me who means what. Especially to me. Arseface," Dahlia muttered the last word under her breath.

Xan chuckled.

This was going to suck on so many levels.

The silence in the car crawled over Athan, snaking its way through his gut. He wished he could shudder and wipe the discomfort away. But it wasn't going to get better. Not anytime soon.

"So, we're all going to the Underworld on a fieldtrip," Xan said. "Since Dahl and I haven't been before, do you want to fill us in? Do we need to bring anything special?"

Athan began to compile a list in his head. "We better stop and get a few things."

Xan pulled off to the side of the road and handed Athan his phone.

Athan tapped on the screen, and the small device piped out new directions for them.

They picked up backpacks and filled them with freeze-dried meals, beef jerky, energy bars, trail mix, and dried fruit. They each took a change of clothes and some toiletries and then stuffed every remaining crevice with pouches of drinking water.

There were many myths about the Underworld. Some were ridiculous stories, like Admetus getting out of dying by letting his wife take his place. Others were laced with half-truths, like Hercules borrowing Cerberus to complete one of his labors. But every single demigod and mortal knew if they ate or drank anything from that realm, their body would absorb the power of the Underworld and, with that, bind them to the realm of the dead, unable to leave without the help of a god.

Athan zipped up his bulging pack. "Here you go."

Xan took it and tossed it in the trunk. "Right. Is there anything else? I don't want to be caught in the Underworld with my pants down."

Athan raised his brows at the other demigod. "You have your blades?"

Xan gave a withering stare. "What do you think? I'm asking if we need to stop anywhere else? Do we need coins for passage or a doggie treat for Cerberus? Does Hades accept bribes? Does he have a favorite wine we could take him? Maybe some pomegranates for Persephone?"

Athan cringed. His pride took a hit with each of Xan's questions, but Athan had never dealt with the goddess of the Underworld. "I didn't think of that."

"Of course not." Dahlia leaned against the car. The wind lifted several dark curls from her ponytail, and they momentarily floated on the breeze. Her dark eyes were onyx, and she folded her arms over her chest.

He knew it was her natural instinct to cause strife. The power from her mother, Eris, would seep into her every action, unless she chose to check it. Athan took a deep breath and tried to release the tension with his exhale. He could be the bigger man. "I'm sorry."

Dahlia curled her lips. "Well, that's all right then. I'm sure being sorry will take care of everything you forget."

He balled his hands into fists as he clenched his teeth to prevent the words that wanted to spill out.

Before he could take a step forward, Xan stepped between them.

"This right here has to stop." He waved between the two of them. "You said the same thing earlier, Dahl. We're on the same team, so no more." He pointed at her. "No more. You hear me?"

"Fine." She leaned to the side, glaring past Xan to Athan. Her gaze shifted back to her cousin. "I'll be back in five."

Without waiting for a response, she stormed off across the parking lot toward the camping store.

Xan turned to Athan. "Don't be provoking her. Hope was her best friend. She's been pretty torn up."

Athan thought back to all the times he'd seen Hope and Dahlia together. They definitely had done things together and seemed friendly enough, but best friends? "So, why does she hate me?"

"She's never liked you since you played Obelia."

Guilt churned in his chest. He was never going to live that down. Yes, he'd been stupid, but his motives were good. "Then why did she yell at Obelia before we left the conservatory?"

Xan closed the trunk. He faced Athan and let out a slow breath. "Dahlia doesn't like you, but she has no respect for Obelia either. Obviously. And Dahl can hold grudges like no one I've ever met before. You know, contention and all that."

"I'm not trying to provoke her."

"Which probably makes it worse." Xan hitched his thumb at the store. "Let's go get her and then figure out what else we need afore we head to the hospital. I want to be as prepared as possible before we go declare war on the gods of the Under-world."

"We're not declaring war."

Xan stopped with a frown. "So says the man leading the invasion."

It wasn't really an invasion. They were going to get Hope back. From the Underworld. Where Skia lived. And Hades ruled. It was more like they were going . . . behind enemy lines. Which could be construed as an act of war. *Skata*!

Athan hurried to catch up to Xan.

They stopped at a temple and traded for several obols and drachma, coins that would buy them passage on Charon's ferry. They decided the beef jerky would be saved for Cerberus, although Athan didn't have much hope that it would actually help. Hades's pet was practically the size of a horse, and any one of his heads could consume all of their meat with one swallow. But the only other idea had been to kill the large dog, which Athan insisted was no way to garner favor with the gods there. As for Hades and Persephone, the demigods stopped at a large market and bought three of the goddess's favorite fruit, and Athan pulled out his change of clothes to fit the pinkish-red globes into his backpack.

He looked up to see Dahlia zipping her bag, her spare pants hanging out of the trunk.

With a shake of his head, Xan told Athan not to bring it up. Curious. But he heeded Xan's advice.

The sharp smell of disinfectant greeted them as they stepped through the sliding glass doors of South Olympian Medical Center. The lights reflected off the dark tile floor in bright cones. At the semicircular reception desk sat three women. A dark-haired, middle-aged woman sat behind the marble top, dressed in a mossy-green matching shirt and cardigan with a lanyard around her neck. The badge on the end of the black cord was flipped upside down, so only the back of her badge was visible. Her features were drawn into a grimace as she eyed her desk mates. The other two women were well into the winter of their years, with hair that matched their season. However, they leaned toward each other and giggled as if young school girls. Their cotton-candy pink jackets were clearly a uniform.

"He thinks she doesn't know. And you know she's going to take him for everything he has," one of the senior volunteers whispered.

"I haven't seen that episode—"

Xan cleared his throat. "Pardon, ladies."

TEN

HOPE

WHEN SHE AWOKE, there were two bottles of water and a package of beef jerky on the ornate nightstand. The canopied bed was draped in dark damask, but the sun neither rose nor set, so Hope didn't understand the need to curtain the bed. Nevertheless, she'd been so exhausted sleep descended swiftly.

But sleep fled as memories of Priska assaulted Hope. Anguish drove her to the bathroom as her physical body churned in protest of reality. Her stomach heaved, and Hope retched over the toilet bowl. When she rinsed her mouth of the sour taste of bile, Hope spit the water back into the sink. She wouldn't swallow anything here. Just in case.

"Did you sleep well?" Thanatos met her on the landing outside her room. The god of death was dressed again in soft grays and deep black, making his slight physique appear even thinner. His slicked-back hair curled around his ears.

She shrugged. "Yes and no."

He tilted his head as he studied her. "Do you want to talk about it?"

Did she? He was an impartial . . . He was a god. "No."

"May I give you a tour of the Underworld?"

His inflection made it sound like he was really making a request of her, but Hope reminded herself it may or may not be a real invite. Nevertheless, it would suit her purpose just fine. "Do you know where my mom would be?"

He paused mid-step. Without looking back at her, he continued down the stairs. As he got to the bottom, he said, "Come on; let's go."

She rested her hand on the door to her room and debated. But there really wasn't anything to debate. She had no one to trust, and at least at this point Thanatos was being . . . accommodating, if not kind. But she didn't trust him. "Okay."

"May I get you something for breakfast? Are you hungry yet?"

Hope closed her eyes. "Will you please stop? I'm not going to eat or drink anything here, so stop offering it to me."

Thanatos chuckled. "You have been well-warned, but that which is from the mortal realm will not bind you here. You have my word."

She leaned toward him and whispered, "Nothing personal, but I don't trust you or your word."

If Thanatos was offended, he hid it well. The only indication of his displeasure was the downturn of his lips.

She straightened. "Now, let's go see the Underworld."

His face cleared, and he extended his elbow.

Hope stared and then slowly brought her elbow up. Was this something she was supposed to know?

Thanatos chuckled. He grabbed her hand and tucked it into the crook of his arm. "You are mixing with a rough crowd if you don't recognize common courtesy."

She couldn't help the blush that spread from her neck to her scalp. Of course. "Well, Skia aren't usually so kind."

His dark gaze made her stomach flip.

"I was talking about the demigods you've been fraternizing with."

She opened her mouth to protest, but he held up his hand. "Please don't defend them. I will not agree, no matter what you say."

She exhaled and dropped her shoulders. "All right, let's go."

They passed several Skia working on various household tasks. One was sweeping the entryway, and another the steps outside the door. So weird to see the vicious killers cleaning.

Thanatos and Hope stepped out of the door, and the heavy, humid air slapped her in the face like a wet blanket. The darkness made the air feel thicker, too. Dense clumps of glowing spots on the rocks above allowed for visibility, much better than had been present at the River Acheron. It was more like dusk than actual night. The air smelled of dirt and loam, the musty stench of a garden shed closed up for too long.

Just outside the front door, in a large circular drive, sat an old buggy. Like from the Old West. Unlike the Old West, the contraption was hitched to a centaur. The creature's body was thick muscle covered in a mouse-gray coat that darkened to almost black on his legs and tail. Across his withers was a transverse strip of the same rich tone that inched up his human back. His skin was a similar pallor as Thanatos's, but the creature's chest and arms were built like a professional wrestler. His thick hair was pulled back with a leather strap, putting his blue eyes on full display.

Hope stopped moving, pulling Thanatos off-balance before he quickly recovered. She pointed to the monster, a deep sense of betrayal welling up from within.

"Did he enslave you?" she demanded of the centaur. If Thanatos had, Hope would kill him. Could you even kill a god? She was going to find out, because enslaving mixed breeds was not okay at all. Seriously—

Thanatos released Hope and clapped the horse-man creature on the back. "Asbolus, how are you, old friend?"

The centaur turned and swatted the god's hand away. "It won't work with her. She's not going to stay."

"Are you certain?" Thanatos asked, tilting his head to survey Hope.

"Quite," Asbolus replied. "But it is good you are doing this."

Hope opened her mouth to ask what was going on, but Thanatos beat her to it.

"Asbolus is an auger."

A seer? She briefly thought of Myrine.

"Are you good?" Maybe he could tell her what to do.

He nodded, the corner of his mouth pulling up into a smile. "I am very good. You should come speak with me before you leave."

Thanatos snorted. "Let's go take a look at the Underworld, shall we?"

He helped Hope into the small carriage then offered her a blanket.

She shook her head. "Is it always so warm?"

"Only because you are still alive, my dear." He set the blanket in a basket attached to the back and then took up the rest of the space on the bench seat. He glanced at his wristband, a device with several concentric circles, as he spoke. "Asbolus, let's start at the inner ring and end at the banks of the Acheron, if you please."

Asbolus extended his arms wide then tilted his head side to side, stretching his muscles. "Hold on," he warned.

The carriage lurched forward, the wheels bumping along the uneven ground as Asbolus trotted out of the gate. The drive was lined with black trees carved from the same stone as the house—in fact, the same stone as everything around them. But vibrant, polished gems hung from the dark limbs, making a lush, jeweled path. The emeralds and rubies glowed from the light, and Hope wondered how the dim lighting could make the precious stones glow.

Asbolus hit a large bump. Hope collided with Thanatos and then was thrown the opposite way, almost falling from the cart. She gripped the edge of the cab, trying to steady herself.

Thanatos held her with one hand and threw the other out in front of Asbolus. And just like that, the ride smoothed out; the bumps seemingly disappeared into the rocky ground. They were still there; she could see them, but somehow Thanatos had made the ride smooth.

When they left Thanatos's grounds, the landscape changed to a never-ending sea of black rock and dark mists, a phosphorus glow from above. Asbolus went from a trot to a canter, and a few minutes later the cart lurched.

The lighting brightened minutely, and the mists were more gray than black. Rock formations towered in the air, dotting the landscape with peaks. The air carried the smell of organic char, and Hope wondered what was burning.

A few minutes later, and another jolt, and the sky had more of the phosphorus glow than darkness. The light cast shadows on the ground, and only an occasional mist scuttled across the rocky ground. There was a distinctive smell of human-ness there.

And then the cab lurched again.

"Do you know where we're going?"

Hope had an idea. "Is all of the Underworld laid out in circles?"

Asbolus nickered a very horse-like laugh. "She's quick, Thanatos. Are you sure you know what you're doing?"

Thanatos frowned at the centaur. "Please stop."

He turned to Hope. "Yes. We are moving into the inner realms, the Fields of Asphodel, Elysium, and the Isles of the Blessed. We will stay in the Isles for only a moment, as those that live there are loyal to Hades. I would hate to have one of them report your presence to him."

"Is that where my mom is?"

Thanatos shook his head. "No. Very few make it to the Isles. They must be born three times and at judgment be granted entrance to Elysium every time to be eligible. The souls that are visiting have been born at least twice. If they are awaiting rebirth, they are servants to Hades or Persephone. All the ones that live there find ways to be of service . . . somewhere."

She knew the minute they lurched into Asphodel. Closing her eyes, she let the smell of people wash over her. She breathed in the air, and her eyes popped open. "Do the dead eat?"

Thanatos chuckled. "Only if they want. There is no need to, but some enjoy the taste."

"Can they get fat? Or too skinny? Can the dead change their body?"

Even Asbolus laughed.

"No," Thanatos answered with a wry grin. "There is no need. You are here as you've always seen yourself."

Asbolus slowed to a walk as they approached a city of dark rock. The buildings were hewn of the same stone as the street, the windows mere gaps in the stone but occasionally covered with fabric curtains.

"How do they get the curtains?" Hope asked as she glanced at the people bustling through the street. Some were dressed as if to go to an office job, while others sat outside a café sipping at large mugs. Two kids played in the street, a game of jumping and giggling with a ball tossing back and forth. They drove past an alley, and Hope caught glimpses of a large open market. "People just . . . live here?"

"What else would they do?"

Thanatos's question made Hope realize she'd never thought about it before. "So they keep on living?"

Asbolus nickered low in his throat. "They can't progress in everything, and some don't really even want to. They live their lives, but no opportunity for children or significant changes. Only the mind will change here."

The cab lurched again, and Hope's mouth dropped open.

The brightness was similar to late afternoon, the phosphorus light a warm glow that lit the rock above like it were the sky. The homes here were farther apart, with plenty of space for yards with fences. The trees were mostly carved from the stone, but they were beautifully done, with details of bark and leaves that almost looked real. The air was barely stale, more like a closed room than actual stagnation. The few people she saw were smiling, laughing, and chatting as they swept porches, polished rock, or in one case, as a man chiseled into a mountain-sized stone. "This is Elysium?"

Thanatos rested his hand on her arm. "Do you like it?"

"It's beautiful." It was like a harmonious community from a dream. She watched as a woman in a checkered apron carried a pie across the street and knocked on her neighbor's door. When the door opened two women embraced, and the one invited the other in. "Is it real? Do they really all get along?"

Thanatos smiled. "This is where the best of humanity end up."

Another lurch and the visual changes assaulted her. They were outside a stone wall, knee-high, where actual grass grew. On the other side of the lawn were orchards, tree boughs hanging low, heavy with fruit. The air smelled crisp with a faint scent of peach blossoms.

"Persephone's garden?" Hope asked. As if it could be anything else.

"And just beyond, Hades's castle." Thanatos pointed at the towering spires.

It was breathtaking. The dark surface of the castle had been buffed to a glossy shine. The light from above was almost at full noon, although there wasn't actually a sun in the sky. Hope closed her eyes, and the chirp of insects sang, confirming life existed in the Underworld.

The sound of a river running, splashing over stones, tickled her senses. She opened her eyes and turned to Thanatos. "Which river is that?"

He raised his brows. "It's the Lethe." Extending his hand to her, he asked, "Would you like to see it?"

ELEVEN

ATHAN

ATHAN FELT THE hair on the back of his neck rise, and he looked up from the faux wood grain to see Xan staring at him. The demigod raised his eyebrows, and Athan shrugged off the questions in Xan's weighted gaze. They were questions Athan had no answers for.

The three demigods were spread out in the wide room clearly meant for two patients. Dahlia lay across the empty bed, as if she were the patient meant to occupy it. Athan sat at the small table situated in the corner of the room. Xan had pulled the other plastic chair over by the bed next to his cousin, but his attention shifted from Athan to the patient in the bed next to them.

Their patient was tall, and if his emaciated frame had been filled out, he would've been a massive man. He was probably several inches over six feet, and a thatch of black hair stuck out from the white gauze on the top of his head. His entire face was wrapped in gauze, as was his left arm, but his right arm was covered in tattoos of snakes, and a jaw of teeth peeked out from the sleeve of the hospital gown.

According to the whiteboard on the wall, the patient's name was Kal Mustonen.

Athan stared at the patient and wondered how he'd gotten burned.

"I'm going to go keep watch," Dahlia said and then pointed to Athan. "You're next, pretty boy, so maybe rest up." She pushed Xan out of the chair and then dragged it outside the door and sat. "Let me know when it's time to go."

Xan closed the door and started pacing the room.

"Does it worry you?" Xan asked, stopping almost midstride to stare Athan down.

Athan refused to be intimidated. He leaned back in the chair, putting his hands behind his head. "Does what worry me?"

"What we're going to lose?" Xan whispered.

Athan glanced away. The thought had been nagging in the back of his mind ever since they'd left Myrine's. But it didn't matter. He steeled his heart. "Why don't you tell me what's worrying you? What is it that you fear losing?"

"Lots of things. My cousin." Xan nodded at the door. "I worry she won't come back or that she won't want to come back." He cleared his throat. "And I don't want to die."

"Then don't come. Both of you can stay here."

Xan's face hardened. "Do you hear yourself? Don't come?" He crossed the small hospital room in two strides and poked Athan in the chest. "You need me. That's what the oracle said." Xan shook his head. "Don't get fear confused with cowardice, Athan. I'm coming. I will do whatever is necessary to get her—"

"Are you saying I won't? You think I don't care just as much as you do?" Athan's anger simmered then boiled, and he clenched his hands, wanting so much to strike out. "Zeus and Hera! You should know—"

"Stop it!" Dahlia poked her head in through the doorway, cutting off their argument.

Silence fell except for the beeping heartbeat of the patient and the rattling of the respirator blowing air into the patient's lungs to keep him alive.

"You two have got to stop," she snapped. "Put whatever it is behind you and focus. This isn't the time for a bloody testosterone battle. Pull your heads out of your arses, both of you!"

Dahlia's gaze flitted back and forth between the two of them, her dark eyes swollen and red. "You need to work as a team, or there's no way we'll get her back." She shook her head. "I am not going to lose anyone else. So stop being ridiculous."

Xan snorted.

"Both of you," Dahlia added.

There was no way Athan was going to admit she was right. Every word she said was like a punch to the gut. Xan was strong and much better than Athan in a fight. And Xan's ability to outthink an enemy was better than any other demigod. Enemies and fighting were both certainties where they were going.

Xan had the decency to look abashed. His lips pulled up into a wry smile. "Sorry. You're right."

Athan felt his entire world shift in that small, sterile room. There was no way he'd heard that right. He looked to Dahlia, who confirmed the impossible.

"Of course I am, but that's not the point." She tugged on the loose curls around her shoulders. "You two need to get your stuff together. Neither one of you is everything we need." She looked at Athan. "Are you even sure you're up to going?"

No. Way. "You'd never be able to get there without me."

She acknowledged the truth of his statement with a frown. "And it has to be now?"

"It isn't going to get easier, Dahl." Xan sighed. "The longer we wait, the colder the trail will be."

Athan chuckled mirthlessly, and both of the other demigods stared at him.

"What's that supposed to mean?" Dahlia narrowed her eyes.

"There is no trail."

The beeping seemed to slow, and the wheezing took a laborious turn.

Athan didn't like to acknowledge this part, even to himself. But it was only fair for both of them to fully understand all the risks. "Once we get there. . ." He thought about Charon, the river Acheron, the Fields of Asphodel, and the likelihood of having to deal with Hades. "I don't know where she'll be, and

I don't know if I'll be able to track her there. I . . . I've never tracked anyone in the Underworld before."

"And you just now thought of telling us this?" Xan glared at Athan. "Now—?"

"Stop!" Dahlia's voice cut through the bickering. "Don't you know what happens?"

Xan stopped his death glare and looked at his cousin. "What happens when?"

Dahlia's shoulders sagged as if carrying an inexplicable weight. "Don't you know what happens when two kids fight over something?"

Xan bowed his head.

Dahlia looked from Xan to Athan, scowling at them both as if they'd committed a heinous offence.

Athan had never had a sibling or even a sibling-like relationship. Except briefly with Xan. But that hardly counted. She was making a big deal out of this.

Xan lifted his head, his eyes full of pain. "No one gets it."

"What?" It was an arrow to Athan's chest, and pain pulsed through him. He couldn't mean . . .

"When mortals fight over something amazing and there is a lot of ruckus"—Xan paused, looking at Athan as if to be sure he was following—"no one gets it. A god always takes it away; they swoop in and steal it. Like what happened with Helen of Troy."

Helen, daughter of Zeus, had been the most beautiful woman on Earth. Several men courted her, fought over her, and then an agreement was made. Of course, they hadn't consulted Helen, and she ran off with Paris. Battle ensued to get her back for her husband, Menelaus, the king of Laconia. Paris was killed in battle, allegedly, but when all the dust settled, Helen was taken to Olympus. The gods claimed it was to prevent further war.

Athan and Xan had talked about it years before, debating which god took her as consort. The gods were selfish like that.

Athan's stomach sank. They'd been there before. Years ago. With Isabel. No one got her. No, he corrected himself. Skia came, and she was now dead in the Underworld.

Athan nodded. "I get it." All the fight spilled away with the words. He wouldn't fight with Xan. Not over Hope. All that mattered was getting her back. One glance at Xan and Athan knew he felt the same.

"Good," Dahlia whispered. "Whatever's between you two stops now. You're going to have to have each other's backs. Once everyone is home safe, then you can unleash your testosterone and strut around like peacocks, okay?" Her anger had disappeared, and her voice was filled with something akin to resignation.

It was so odd that Dahlia, daughter of the goddess of strife, had put an end to their dispute. Odder still was the shifting of her carriage. Dahlia always looked like vengeance was about to be unleashed. Pride usually exuded from her very being. But minute by minute, the warrior girl looked like a flower wilting.

"Okay, Dahl, deal." Xan held out his hand. "Truce?"

Athan took a deep breath. The smell of decay filled his nostrils. Death was close. With no enthusiasm, but knowing the wisdom of Dahlia's words, he put his hand in Xan's and shook. "Truce."

Dahlia snorted, and a spark of her old fire flared. "Are we ready to go?"

The beeping of the machine grew slower and slower. The wheezing breaths rattled with the impending inevitability.

"Are you sure no one is going to pop in afore he crosses over?"

Athan shook his head. He wasn't sure. But it was extremely unlikely. And this was their best shot. "There was no next of kin listed."

The shadows in the corner shifted, the grays deepening into the inky murkiness of the Underworld.

Silence. Then the startling ringing of an alarm. A small, white light on the wall flashed, and then over the speaker in the hall came a panicked voice announcing a code green.

The darkness pulsed, and the rancid smell of the Underworld oozed from the shadows.

Rushed footsteps outside passed by the door, but no one entered. There must be a more pressing emergency than this expected death.

The smell intensified, even as the center of the shadow blackened. A tarry pitch spread, dripping its darkness into the void of a portal.

"Oh, gods, that smell," Dahlia muttered.

Figures emerged from the shadows. Two and then three and then three more. But still more came. The unnatural sallowness of their skin announced the harbingers of death. The creatures were all sizes, wearing the telltale leer, and each one of them holding black blades of death.

Athan froze. His heart, his thoughts, his hands all motionless as death moved toward him.

They were outnumbered. It would be a massacre. Flashes of the pain he'd endured quickened his pulse. His hands, slick with sweat, fumbled to grip his own immortal blades. And even though his mind screamed at him to move, his body was frozen, his fight-or-flight overridden by sheer terror.

Xan swore, and then suddenly he and Dahlia were in front, blocking the path of the Skia.

Xan dodged and countered with the same practiced movements Athan had seen a hundred times. Only so much faster. Xan was a blur of fury, and he stabbed and punched and kicked without pause.

Bursts of bright light indicated the death of a Skia, and Xan seemed to wield a sparkler. Dahlia moved beside him. She grunted and swore at the creatures as she struck with her blades.

It was only seconds later that he heard the demigod son of Ares yell, and the silver blade with the ruby hilt was pulled from a shadow-demon's chest. Light erupted from the gaping wound. Athan turned away.

And faced a demon of his own. Athan stepped back, and the Skia opened his mouth in a rasping chuckle.

With a deep breath, Athan brought his blades up and faced his attacker. He couldn't fail, or Hope would die.

The demon swung wildly as he advanced. Athan stepped back in an arc that brought him behind the Skia. Athan stabbed the creature in through the ribs and spun to meet the next one.

This one, too, drove forward, his movements jerky and uncertain. Athan leaned back, dodging a swipe at his face, and then stepped in close to stab the demon in the stomach. He pulled the weapon out, and it released with a wet sucking sound, making Athan cringe.

He turned to see Xan wiping his blades and Dahlia engaged with the last spawn of Hades. She blocked a jab with her forearm then shifted in toward the Skia. Her arm came back, and she pushed her dagger into the demon's chest.

She spun back and hissed with a shake of her arm.

The golden hilt inscribed with Eris's apple of discord stuck out from the monster's chest. Light seeped around the sides of the blade.

Metal clanged to the floor, followed seconds later by another.

Hades's minion opened his mouth in a silent scream as the light devoured him.

"Bloody Hades," Xan swore and pushed Dahlia over to Athan.

Dahlia stooped down and grabbed her immortal weapon from the floor.

The dark blades of the Skia faded until they, too, were no longer in the mortal realm.

"A little heads-up would've been nice, Athan. Are there always so many?" Xan asked as he sheathed his knives.

"I've never seen Skia when we escort the dead," Athan responded. Was it because his father was with him, or was there something more?

Xan shrugged, dismissing the matter as he stepped over to his cousin. "Are you all right?"

Athan ignored them and turned to assess the rest of the room.

There by the bed stood an apparition of a man. He was tall and solidly built. He wore slacks and a short-sleeve, button-down shirt. His left arm was badly scarred, as was his neck and the left side of his face. His left eye was cloudy, as if injured, but his right eye was so dark it was almost as black as his thick hair. He would've once been considered handsome, but the scarring had affected his angular features, making him pitiable. The front of his yellow shirt had three holes and was scorched on the ends. Shot and burned.

The man blinked as if in disbelief as he stared at the three demigods, and his gaze shifted to the floor and back. Behind him lay the inert figure of his mortal body, now still in death.

"He's dead."

"Of course they're dead," Dahlia shot back. She examined her sleeve, pulling back the black stretchy fabric to expose her arm. With a frown, she yanked the sleeve down and turned to

Athan. "You've really got to get yourself together. We can't afford—"

"No, the man . . ." Athan looked to the portal. The gaping blackness leading to the Underworld was slowly sinking in on itself. "*Skata!*"

Grabbing Xan and Dahlia, he moved to the darkness.

"What the Hades, Athan? Don't run me into the wall!" *Dahlia bounced off the portal. She put* her hand out to steady herself, and it rested through the darkness on to the wall of the hospital room. "What's wrong with you?"

He had only seconds to figure it out, and his mind ran with the implications.

"Come here." He waved at the dead man's soul.

"Who are you talking to? Oh, oh! You can see him?" Dahlia pointed at the still body on the bed.

The spirit hesitated, his glance darting from one demigod to the next.

Athan reached out and grabbed the man's arm, but he flinched and pulled away. Athan had grabbed the burned one. "Sorry," he said to the man and pointed at his tattooed wrist. The man extended it, letting Athan grab hold. "Xan, Dahlia, come here."

Xan frowned. "I can't even see what you're holding. Am I supposed to touch him, too?"

Athan had no idea. He'd always been with his father when he escorted the dead to the Underworld.

"Just hold on to me." He pulled the dead man and pushed him toward the portal. The man stumbled, clumsy in his movements. Perhaps there were more injuries his clothes were hiding.

The man glanced back at his body, his mouth working in silent protest.

Why would he want to go back? No one had been to see him in the week since he'd been admitted, according to the volunteers.

Athan pulled and pushed, until the man's leg was swallowed up in the blackness, followed by his torso.

Dahlia slid her grip down Athan's arm until she was holding his wrist, just above where he was grasping the dead's arm.

She inched forward with her foot, and her leg disappeared into the inky darkness.

"Shite." Xan let go of Athan's sleeve and stepped back. Emotions warred across his face, and then he moved forward, extending his hand to where his cousin was being sucked into the void.

But his hand didn't disappear; instead, there was a *thunk* as it rapped against the thin hospital wall.

"I told you to hold on," Athan said as he stepped toward the portal.

Dahila passed through the veil, standing in the barren waste of the in-between.

The man pulled against Athan's grip.

"Are you coming?" Athan wished Xan would accept defeat and stay behind. Dahlia was just about as tough as her cousin. Surely they weren't both necessary.

Xan gritted his teeth.

"If you're scared, you can stay behind. I'm sure we'll be fine." And Athan meant it. If Xan wasn't fully engaged, it would be more dangerous for all of them.

"You'd be daft not to have fear." Xan grabbed Athan's shoulder and shoved him forward. The two men stumbled through the portal and into the Underworld.

The cool air hung heavy with the stench of rot. Dark mists shifted and scuttled over the firm, barren ground. Pale phosphorous light danced across the rocks. Desperate moaning carried on a slight breeze. The barren waste was washed in gray.

"Bloody Hades." Dahlia covered her nose. "Is it all like this?"

"Where next?" Xan asked as he dropped Athan's arm.

Athan took a deep breath, letting the ache of the Underworld fill him. He pushed his mind past the crumbling decay surrounding them and searched for the lapping water from the river Acheron. A shriek from Tartarus splintered his concentration, but he'd felt the pull.

"It's this way." He hesitated, fighting the despair in the mists, before blinking his eyes open.

Dahlia stood next to Xan, rubbing her forearm through a split in the black fabric. Her wide eyes scuttled over their bleak surroundings.

"Did you get cut?" Athan asked.

Xan froze.

"No. No. It didn't break the skin. It's fine." The words spilled out, and her gaze darted between the two demigods. "I'm fine."

Athan acknowledged her with a nod. "Okay then, let's roll."

The dead man pulled from his grasp and, without any direction, shuffled into the mists.

TWELVE

HOPE

SHE PUT HER hand in his cool one, and he tucked it back into the crook of his arm. They strolled through the garden and down a stone path.

Another wall greeted them, this one chest-high with shards of broken crystals lining the top. "Why is it blocked off?"

Thanatos pointed to a wrought-iron gate. He pulled a ring from his pocket and selected an old key from the countless ones there. Inserting it into the lock, he twisted, and the clang of the metal lock withdrawing screeched in her ears.

"It is the Lethe."

The river of lost memories. Those that drank of its waters would allegedly forget.

She walked through the gate and looked down the steep hill to the river below. Liquid diamonds splashed over the dark rocks, prisms of light dancing within the water. The air was cooler, crisp and clean, and it pulsed with promise of new possibilities.

"It's beautiful," she breathed. She stepped toward the river, and Thanatos grabbed her arm.

"Let's use the steps, shall we? The hill is quite steep, and you definitely don't want to fall in."

She followed him down the stone stairs, her gaze wholly absorbed on the dancing rainbows, and bumped into him when he stopped at the bottom. "Sorry."

He turned and faced her, his proximity making her breath catch.

"No need to apologize, Hope." His smile softened the sharp angles of his face, making him look human. Almost.

She stepped back.

"Do people really drink from there?" She pointed to the water, hoping to direct his penetrating gaze elsewhere.

He obliged. "Yes." His gaze went up the river toward a large mountain. The river seemed to come out from underneath the towering rock. "My brother lives there in that cave. Do you see?"

"Hypnos."

He chuckled. "Yes. It's fitting, really. He is the god of sleep, but dreams have the potential to dredge up unconscious memories. He will drip some of the river into an individual's mouth if the memory is too painful."

"He can do that?"

"You don't think it's right? He helps them let go of their pain. It is a mercy."

She shook her head. It was like stealing a part of a person's mind. "I get that some people have bad memories and things"—she thought of her mom, Apollo killing his sons, Skia attacking Athan—"but that's wrong. And the dead can come here and drink from the Lethe? Isn't that like giving up a part of who you are?"

He took a deep breath. "You are still young and perhaps a bit . . . idealistic. For some, the burdens are so many they actually consume them. This allows souls eternity without having to carry those burdens anymore."

He squatted at the river's edge and dipped his hand in the water, cupping the liquid in his palm. "One drop can erase a recent memory, if someone had been murdered or worse. A cupful would eliminate several days, possibly weeks depending on the mind. The more a person drinks, the more they would forget. Some choose to drink away the pain of hurt, betrayal, or loss with the water of the Lethe. But it is only an option to those who can make it to the banks of the river."

The river flowed only in certain parts of the Underworld. "So only those who live a life worthy of Elysium or the Isles can drink of it?"

"It is a privilege." The water trickled from his hand. "Don't judge others whose shoes you have not walked in. You know not what pains them."

Guilt stabbed her. She was being a hypocrite. "Of course."

She reached out and let a drop from Thanantos's palm fall into her hand. The water was delightfully cool, and desire to lick it pulsed through her. It wasn't just desire. No, the longing became a craving and then morphed into a need. She needed to drink it, to wash away the horror of Priska's death. She raised her hand . . .

Thanatos emptied his palm and then grabbed her wrist, twisting it to release the single drop back into the water.

"I guess you have some pain you'd like to be rid of after all?"

Hope shook her head, not in denial, but in an attempt to clear it. "Why did it do that? Why did I suddenly want to drink it so bad?"

Thanatos gazed out over the wide river. "It measures your pain and makes you want to consume an amount equal to your anguish. Don't touch it unless you plan to drink."

Hope stepped away from the bank of the river. "I'll remember that."

Thanatos extended his elbow, but Hope suddenly wanted to distance herself from the god, and she swept past him to the stairs.

They rode at a more leisurely pace back through Elysium. Hope asked if her mother was there, but the god of death only shook his head.

They crossed into the Fields of Asphodel, and at the slower pace, the area reminded Hope of downtown Seattle. It was crowded, busy, and loud. She again asked about her mother, and again Thanatos shook his head.

Which left only the Isles of the Blessed or Tartarus. But when she asked Thanatos, he yet again shook his head.

By the time they arrived back at his home, darkness had descended and frustration drove her from the open carriage and to her room.

When Hope got out of bed the next morning, her head spun. Her dry tongue felt like sandpaper to her parched lips. Two bottles of water sat on her bedside table, taunting her, and in addition to the package of beef jerky, there were now two chocolate bars. She didn't even like chocolate, but she picked up the bars and smelled them.

"Hope?" Thanatos's muffled voice came through the door. He tapped at the wood.

She shuffled to the door, holding the wall, just in case.

"Coming," she choked out, horse and indecipherable. She tried to clear her throat, but there was nothing to clear. Her stomach churned, and the floor started to rock. She was going to pass out, and she mentally braced for the impact.

"Foolish girl," Thanatos whispered as he caught her. He carried her to her bed and then sat beside her. "You are still living." He grabbed a water bottle, uncapped it, and extended it toward Hope.

She tried to shake her head, but it lolled to the side.

"Find something else to be obstinate about," he said, as he dribbled water over her lips.

She closed her mouth before the liquid could pass. She would not be damned.

Thanatos growled, and the sound rumbled in her ear.

"I swear on the River Styx that this is from the mortal realm. It will not bind you here." Thanatos lifted her head and held the plastic bottle to her lips.

He could be lying, but even if he were, she needed the water. Greedily, she gulped the first bottle down. Her stomach flipped, but the water stayed down. "Gods, I'm so stupid."

Thanatos didn't argue with her. He held out the second bottle. "Drink it all. I'll go get you more. And eat that dried meat, or at least suck on it. You need the salt."

Just before he closed the door, he glanced over his shoulder at her. An entire storm brewed in his eyes.

The door clicked shut, and Hope closed her eyes. Her mind was just alert enough to scream in protest. The gods didn't do favors. What did Thanatos want with her?

"Feeling better?" Thanatos held out another bottle of water.

Hope pushed him away and scooted to the edge of the bed. She needed to use the restroom . . . right now. "I'll be right back."

The bathroom was all black and crystal. On the polished counters was another clean set of clothes, a faded vintage T-shirt and jeans. As she washed her hands, she wondered how the god of death knew what size she was. Or even what styles to get. She poked her head out of the door. "Do you mind if I shower?"

He raised his eyebrows. "Be my guest. I'll be downstairs in the study." He set the bottle of water down next to two additional sealed ones and a basket of packaged snacks. "Be sure you eat something, too, please."

It was the *please* that touched her heart. Because even if he was trying to use her, he was being so kind about it.

"I'll be down shortly." She closed the door and continued to let her questions flow through her mind. She did feel better, only weak, and food would take care of that. Could she starve to death in the Underworld; was that possible? How long had she been here? What could the god of death want with her, a cursed monster?

When she was clean, dried, and fed, Hope made her way to the study, only flinching when she passed several Skia, but they completely ignored her. She wanted to trust Thanatos, but could she?

He stood as soon as she entered. Crossing the polished floors, he stopped in front of her and clasped her hands. "You gave me quite a scare. Even cursed, you have physical needs, something we will need to bear in mind."

"How do you get the food and water?"

A slow smile spread across his face, and his dark eyes twinkled. "Hermes is not the only psychopomp. I'm quite pleased that hoarding a few mortal items has paid off, and my Skia help when I need them to."

She pulled at the T-shirt. "And the clothes?"

He shook his head. "They are clean. I promise."

Something told her she didn't really want to know.

"Come sit down," he said, pulling her toward the plush chairs. "You will take a day or two to recover from your self-imposed fast, I reckon."

Self-imposed fast. Right. "Can I die here?"

Thanatos tilted his head as if considering her question. "I honestly don't know. I looked for your *Book of the Fates,* hoping there was a copy here, but I can't find it. I've asked the Moirai to grant me an audience, but they haven't responded yet." Irritation flashed across his face. "I need to know the terms of your curse to be able to answer that."

He'd asked the Fates for an audience, but they hadn't attended him? Did he know about her mother? What about her grandmother? The biggest question, and the one most pressing, was whether or not she could trust him. And she had no idea. But did she even have a choice? She had no other options. None.

"My great-grandmother was the daughter of a shepherd and the goddess, Hera."

Thanatos sucked in a breath, and his eyes darkened. "Hera is the goddess of marriage and fidelity. If you don't want to tell me, fine. But, don't lie to me."

THIRTEEN

ATHAN

THE MISTS SKITTERED and rolled over the dark rock at their feet. Misery mixed in the dark vapor, scuttling over their shoes and legs, a tangible emotion with spindly limbs. Unease crawled over Athan, an itch just under the skin that refused to relent. The sulfuric stench of rotten eggs clung to them, and the sound of lapping waves was louder, yet they still hadn't reached the Acheron.

Several hours later, Athan called for a rest.

"Please tell me we're almost there." Dahlia's eyes were wide, her face glistening with moisture.

Odd, it wasn't hot in the Underworld as many humans thought hell would be. Not that it was cold either. The dank, musty air was warm but barely uncomfortable.

"We should rest," he said. Athan thought back to the other times he'd been in the Underworld with his father. Had it ever taken this long to get from a portal to the River? He pulled the dead man's sleeve. "Stay here with us."

The apparition narrowed his eyes. Amongst the mottled scar tissue from his burns, an angry scar ran from his temple to his jaw. His mouth opened, but whatever argument he had was lost to them in silent movement.

"Your voice is lost until judgment," Athan told him.

The man flipped him off and then sat, the lower half of his body disappearing into the thick vapor.

"It looks like your charisma doesn't carry to the dead." Xan chuckled to himself, as he swung his pack to the side and pulled out a pouch of water. With his teeth, he tore the corner and began to drink.

Athan wanted to flip *him* off. "I guess not."

But it was more than that. There was something dark about this man's life force. Something that made Athan uneasy.

Dahlia wiped her sleeve across her face. "Do you guys feel that?"

She pointed at the haze moving across the barren landscape.

Xan paused, holding the pouch of water inches from his mouth. "Feel what?" He kicked at the mist, and his pack swung forward. The vapor swirled away from his boots, exposing the packed gray earth. "What do you feel?"

Dahlia shrugged her pack off her back and set the canvas bag on the ground. She fumbled to open the side pocket, the zipper snagging on the fabric.

"Bloody Hades," she swore, her voice cracking with emotion. She tugged at the corner of a water packet. As the pouch broke free of the pack, she stumbled back and landed on her butt.

"Shite!"

"I'm fine." But the warble in her voice betrayed her lie.

Athan extended his hand. He'd let her keep her pride. "Of course."

Her skin was cold and clammy, and he could feel her desperation and fear.

She snatched her hand back. With a swallow, she rubbed at the skin through the broken fabric. Her normally warm, russet skin was a blotchy gray around the tear. "I said I'm fine."

Athan's protest died on his lips as Xan stepped up next to them and whispered, "I'm not worried that Dahlia fell. She could kick your arse any day, pretty boy." He pointed to where Dahlia's pack had dropped into the mist. "Something's not right."

The dark eddies covered any trace of the bright orange fabric of her pack. Dahlia leaned over to grab her bag, but her hand swung through the haze and came up empty. "What the—?"

"It's gone."

Dahlia's hand sunk into the darkness, and she shuffled around in circles until she was far away from where she'd dropped the pack. Athan stooped low and joined her, his own pack making his movements awkward and unsteady.

"I said it's gone." Xan pointed at the center of their search area. "As soon as you let go, it disappeared."

Athan stood and pushed back the panic crawling in his chest. "It's okay. It's okay." They'd just need to ration more strictly.

Dahlia stood, her shoulders slumped in defeat. She wiped at her face again. "Bloody Hades."

Xan wrapped her in a hug. "It's fine, Dahl. We can get by on a little less."

Exactly what Athan was thinking. Not that big of a deal.

Her dark curls covered her face as she buried her head in Xan's chest. "I'm sorry."

There was something so wrong about watching Dahlia cower. Worry gnawed at his heart. "Do you want me to take you back?"

He wasn't even sure how to get back at this point, but there was no doubt Dahlia had been injured by the Skia blade. He had no idea how the wound would fester here in Hades's domain, but Athan wasn't going to take chances. He couldn't live with anyone else dying.

Dahlia seemed to move in a blur. She was away from Xan and holding Athan by the front of his shirt in the blink of an eye. "Are you saying I'm not good enough to be here? Do you think I'll slow you down?"

Athan drew back from her vehemence. "I . . ."

He looked at Xan, but the son of Ares just shrugged. Great. Of course the war god's son wouldn't help.

Athan took a deep breath. "I know that blade touched your skin."

"Bloody hell!" Xan surged forward and grabbed Dahlia's sleeve. Before either of them could protest, he poked his fingers through the tear in the fabric and ripped it through to the hem. His thumb ran over her skin, and then he glared at Athan. "It's fine. What are you talking about?"

Athan looked at his companions, and pointing at the ashen skin of Dahlia's forearm he asked, "You can't see it?"

Xan shook his head even as worry crept over his features. His gaze went to his cousin, and he tugged on her arm.

Dahlia said nothing, but grimaced when he brushed over the wound again.

Athan pulled her arm away from Xan. Cradling it, Athan ran his fingers over the dusky patch of skin. The cold bit at him. Searing pain like a Skia blade stabbed at his fingertips, and he jerked away.

Dahlia flinched and pulled the ends of the fabric together. "It's not broken."

He pinched his lips together. Strange. "But you can feel it."

She nodded.

He let out a slow breath. "I can feel it. Somehow it's in your skin. Just as if he'd cut you."

She nodded again.

"Shite!" Xan pushed Athan out of the way. "Seriously? Why didn't you say something?"

She gritted her teeth and set her shoulders. "Because I wasn't going to skive out on you. We're here for Hope. I'm fine. I'll be fine." She looked around the darkness and pointed into the mist. "That gormless arse is wandering off, Athan. Go get him, and let's go."

Athan jogged after the apparition, even while something about Dahlia's words nagged at him. The dead man continued to pick up the pace, and Athan had to push himself to keep the man in sight. Thoughts turned to panic. If the man escaped, there was no way they'd get across on Charon's ferry. He pushed himself harder, going from jog to run, to an all-out sprint when the man disappeared into the blackness.

The sounds of waves lapping against a shoreline grew, and the ground seemed to crumble beneath Athan's feet. He tripped forward and stumbled, barely catching himself before he fell into the water.

They had arrived at the Acheron.

Death smelled like overripe fruit and mold. A bitter tang wafted off the river, causing an ache of despair to swell in his chest. Athan stepped away and looked around.

There, in the swirling mists, were dozens and dozens of dead milling around at the water's edge. The color leached from their skin, their paleness much like a Skia's, but their eyes lacked the total blackness of Hades's minions. If that weren't enough, the confusion, worry, and in some cases fear etched on their features eased any concern about them being Skia.

Expressions were the only way to determine what they were trying to communicate. Some looked to be pleading; others emanated anger. Somehow the apparitions were corporeal to one another. Two men shoved a third toward the water's edge.

Athan watched as the man stumbled into the river, his face morphing from anger to horror. Hands, dozens of them, broke the surface. Bony fingers, meaty hands, scrawny arms . . . all the same pallid color, clamoring, reaching for the dead man's soul. The water surged, and bodies crawled over top of one another. Gruesome creatures, once human, clawed at anything in their way as they tried to pull the man into the water.

Athan's stomach turned.

The apparition's mouth opened in a silent scream as he struggled to free himself.

The water surged again. A bald head broke the surface. Loose skin flapped over his ear, the bone of his skull punctured through, with gray matter oozing from the wound. His emaciated frame pulsed with power in a stark contradiction to his physical appearance. The zombie-like monster opened his mouth, revealing rotten, broken teeth. The flesh from one hand was gone, only the bones remaining, and the other hand was nothing more than a stump of rotting meat. The creature leaped and wrapped around the man. The water-demon's broken arm encircled the doomed man's neck, and he brought his mouth down in a hard bite below the ear. Black blood spurted, and the frenzy of river creatures surged.

Athan dropped to his knees as he retched. He closed his eyes, the splashing waves the only indication of the violence ensuing in the river. The bitter smell of ash singed his nostrils. He looked at the ground, only to see round river rock washed smooth over eternity. The rocks were darker underneath, darker with moisture from the river Acheron.

He jerked up and saw Xan's face washed with revulsion. He brought his hand to his mouth and turned away. If Xan couldn't take it, Athan knew he couldn't either. Keeping his eyes on Xan's back, he moved toward the other demigods.

Glancing at Dahlia, he cringed. Her head was tilted to the side, her eyes narrowed and her lips pursed.

A heavy splash came from behind, and Athan scurried forward.

"What the Kracken are those?" Xan faced Athan and glanced back at the river. "Are those zombies? Hera and Zeus. And what were they eating? Was it one of the dead?"

Weird. "You could see those sea-zombies, but you couldn't see what they were eating?"

Xan raised his eyebrows. "That's what I said." He turned to Dahlia. "Could you see what they were eating?"

She shrugged and pinned Athan with a glare. "You've never seen them before?"

Athan opened his mouth to respond, but Xan beat him to it. "Don't go swimming, Dahl."

Her glare shifted to her cousin. "At least I can swim."

No way. They were in the Underworld, at the banks of the river of death and . . . "You still can't swim?"

Xan rolled his shoulders, but the feathering tic in his neck gave him away. "I really never thought it would come to this."

Athan chuckled. "Don't fall in."

Dahlia snorted. "For real."

"I wasn't planning on it," Xan muttered. "Is our dead guy around here?" He waved his hands, and a few spirits flinched as he moved through them.

Athan scanned the crowd now milling around with somber faces. The hostility had faded, but anxiety pulsed off them as their gazes darted to the river. He glanced through the pack of deceased trying to find their patient, but couldn't . . . Ah, there he was. Holy. Hades. What was he doing?

"Do you see him?"

Athan closed his eyes and swallowed. He glanced back at the river and cringed. "Yes. I see him."

His palms tingled, and he met Xan's gaze. With a wave Athan said, "He's over there."

Athan watched Xan's features morph into incredulity.

"He's at the bloody river?" His narrowed gaze went from Athan to the river and back again. "For real? Do the dead not see . . . that . . . those zombies?"

Athan nodded. "Yes, they can see them."

Xan's pale skin blanched further. "I'm so glad I can't touch the dead."

Right. There must be something seriously wrong with this man's soul for him to be drawn to the river.

FOURTEEN

HOPE

HOPE HELD UP a hand. "I still have my *Book of the Fates.* Remember how I recognized that handwriting? That's why. And that's why you can't find it here. It's in a hotel room in the mortal realm, where I left it."

She couldn't believe she had left it, the statue of Hecate, and all of her possessions in the dingy hotel room. How long had Priska paid the bill for? Gods, what if it was stolen?

"You have your *Book of the Fates?*" He nodded as if accepting what she'd told him. "And you are of the lineage of Hera?"

Hope nodded in confirmation. "Phoibe refused Apollo's advances, and on the night she gave birth, he showed up and cursed her offspring, then killed her and her husband. Phaidra was her daughter. She was the Sphinx in Egypt, Thebes, and everywhere else that had Sphinxes. She made a bargain with the Graeae, which is how we have our human form, except on the new moon, when Apollo placed the curse, or if we are on the land where he placed it. But I don't know if that is all of Europe or just ancient Greece. I've only ever been in North America."

Thanatos leaned toward her. "And what fulfills the curse? Why does Apollo have the Sphinx killed?"

"It has to do with what constitutes a family. Way back when Apollo killed Phoibe, a family was a husband, wife, and their children. If we refuse Apollo and marry someone else then have children, making a complete family, it fulfills the curse. I want to find a way to break it. I don't want to have my choices limited just because some god got thwarted. It's ridiculous."

"Yes. I could see why you would feel that way."

Disbelief made her frown. "You understand?"

The god of death stood, towering over her. Anger flashed in his eyes. "Do you think you are the only one affected by curses? Even gods can be bound if enough power is exercised. Think of Cronus in Tartarus. Do you think he voluntarily went there? He would love to escape, but he is bound by the power of the gods. Do you think I enjoyed killing your mother? I. Had. No. Choice."

Her mind raced as she put it together. "You are bound?"

"I serve Hades." He sat back down, almost collapsing in on himself. "And yes, I am bound."

Sympathy pulsed through her chest. She'd never even considered that the gods could be bound. Or that they wouldn't like it. Of course they wouldn't like it. Who would? "Are you trying to break your curse?"

He took a deep breath and squared his shoulders. "One day, my dear, I shall. And it will be glorious."

That was exactly how she felt.

"So how are you to break your binding to Apollo?" Thanatos relaxed back into his seat. He rubbed his hands together as he studied her.

"I don't know." Hope explained how she'd gone to the temple of Artemis, the conservatory, read a few *Books of the Fates,* and then had put together that she needed to come here. "None of my mother's history is recorded, and you said yourself that the dead can't lie. I need to know what I can do to break the curse, and everything has pointed to coming here."

A dark curl fell across the god's forehead, and he brushed the ebony lock back from his face. "I will help you. Together, I'm confident, we can see an end to this."

She should have been ecstatic with his declaration, but a foreboding sense of unease unfurled in her belly. Hope pushed the worry away. It was only because of what he'd done to her mother. Of course distrust lingered.

Over the next two days—that was how Hope preferred to think of the time she was awake, although she had no way to measure time—she and Thanatos discussed every detail of her understanding of the curse. Not being able to reference her *Book of the Fates* was incredibly frustrating, and there were a few times she had to admit a dead end. When she wasn't with the god, she would sneak into the library and read the *Books of the Fates* from others who'd been cursed. But no matter how many she read, she still hadn't found a way around a god's binding.

She ate prepackaged food until she couldn't stand to look at a granola bar or fruit cup, and even beef jerky and canned chicken held no appeal. But the food and fluid had done their trick, and she felt strong and energized once again.

Hope sat in bed, counting the days on her fingers again and again. Even if time moved slower in the Underworld, she should've changed by now.

When she brought it up to Thanatos, he looked like he'd won the lottery. "I was wondering about that, too. I had my suspicions, but I didn't want to give you false hope."

She tried to connect the dots, but then that meant . . . "It doesn't work here?"

"Curses from one realm don't usually carry into the next, unless the god has powers in both realms. Apparently, Apollo's power has no effect here."

"You mean I'm human?"

Thanatos shrugged. "You are whatever you would be without the curse. You still have blood from Hera, so not quite human, I would say."

Which would explain why she'd been able to go as long as she had without water. Several days, according to Thanatos, who had informed her that time did not work the same in the Underworld.

"Let's go find your mother today, shall we?"

She'd been about to ask, and something about the fact that he had extended the invitation made her happy. The longer she was with Thanatos, the better she thought of him. He wasn't traditionally attractive like Athan or Xan; the god of death was too thin, too pale, and too angular to be considered handsome. He didn't have the same terrifying beauty of Apollo, either. But Thanatos was kind, which softened his sharp features. He was a god and still had that striking quality, but over the course of the time Hope had been in the Underworld, she'd come to consider him a friend. A *tentative* friend.

"Yes. That sounds fabulous." She stood and accepted his arm as they made their way out to Asbolus.

The centaur stood hitched to the carriage, a scowl on his face.

"Hi, Asbolus." Hope practically sang the greeting. "How are you today?"

The creature turned and glared at Thanatos, making Hope falter in her steps. "This is wrong, Thanatos."

Thanatos held up his hand. "What you see is not set in stone, Asbolus, and we both know it. I *will* do this . . . for Hope."

Asbolus snorted then turned to her. "Be on your guard, little one. Truth can be a painful lesson."

"Enough," Thanatos said. He helped Hope into the carriage and then stepped up to Asbolus. "You would do well to remember I choose where my kindness falls. I will not bow to Hades forever."

Asbolus inclined his head to the god but said nothing.

They lurched through the first rings of the Underworld, the barren waste passing by in a blur of grays. Asbolus slowed to a trot as soon as they crossed into the Fields of Asphodel.

Hope looked around as if her mother would appear, but when Leto didn't appear, Hope turned to Thanatos while asking, "How do we find . . . ?"

The words died on her lips.

Thanatos grimaced as if in physical pain. The muscles of his neck bulged under whatever strain he was going through. His eyes were closed, his jaw rigid, and he shuddered and trembled from the invisible force.

Hope reached out to the god but hesitated to touch him.

Just before contact, he opened his eyes. With a hiss, he withdrew from her. "Don't," he said. His eyes bore into her, and his intense gaze held her captive. Through clench teeth he said, "I must go. I will return as soon as I can. Asbolus, take her home."

And he disappeared.

Fear simmered and boiled, making her skin crawl. "What just happened?"

Asbolus trotted around the fountain in the square. "He has been summoned, and he cannot refuse."

"Who would do that?" But there was only one lord of the Underworld, so only one logical choice. "Why?"

Asbolus's muscular shoulders rose and fell. "It is not Thanatos's place to ask why." The centaur glanced away. "I'll take you back."

"No." She wasn't going back. Now that they were in the Fields of Asphodel and she could actually start looking, she was determined to make use of it. "We can still look, right?"

But Asbolus continued to make his way through the crowds of people.

All thoughts of Thanatos fled, and her goal of finding her mom suddenly seemed to be slipping through her fingers. "Stop!"

But the centaur didn't even glance back at her.

She reminded herself that she was not going to be a victim. She stepped to the edge of the buggy, and with a deep breath, she jumped. As soon as she hit the dark rock, she rolled. Pain exploded on her left side, but she stood and ran back toward the square. There had to be someone who could help.

"Hope!" Asbolus yelled after her, but with the cart hitched to his back, he would have to find a space to turn around.

She knew searching for her mom would be like the needle in a haystack analogy, but at some point, she had to start looking.

FIFTEEN

ATHAN

THEY FOLLOWED THE river. Athan figured there would be more souls closer to a dock, so they walked into the crowd and down the shoreline, hoping to run into a port for the ferryman, Charon. But the number of souls diminished and then disappeared until it was only the three demigods and the spirit of the patient.

"Please tell me we aren't walking in circles," Xan said.

Athan looked at his watch. They'd been in the Underworld for more than fifteen hours. Athan's eyes ached with fatigue. He'd passed tired several hours ago, but he refused to give into exhaustion.

"You don't know what you're doing, do you?" Xan stopped walking and crouched to the ground, his movements graceful like a panther. He pulled his pack off, and careful to keep contact with it at all times, he opened a pouch and pulled out a protein bar. He tore the wrapper off and dropped it on the ground, watching as it blinked out of existence. After taking a big bite, he looked up at Athan. "What? Don't tell me you're not famished." Xan held out another bar to his cousin. "Dahlia, you want one?"

Athan turned away from the snacking and stared out at the Acheron. He was doing something wrong, or rather, not doing something right. He could feel it.

"It's all right to admit you don't know." Dahlia held out her half-eaten bar.

Athan waved it away.

She spoke between bites. "Xan's just pissy because he hates not being able to fix something. But I reckon you remember that about him."

No. In fact, he hadn't remembered. Like so many memories he'd pushed to the recesses of his mind, he'd forgotten. Athan closed his eyes and listened to the water lap at the shore. He probably should eat something. He let his mind wander, ignoring the grumbling from his stomach.

Hadn't Charon been waiting when they'd come to the river?

"Skata," Athan muttered. His eyes blinked open, and he looked out at the endless gray river melting into the horizon. He dug into his pocket, grabbed several drachma, and strode to the water's edge.

"Charon," he yelled. And then he threw the coins. The money broke the surface of the Acheron with several *pilps* and *plops*. Athan gritted his teeth and waited.

"What. The. Kracken?" Dahlia breathed from behind him.

A small skiff cut through the murky fog. The square bow appeared weathered by elements that didn't exist in the Underworld, at least not that Athan had seen. The worn wood was pocked and splintered, and the imposing figure standing at the stern pushed the ferry through the water with a long, dark pole.

Athan looked around for the dead man, but he was right there, his gaze riveted on the approaching vessel.

"Holy Moirai," Xan swore. He stepped next to Athan and then pulled away with a shudder. "The dead bloke is right there, isn't he?" His hand went through the man's shoulders before connecting with Athan.

Athan's jaw hung loose as he faced Xan. "You can feel him?"

Xan frowned. "Aye."

The dead patient stepped away from the living, pulling back behind them. Athan turned and grabbed the man by the wrist. "Don't think you're going anywhere. We need you to cross."

The man leaned away and his mouth moved rapidly, but still there was no sound.

"That's creepy—"

The boat scraped up onto the shore, and all four of them turned to the sound.

Charon remained at the back of the skiff, his black robe almost completely covering him. His hood hung low over his face, and his chin and neck were hidden in shadows. The ends of the garment puddled on the bottom of the god's ferry.

The sleeves, however, gaped open over pale thin wrists, and clutched in his bony fingers was the dark wood pole he used to push through the river Acheron.

Charon pulled the shaft from the water and knelt as he reverently set the rod in the skiff. With movements fluid and oily, he floated out of the boat and onto the rocky shore.

"Why are you here?" His voice rasped from inside the hood.

Athan pushed down his panic. "I've come to deliver this man's soul."

Charon laughed, the ghostly chuckle an unnerving cacophony of sound that chilled Athan's bones.

The river seemed to swell, the mists surrounding the Acheron darkened, and the scent of carrion and rotten fruit ballooned around them.

Dahlia swore, and either she or Xan retched. Athan's stomach flipped and turned, and he was glad he hadn't eaten the protein bar after all.

"Liar," Charon hissed. "Your father has not required this."

The trick to lying was telling as much of the truth as possible. "I never said he did."

The air pulsed with energy. A magnetic force pulled Athan's gaze toward the god. He willed his features into neutrality, but Athan's heart pounded in fear. "Do you require more than an obol per person for passage?"

Faster than a pulse, Charon's bony fingers clutched the collar of Athan's shirt and pulled him close. The coppery smell of fresh blood wafted from under the god's hood, and when he spoke the sharp tang became stronger. "Don't toy with me, Son of Hermes. I owe you nothing."

Athan's heart thrummed a racing tempo of fear. The ferryman of Death had unnaturally pale skin, similar to that of the Skia. His irises and pupils were as dark as pitch. His prominent cheekbones jutted out, making him appear malnourished and gaunt. But most disturbing were his lips. Stained the color of fresh blood. And then his tongue wiped—no, licked the blood off, as if his dessert had been interrupted and he'd taken a hurried last bite that had smeared across his lips.

"You are in my domain right now. Don't tempt—"

"We're here for Hope."

Charon sneered. "There is no hope in the Underworld."

"No," Xan corrected, coming forward. He tapped Charon's bony hand with the tip of his immortal dagger. "We're here to get Hope, the Sphinx, out of the Underworld. She's not dead, so she doesn't belong here."

Charon's sneer became a smirk. "Yes, she was here, this monster of whom you speak." He pulled his hood off to reveal a pasty, bald head, eyes sunken deep in their sockets, and skin pulled tightly over his bony skull. "Is she why you've come?"

Athan shot Xan a look, trying to tell him to shut up.

Xan didn't even look his way. "Yes, Lord. We would petition for your aide."

Athan wanted to hit him. You didn't petition gods for aide. Gods were selfish. It was always a bargain when dealing with them.

"I see." Charon looked back and forth between the two demigods. And then his eyes lighted on something behind them.

Athan turned to see Dahlia staring at the divine ferryman. Her eyes were dilated, and her lips parted as her breath came out in shallow gasps.

"She has been marked by Thanatos's guard. You will have a difficult time getting her out of the Underworld."

Xan sucked in a low breath. "Nothing that happened would require her death." His voice was low, as if to spare his cousin the words.

"True, but Death has called her for some time."

What was he saying? Dahlia?

"What of the Sphinx?" That was why they were here. Everything, everyone else, would have to wait. Even the rest of Athan's team.

"Yes. Your riddle." Charon licked his lips and turned his dead eyes back to Athan. "She crossed here. Thanatos was her guide. I do not think things will end well for her."

Thanatos, the god of death. Athan had seen him rip the soul from Hope's mother. Why would Thanatos help Hope? And why would Hope allow Thanatos to help her after he killed her mother?

"We would like to stop him." Athan remembered the animosity between the two gods of the Underworld.

"Aye," Xan agreed. "Will you help us?"

Charon frowned as if mulling over the proposition. "You have a soul?" He pointed to the dead man in the hospital gown. "Did you bring him through the portal?"

Athan nodded. There was no need to tell him about the Skia they'd fought.

"Then you may pay me for passage. I will take you across the river Acheron." Charon turned and glided back to his ferry.

Athan grabbed the dead man, and Xan went to get Dahlia.

The boat rocked as they climbed aboard. What had appeared as a small skiff, large enough for one, elongated and easily accommodated the five of them.

Xan sat on the only bench, just below Charon's feet, jaw clenched. The dead soul stood at the bow, staring over the edge, his milky eye frozen on the deadly water. Dahlia stood behind him.

Athan braced for the movement as Charon pushed back, the bottom of the boat scraping along the rocks until the river sucked it away. A painful moan bubbled through the water, and a claw-like appendage broke the surface and scrabbled at the edge of the boat.

With a crack, Charon smacked the already mangled fingers, and they released their tenuous grip before sinking back into the darkness.

"Don't fall in," Dahlia told the soul and pulled him back from the edge. She held his wrist loosely, as if abhorring the touch but knowing the necessity of it.

Charon hissed something unintelligible from under his hood.

Foreboding clawed its way up Athan's chest into his throat, making it difficult to catch his breath. Something about Dahlia being cut by a Skia blade. And now she was able to see and touch the dead? That wasn't right. Xan would never forgive Athan if something were to happen to Dahlia.

The fog rose from the river and swirled around them in small eddies. Charon pushed his pole through the dark water of despair, and the scraping continued. A faint scratching that made Athan's skin crawl. How had he not heard the scraping before?

Charon delivered another thwack to an interloper, and bile burned the back of Athan's throat as he watched a mangled head sink below the surface.

"Someone say something. That grating is going to drive me insane," Dahlia said.

"Those monsters are the creepiest things I've ever seen."

Dahlia snorted. "That's not really helpful."

Athan looked between the two of them. "I've never heard it before, not until this trip." He glanced back to Charon. "Why is that? And what are those things?"

"The dead," Charon said.

Athan gritted his teeth against the snappy reply. The god said nothing more, and Athan wanted to rip the hood from his head and yell at him. Why was he being so obtuse?

"But why are they in the river?" Xan asked.

The boat rocked. Athan shuffled to try to regain his footing. Dahlia screamed, but the sound was cut short by a large splash.

"Shite!" Xan scrambled past Athan to the edge of the boat.

Dahlia thrashed in the water as hands, arms, and bodies clamored over each other, clawing at her. She screamed, but the sound was cut short once again as the pale-fleshed monsters pulled her under.

SIXTEEN

HOPE

"**Excuse me?**" **Hope** asked one of the men behind a stall. She'd picked him because his tables were filled with bright toys. As she drew closer, what at first appeared to be dolls, seemed to morph as she studied the small figures. The heads were the same rock as the rest of the Underworld, but the faces painted on the black stone were grotesque caricatures of pain. The bodies were stuffed, and deep red stained the fabric in the spots of vital organs.

"Yes, girlie? You want to buy a haunt for someone you left behind?" He continued to sell her. "These have been sanctified by the goddess Hecate. Sure to bring chaos to whomever betrayed you."

She shook her head. "I'm looking for someone. How do you find someone here?"

The merchant narrowed his gaze. "Who you be looking for?"

"It's time to go, Hope." Asbolus grabbed her arm and pulled her away from the stall.

The merchant's gaze went from curious to cunning. "A centaur is watching her. She is still aliv—"

"Stop now, or I'll have Thanatos put you in Tartarus."

The man chuckled. "I fear Hades more than the god of death. See here, is this the—?"

"Halt!"

Hope turned and her heart skipped a beat. Three men, pale skinned with eyes dark as the rock beneath them, advanced toward her. Skia. Perhaps Thanatos sent them for her.

"Hades would have a word with you," the one in front called.

Oh gods. She reached for her blades, but of course she didn't have them. Her heart pounded against her ribs, demanding that she run. Hope backed away, inching toward a side street leading out of the square.

"We will not hurt you, monster."

Right. She didn't believe them at all.

"Stop right there, Marcus," a familiar voice hissed.

Hope glanced to her right, and she froze in panic.

Darren.

Darren was there. The Skia that had attacked her in Goldendale was flanked by a half dozen other men all with the same pasty skin and black eyes.

Time slowed.

"We found her first, Darren. Y
know. We'll bring her in."

Darren laughed. "Who said a
in?"

The first one, Marcus, scrunch
a black blade buried itself between his eyes. The creature fell
backward, sending the other two behind him scrambling for
blades. But they were outnumbered and clearly caught by surprise. In seconds there were three bodies on the ground.

By the time the third body fell, the merchant had disappeared. There was screaming in the background, peripheral
noise, indicating Hope's fear was well grounded.

"Little monster, you've come to my world." The telltale
leer widened into a sickening, distorted grin.

"What do you want?"

Darren pulled a blade from the other Skia's body and held
his arms wide as black blood dripped to the dark ground. "Ret-
ribution."

He leapt forward, closing the distance between them. As he
drew the blade back, Hope grabbed his wrist. Turning into his
body, she kneed him in the groin.

Darren laughed, a wheezing sound of death. He pulled her
close until her body was flush with his cold one. "I'm dead.
That doesn't hurt anymore."

She still held his wrist and used her body weight to pull his
arm down as she dropped to the ground. As he bent forward

...ntum, she jumped up, driving her elbow into his ...et go of his hand, and scooting away, she shifted into ...sive stance.

"You've gotten better," Darren hissed as he wiped black fluid from his face.

She counted six Skia. Far too many for her to defeat on her own . . . unless she had blades.

Hope ran to the fallen bodies. She pulled the blades from the dead Skia's body, and a cold liquid black as pitch ran down the blades onto her hands. With the practiced aim Xan had taught her, she threw one blade and then the other. One Skia dropped, and then the second went down.

But then Darren was in front of her again. "You've gotten much better."

He swung with his blade and followed with his fist. She ducked and blocked, countering with a fist of her own, before dancing back away.

"Your style is different, too."

She couldn't run until she'd killed them. Not unless she was much faster . . . "Asbolus!"

There he was in the alley on the other side of the square. Despite being muscular and strong, the centaur was avoiding the fight. What was wrong with him?

She didn't have time to think about it. Two more Skia circled in. Hope paced back, shifting her position until both attackers were coming from the same direction. One threw a knife, a sad attempt really, and she ducked. Grabbing a handful of the gruesome dolls, she threw them at the Skia. It was only enough to make him flinch, and she grabbed his wrist and twisted his arm as she stepped behind him.

She moved just in time. The second Skia drove his blade right where she'd been standing, into the other Skia's chest. His grip on his blade loosened, and Hope wrenched it free and shoved it into the second Skia's eye.

Three left.

Another Skia charged her. Hope had just enough space to arc step behind him, but as she pushed her acquired blade between his shoulders, she saw he'd been a decoy.

"Drop it," Darren hissed, his blade at her throat.

She let go of the blade buried in the Skia's back. "You cut me before, and it didn't kill me," she taunted with bravado she'd learned from Xan. "This is not the end for me."

"You're in my world, Hope." His arm came around her neck in a choke hold. "And you've lost all your power."

Hope tucked her chin, trying to prevent the pressure from cutting off her blood supply to the brain. She stomped on his foot and clawed at his arm, but his grip was too much.

There was a crash, and Hope was thrown forward.

Someone yelled, and Asbolus was up on his back legs kicking a Skia in the chest.

Another voice, this one softer, and someone pulling her body. Her vision tunneled, the edges darkening with her mind, demanding escape. She was going to black out. As her vision swam, she saw Thanatos appear. He raised his arm and blasted—literally blasted—a Skia. It was like shards of darkness scattered as another Skia disappeared with the god's force.

And then darkness took her.

SEVENTEEN

ATHAN

As ATHAN SEARCHED the waters for Dahlia, all he could think was Xan didn't know how to swim. How could he not know how to swim? Why hadn't he learned?

Athan kicked off his shoes and pulled out his daggers. With a silent plea to his father, he jumped over the edge of the boat.

Icy fingers clawed at him, terrifyingly cold like that of a Skia blade, and Athan lashed out with his blades instinctively. He opened his eyes and saw human bodies in various stages of decay surrounding him, leering at him. One reached out again, but withdrew as soon as Athan pulled his blades in front of him.

A frenzy of activity indicated Dahlia's most likely position, and Athan kicked through the sludgy river. He slashed forward with his immortal blades and then back, the silver knives seeming to glow in the murky depths.

Skeletal bodies emaciated with hunger opened their mouths in silent screams, exposing their rotten insides. Stringy hair floated around him, and he cut through the strands and continued to push forward to the thrashing movement ahead.

Time seemed nonexistent. Seconds felt like hours. Hours of cutting through bodies. The mangled limbs floated by, only to be grabbed by one of the water demons, hunger flashing across its face. Athan kicked upward and gulped a mouthful of air, and an earful of Xan's profanity, before something pulled him under. Again he lashed out with his knives.

And then Dahlia was in front of him, eyes wide with terror, and her hair writhing in the darkness as if it were alive. Her clothes were torn, her skin scratched and scraped.

The dead man was nowhere to be seen.

Athan pointed her toward the surface, and she shook her head.

What could that even mean? Keeping his blade locked under his thumb, he grabbed her arm and pulled. As soon as the immortal blade touched her skin, anger replaced the fear in her expression, and she reached to her waistband, withdrawing her own divine blades.

As they rose through the Acheron, something hard smacked Athan on the head, making his eyes water. They broke the surface, and Xan was at the bow of the boat holding Charon's pole.

"Bloody Hell!"

Both Athan and Dahlia reached for the pole, and Xan dragged them back to the boat. Xan reached over the side and pulled Dahlia up over the lip of the skiff.

Athan kicked at the sludge, and then sharp pain stabbed him in the calf. Darkness exploded across his vision, and his mind emptied of everything except pain. Gods, the pain. He . . . couldn't . . .

He was sinking. And even though he knew that was bad, so bad, he couldn't stop it from happening. Weightlessness cradled him for a moment, and then air whooshed by and he landed with a thud on his back.

"If you die, I will be so pissed." Xan's voice scratched through the blackness.

All the motion made Athan's stomach churn, and he rolled onto his side and threw up. Sludge from the Acheron gushed from his mouth, tasting of blood and beef. He retched again, and when he saw a partially decomposed stump of a human digit, he vomited until his throat was raw and nothing more would come out.

The words surrounding him made no sense, and Athan stared up at the blackness above. The faint phosphorus lights almost looked like stars, but the smudges of light refused to come into focus. A dull throbbing in his left leg reminded him of his near death.

The noise snapped into clarity.

"If you'd told me Skia had come for him, I would've warned you. He was to be damned, and nothing was going to stop it." Charon's pale features were contorted in rage. "Foolish demigods."

"How were we supposed to know—?"

"There are no secrets in the Underworld. None. There is no need for lies or deception." Charon's bony finger prodded Xan in the chest. "Consider this your lesson. You are lucky they are both alive . . . still."

Athan wasn't sure it was luck.

The boat stopped, and Athan lifted his head. A familiar sensation tugged at his mind, and he recognized the dock he and his father had used when the Fates told him about the Sphinx.

As they disembarked, Charon held Athan back.

"Make sure you thwart Thanatos, Son of Hermes. That was our agreement."

Athan nodded. If Thanatos was trying to harm Hope in anyway, Athan would thwart all he could. He stepped off the boat and onto the solid dock, his clothes in tatters.

"And do not confuse your despair with reality," Charon called as he pushed the boat away from shore. Before Athan could form a reply, Charon and his ferry disappeared.

Athan let out a breath, pushing away his worry and concern. They had crossed the river Acheron, and now they had to make it through the Underworld and get Hope.

Failure was not an option.

E I G H T E E N

HOPE

SHE WAS BEING carried. The movement was jarring as they shifted her in their arms. She wanted to protest but couldn't find the strength to open her mouth.

Voices whispered vehement words, and Hope caught bits and pieces of the conversation.

"Not what we'd agreed . . . actually hurt her . . ." The voice was familiar and had the inflection of the divine. But he was angry.

". . . would've healed . . . or are you pretending?"

The man carrying her sucked in a breath and swore.

Hope wanted to tell the other person that the pain wasn't pretend. There was no way to pretend this much. But she decided she didn't care enough to expend the effort.

When she opened her eyes, the first thing Hope saw was the god of death sitting at her bedside. His gray T-shirt was rumpled, and his angular features were distorted in a grimace. As soon as their eyes met, the frown disappeared.

"Did you rescue me?" She cleared her throat and accepted the bottle of water.

Thanatos waited until she'd finished all of it and then threw the empty bottle into a waste bin in the corner. He ran his hand through his hair in a very human gesture of frustration. "What were you thinking?"

Hope pulled herself up, groaning as every muscle in her body protested the activity. As soon as she was upright, Hope leaned back against the upholstered headboard, exhausted by her puny effort.

"This world . . . It doesn't run the way the mortal realm does. You are not invincible here." He dropped his head to the edge of the bed. He took a deep breath and then looked up and met her gaze. "I don't know the limits of your curse."

"Could he kill me?"

Thanatos shook his head. "I don't know." He clasped his hands together. "Please don't wander around unprotected."

She nodded. "But I need to find my mother."

He closed his eyes and pinched the bridge of his nose.

She hated that it felt like she was trying his patience. He'd been so kind, and she hated that she was such an inconvenience. "Would you rather I just go?"

He opened his eyes and frowned. "That's not the problem, Hope." He stood and crossed the room. "Try to get some sleep. I'll be back tomorrow."

She turned over her relationship with Thanatos as she waited for sleep to claim her. His interest in her was obvious. He wasn't as forward as Xan in his declaration, but it felt like he was trying to, what was the word her mother used . . . court her? As sleep crept over her, she wondered if the god's interest was driven from loneliness. Was it her, or would anyone do? Could she be reading him wrong and all he wanted was friendship? Was he driving for something more?

It didn't matter. She could only offer him friendship.

Thanatos hadn't returned when Hope awoke the next day. She mulled over her options only for a moment before deciding. She wasn't reliant on him, and as much as she appreciated his concern and all he'd done for her, she wanted to get out of the Underworld. Which meant she needed to get information about her curse.

As she descended the stairs, Hope passed several more Skia and wondered at the vast number of them. There had to be several dozen here in Thanatos's home. Like servants or bodyguards. Why would the god of death need so many bodyguards?

Hope dismissed the thoughts as she raced outside to find Asbolus.

The dark rock extended as far as she could see. Behind the mansion-like home of Thanatos stood an outbuilding of the same black stone. The structure had bright white Xs over the doors and in panels below the windows, a pattern very reminiscent of a barn.

"I need you to take me to the Fields; that's it." Her last visit flashed through her mind. "And some immortal blades, just in case. Do you have access to blades?"

Asbolus stood at the front door, his arms crossed over his bare chest, his hooves clicking on the stone as he shifted uneasily. "What you're proposing is madness."

"Me being here is madness, but I'm here nonetheless." She narrowed her gaze and offered a patronizing smile. "Didn't Thanatos say you were an auger?"

He stepped out of the door. "He did."

She threw her hands up. "Then you know if anything is going to go wrong."

Why couldn't she catch a break? Why couldn't one single thing go her way? Was it really too much to ask?

"Fine." Asbolus leaned over her. "But you won't need blades."

She stared up past his chiseled torso to his clenched square jaw. She felt a little bad about how hard she was pushing. It was probably rude, but being nice sure wasn't getting her anything. "Good. Let's go."

As if reading her mind, he stepped back into his home. "I'll be out shortly."

He closed the door in her face. A few minutes later, Asbolus came around from the back of the house carrying a saddle.

"We're not taking the cart?"

He chuckled, a deep throaty sound that was more human than horse. "For just you? No."

Was it weird that she was having a bit of a panic attack? "I've never ridden a horse before."

Asbolus stopped walking toward her and raised his brows. "Then it's a good thing I'm not a horse." He told her how to fasten the saddle. "Then you just have to hold on."

Was he kidding?

Again, as if he could read her thoughts, he responded, "It's like embracing someone while riding a motorcycle."

"Yeah," she muttered, "if the guy is naked."

His laughter was rich and deep, and his abdominal muscles tightened with the force of it. He finally reined in his mirth and, with a twinkle of mischief and a wink, said, "Go ahead and mount up."

Hope's face flamed with embarrassment, but she said nothing as she pulled herself into the saddle.

"You are going to have to hold on," he chided. As if to demonstrate the necessity, Asbolus trotted a few steps and then cantered a few more.

Hope hung on to the saddle and gritted her teeth. Then, with a lurch, she flung her arms around Asbolus's waist as he broke into a run. It was almost as good as flying. The air tickled and teased at her hair, pulling the golden strands back away from her face.

The second Hope and Asbolus were off Thanatos's grounds, the air became dank and heavy with a biting chill. The wind buffeted them, screaming a song of pain and the anger of betrayal. Despair crept into her heart, and Hope wanted to weep with the futility of her purpose. There was no way she would succeed, and worse than that, she would be a disappointment to everyone who had ever known her. A wave of hot betrayal hit her, and she wanted to lash out. She should make Sarra, Krista, and Obelia pay. In fact, now that she was in the Underworld, she should track down Apollo's sons and make sure they were receiving ample punishment. Perhaps there was a way for her to seek revenge, even here . . .

Asbolus lurched, and the bitterness was gone. The dank air, while still heavy, was filled with a sense of acceptance. It was blessedly silent.

"What was that?" she yelled to him. It couldn't have been natural.

"Tartarus," he hollered back at her. "I'm sorry. I should've warned you." He slowed to a brisk trot and looked over his shoulder, his gaze appraising her. Whatever he saw must've been reassuring, and with a nod he faced forward and resumed his gallop.

With another lurch, they were inside the realm of the Fields of Asphodel. Hope recognized the smell before she even saw the buildings. But Asbolus didn't stop. He continued his run through the vast fields, and they lurched into another in-between.

"Why the space in-between? And why didn't I see that before?" First the awfulness of Tartarus and now the in-betweens? "Why is it different?"

"I'm no god. I can't shelter you from the realities here."

"Thanatos changed what I saw?" The sense of betrayal spiked, and this time it was all her own. "How dare he!"

They lurched again, and the air was sweeter. Asbolus slowed his pace as they came into the beauty of Elysium. The polished stone houses were spaced farther apart, and the yards had various adornments of colored crystal.

He pointed to a large black tree, the green crystals cut as leaves. Red globes the size of cherries hung from the limbs, and the phosphorus light glinted and fractured off the faux fruit. "It's very beautiful, is it not?"

"Yes. Where do they get the crystals?"

Asbolus chuckled. "Crystals? No. They are gems, mined from here in the Underworld. Or did you forget Hades is the god of the riches of the ground?"

Hope turned to look back at the cherry tree. "For real?"

He laughed again and tapped her hands after coming to a stop by a garden of sculptures. "Yes. One of the rewards of Elysium. Now here you go."

Trees and bushes of jewels extended as far as she could see. A low wall separated the road from the pathways of the park.

"Where am I going?"

"They will meet you in there."

Hope slid from the saddle, surprised at how wobbly her legs were. She held on to the horn of the saddle, and the ground seemed to solidify as her legs adjusted to standing. "Who will meet me? My mom? Priska?"

Asbolus stared across the vast park. He turned, his hooves clopping against the stone. After a deep breath, he met her gaze. "The Fates."

He nodded once and left.

Hope stood rooted to the ground. She heard Asbolus's retreat and had a fleeting thought of running after him. She let out a slow breath and then another. Straightening, she squared her shoulders and went to meet the Fates.

NINETEEN

ATHAN

SOMETHING WASN'T RIGHT. It wasn't that Athan considered himself a particularly optimistic guy, but this was different. As they trudged through the barren waste that separated the river Acheron from the Fields of Asphodel, Athan wanted to scream in frustration.

The last trip in the Underworld had taken less than an hour. How was it even possible that they'd been trudging through the abyss for over forty hours?

Hours ago, Xan had called a halt to the march, declaring a need for rest. He'd insisted they tie a rope around each of them, connecting them to each other in one straight line. Just in case, he'd said.

Athan argued it would impede them in a fight, and he expected Dahlia to side with him. But his argument fizzled when the demigod daughter of Eris merely picked up the end of the rope and tied it around her waist.

"Don't let go of the bedroll, Dahl."

"Do you hear them?" she whispered. "Athan? Can you hear them calling us?"

He swallowed his denial. The screams from Tartarus broke the silence, and the echoes pulsed through the air. In the distance, a red haze rose into the sky.

The air ached with a palpable wanting, and the hair on Athan's arms stood on end. It was as if the atmosphere called to him, whispering at him to give up, that he would never win. Never get Hope. That no matter what, he would never, ever get out of the Underworld alive.

"No," he lied. "I don't hear anything."

Dahlia frowned, and her face clouded with confusion.

"Come on, Dahl. Come lay down." Xan beckoned her over.

Athan pulled his sleeping bag out of his pack and sat down. He discarded the torn T-shirt and put on his spare.

"How much longer do we have in the in-between? How close are we to the fields?"

Athan shrugged and then remembered Xan wouldn't be able to see him. "I don't know. I . . . It's never taken this long before."

Xan didn't respond, and Athan wondered if Xan was silently cursing him.

Xan got Dahlia to lay down on his sleeping bag and then came to stand over Athan. "There's something wrong with her. Something happened in that water, and it's affecting her."

"I know," Athan admitted. His leg still throbbed with an ache all the way to the bone. But that wasn't the worst of it. Despair, dark and deep, would pulse through him when the pain was at its worst. "Did she throw up after she got out of the river?"

Xan shifted, rolling his shoulders back. He grimaced as if the pain his cousin struggled with was gnawing at him, too.

Athan averted his gaze back to the glowing rock above.

"No," Xan whispered as he went back to Dahlia. "No, she didn't."

DAHLIA DIDN'T WAKE up. She'd thrashed all night, her whimpers and cries keeping Athan from any significant rest, and judging by the dark circles under Xan's eyes, he hadn't gotten much sleep either.

Athan sat on his sleeping bag, alternately eating a protein bar and drinking another pouch of water. When he contemplated opening another bar, he instead grabbed the garbage and shoved it in his pack. He couldn't put off the inevitable, no matter how much he wanted to. Shouldering his pack, Athan tried to think of a delicate way to broach the subject.

"She's not going to make it," Xan said. He scrubbed at his face and then ran his hand through his hair. "We can move her, but . . ."

But they wouldn't be able to maintain their pace, and they didn't know if she would ever wake up. But then what were their options? They couldn't leave her. Dahlia lay on the second sleeping bag, Xan sitting on the edge. The second backpack was open, and the remaining supplies were in two separate piles: needs and conveniences.

Almost as if reading his thoughts, Xan answered the unasked question. "You could go ahead, and I'll stay with her."

Athan considered for only seconds. "No. Even if . . . I'm not sure I could find you again."

"I understand that risk. But we can't all stay here. We're losing precious time. You need to get Hope."

The mist scuttled over Dahlia, and with a scream she sat up. "They're here," she rasped, her eyes wide and glassy.

"Shite." Xan jumped up and drew his blades.

The mists around them dissolved, revealing dozens and dozens of Skia.

Athan's heart sank. It had taken all three of them to kill the Skia at the hospital, and even then Dahlia had gotten injured. This? There was no chance. He stood slowly as he pulled his silver blades from his boots.

The harbingers of death advanced.

Athan backed up and watched in dismay as his sleeping bag disappeared. He stood next to Xan and waited.

Dahlia started crying, racking sobs of despair. "No. No, no, no," she choked out.

Athan glanced down and saw the beautiful girl, head in her hands, weeping. He looked back up, and the Skia were upon them. He blocked and stabbed. Darting in and jumping out, a desperate dance.

These Skia, like the ones in the hospital, were not well trained. Their movements were poorly timed, their swings projected by their body easily anticipated and just as easily blocked. One by one they fell. Even if the strike were not a deathblow, the shadow-demons withdrew after any contact from Athan's or Xan's blades.

But even so, there were so many.

Xan grunted as he fought alongside Athan. He pulled his blade out of one body, only to plunge it in to another. His arms were tiring, the adrenaline running its course; he would not be able to keep up the pace.

And still they came.

"Halt!" a woman called.

If he remembered anything from training with Xan, it was you never stopped before the threat was exterminated. Athan stabbed another monster in the chest, and the creature dissipated within a burst of light.

A blast of power blew over him, hitting him in the stomach as strong as any physical blow. The skin on his stomach singed, and he stumbled back and landed on his butt. He shifted then stood, half-crouched from the pain. Still, he held his blades out in front of him, waiting for the next attack.

The Skia were gone.

"They are not your enemies." The goddess stood tall, dressed in a black flowing chiton, a gold clasp at her shoulder. Her wavy hair, a maroon-red that reminded him of blood, was pulled away from her face in a low ponytail, accenting fair skin dusted with pale golden freckles the same color as her clasp. Her blue eyes blazed.

Her extended hand opened as if to blast him again, but instead a warmth spread from his chest to his toes, and his eyelids drooped with fatigue. He fought to keep his eyes open and watched as Xan was hit by a blast of magic the color of honey.

Xan swung his blades in low arcs and then paused. His eyes closed, but Xan's muscles remained taught. A whisper of movement from the goddess, and Xan struck out again. Closer this time. Another pause. Xan looked like he'd been hit with the slow-motion fatigue Athan felt. As if he was moving through honey.

Athan struggled to stay awake. It was becoming more difficult to even keep his eyes open, let alone stay alert. When he blinked, Xan was falling, his body collapsing in a heap on the dark-gray stone ground. Two women dressed in black, like the goddess, were there with a litter as if waiting for the inevitable.

Another pair of women loaded Dahlia onto a litter of dark fabric between two poles of gold.

Athan turned, and the goddess with hair the color of blood stood in front of him.

"Do you know who I am?"

Her name had eluded him until now. "Hecate." Goddess of magic, witchcraft, crossroads, and chaos.

Her eyes narrowed, and he wondered if he'd said it all out loud.

"You will come with me." It was not a request. Not that it mattered. It wasn't like there was an option of refusal. And she had saved their lives.

Athan shuffled forward a step, and then the sensation of falling overtook him. It was going to hurt when he hit the ground, and he mentally braced for it. But the pain never came.

TWENTY

HOPE

THE PARK WAS stunning. There was no other word to describe it. Gems of all shapes and sizes were on full display in the light. Bright cardinals and vivid jays were spotted amongst the jeweled fruit and flowers. Hope stopped to admire a cluster of Gerbera daisies cut from a startling orange-colored gem.

"Do you like them?" The lilt of the voice announced the divinity of the feminine speaker.

Hope turned, expecting to find three women, but instead stood face-to-face with Artemis.

The goddess had her silver hair pulled back in a low ponytail. Her dark, fitted clothes were rumpled and stained. But what made Hope's heart stop were the red-rimmed eyes of a woman who had spent a significant amount of time crying.

Hope swallowed. "They remind me of her."

Artemis nodded. "Gerberas were her favorite."

The goddess's hand rested on the hilt of a silver blade. "Did you know when a demigod dies, their immortal blades are returned to their parent?"

The lump in Hope's throat thickened, and her eyes welled with tears. She shook her head.

"Did you know it was I that charged her to take care of the cursed Sphinx? I thought it a kindness to the monster that my brother had created, but it also gave her purpose. She looked at Phoibe as if she were her own child."

Artemis pointed to a bench, and Hope followed. They sat on the dark stone, and Hope was struck that it seemed to radiate heat from within. She wanted to curl into that warmth as she distanced herself from the bitter look of the goddess next to her.

"I'm sorry," Hope whispered.

Artemis nodded. "You're sorry. As if that will make any difference." She looked up at the sky. "Did you know Priska lost her husband and daughter long before your great-grandmother was born? She mourned them unlike anything I'd ever seen. She tried to take her own life. Again and again and again. At one point I questioned the wisdom in stopping her, but every single time I couldn't let her go. And then Phoibe seemed the perfect answer. An unwanted daughter of the gods. She would live forever. Hera was too stupid, or too blinded, to want to keep her only demigod daughter, and she gladly relinquished her rights to me. And then my brother . . . Of course I had to step in. But now? This is how you repaid me for my infinite kindness?"

Tears dripped down Hope's cheeks. "I didn't know she would do that."

"Of course not." Artemis's hand rubbed the black stone. "You are still far too young to understand the sacrifices one makes for love"—she sniffed—"or duty."

The words were a dagger to Hope's heart. "Was that all I was?"

Artemis stood and pointed at Hope. "She was too good to have been wasted on this. You'd better hope our paths don't cross again, monster. I won't be so kind if they do."

Hope wanted to say she would make it right, that somehow she would make up the loss. But she had nothing to give. Nothing to offer the goddess. Hope bowed her head and let the tears fall. It didn't matter what she said. Nothing would be good enough. So she said nothing.

Doubt crept in. Was all of this truly selfish? Was it selfish to want to be free from a curse? Maybe it was.

"It's not," a woman said, taking the abandoned spot next to Hope.

Hope wiped her eyes. The girl sitting next to her was dressed in a pale blue chiton edged in silver. She held an odd walking stick with markings in ancient Greek that ran the length of it. Her thick brunette curls cascaded over her shoulder, covering the strap of the leather messenger bag at her hip.

Standing beside the bench were two other young women: one blond with fair skin, who was clacking two knitting needles together; the other, with dark, cropped hair, appeared macabre with several pairs of shears hanging from leather straps.

"Don't lie to her," the dark-haired one snapped. "It is selfish."

"But that doesn't mean it's wrong," the blond said without looking up from her needles.

The brunette smiled at Hope. "Don't mind my sisters."

They looked nothing like sisters. Oh! Oh, gods! Literally. "You're the Fates?" The shears. The measuring stick. The knitting. Of course they were. Hope looked at the blond goddess. "Is that really the thread of someone's life?"

Atropos leaned over Hope. "Do you really think you have the power to cut someone's thread that wasn't meant to die?"

Hope shook her head.

"That's right. You don't." The goddess who measured life stepped back and grabbed the blond by the elbow. "Come on, Clo. Sit down. Move, Lachesis."

Lachesis laughed and stood. She extended her hand to Hope in invitation. "Let's go walk through Rhadamanthus's garden."

Hope stood, mostly to clear the bench for the other Fates. "Will he be upset we're in here?"

Atropos snorted, and Lachesis laughed again. "No. He won't mind."

Hope followed after the goddess who measured man's life. Hope had so many questions, but her mind blanked on every single one.

"You want to know how to break the curse." Lachesis walked past the daisies and onto a well-used path through the jeweled garden. "But you already know that it's impossible."

Disappointment churned in Hope's stomach. "Then why did I come?"

The goddess fingered a thin branch, and the dangling stones shook and swung. "Answer your own question," she prompted.

Why had Hope come? "To talk with my mother. To find out if there is anything else I can do."

"Would you bargain with another god to make the curse shift or change?"

Hope's first instinct was to say yes. If she got to choose the terms of the agreement, she would make a bargain with another god. But then, that would enslave her to that god. She didn't want to owe anyone anything.

"What if I offered you aid in exchange for a service?"

"No matter what, I'm going to owe someone something, right? Is that what you're saying?"

Lachesis let go of the branch, and the entire shrub shimmied. "No. Do you feel indebted to Athan? Or Xan or Dahlia? Do you think they feel indebted to you?"

There was no reason for any of them to feel indebted to her, and she said as much.

"Do you feel you owe Priska something?"

"She's the one who made it possible for me to come here, and she died. Of course I feel like I owe her."

"Do you feel like she owed you something?"

"No."

"Really? Your grandmother gave her a purpose to live when she had none. She gave her joy. Because she continued to live, she found love again and again. And not just romantic love, although she did find that again, right?"

"But it was still my fault she died," Hope choked out.

"Did you ask her to?"

"No."

It was a difficult concept to wrap her head around. She couldn't help the guilt that hung heavily in her chest. Hope wanted to push it away or ignore it. Not have a conversation about whose fault it was.

"What if I told you she did it because she felt guilty about not being there for you, like she'd promised to you all those years ago? What if her death was an attempt to make it right by you?"

"Why would she do that?"

Lachesis pursed her lips. "Don't take Artemis's words to heart. She is hurt and mourning her only daughter's death. Even so, if there comes a time where you could do a service for the goddess of night, you might consider it an olive branch. The gods have long memories."

"So, I do owe her?"

Lachesis turned to Hope and pointed at her stick. "You don't owe anyone anything. Life doesn't work that way. If you are constantly trying to keep track or keep a tally, you will miss out on the opportunities to be an influence when it actually matters. I'm the one that measures worth. No one else, not god nor mortal. However, if you want someone to be on your side, it never hurts to help them achieve their goals, either. Maybe give them a reason to like you. Especially true when you're dealing with gods."

"So I don't have to, but I still *should* give her something if I can?" Wasn't that the same thing? Hope felt like the conversation was going in circles, and she couldn't keep up.

They continued down the path, only to see Atropos and Clotho ahead of them on the bench.

"Your choices are yours, and you will have to live with them. Be careful whom you trust, and always be polite."

"You sound like my mother," Hope said with a wan smile.

"Yes. Let's go see her now." Lachesis grabbed Hope's wrist, stopping her on the path before the bench. The ground seemed to drop out from under them, and Hope stumbled to gain her footing.

TWENTY-ONE

ATHAN

A LOUD POP like the crack of gunfire awoke Athan, and he sat up. A coarse black blanket fell from his shoulders, and a chill skirted over his bare skin, giving him raised goose bumps. A roaring fire burned on the other side of the room in a roughly-hewn fireplace, and another snap of the wood told him what had awoken him. Rough walls of dark rock surrounded him, and the ceiling was the same black stone of the Underworld. If the cave wasn't so high, he'd feel buried alive. There wasn't even a window, only a single opening into the darkness of what he assumed was Hades's realm.

A glance around the room told him he was alone, and he swung his legs over the side of the cot and waited for a wave of dizziness to pass. On the other side of the space, four bunk beds the same gold and black as the litter and his cot lined the wall. Shelves were carved into the stone, making cubbies that appeared to be filled with clothes and other linens.

Where were Xan and Dahlia? And why hadn't they put him in a bed?

Athan stood, and the blanket pooled at his feet. Cool air skirted over his bare skin, and he shivered. Who had undressed him, and why? Not that he minded his boxer-style briefs, but he didn't want to wander around the Underworld in his underwear.

He wrapped the blanket around his waist and toured the room. The clothes were all chitons, far too small for him, and bedding was folded and stacked in the corner, likely for the inhabitants. Over by the bunks, pictures were stuck to the rough stone: girls smiling, their arms thrown around each other. They weren't sisters—there were too many different races for that to be the case—more like a sorority, as they were all similarly dressed in fitted black clothes or drapey chitons.

Dahlia would fit in well with the group. Maybe. Except Dahlia didn't wear dresses or have friends, except for Xan and Hope.

"You're up."

Athan turned and faced a redheaded woman, somewhere in her late teens, standing inside the opening to the cavern. She was dressed in a black robe, a blue clasp at her shoulder.

"Hecate will see you." Her words were clipped, as if well rehearsed, and her accent was similar to Xan's brogue when he got angry or drunk.

"You're from Ireland?"

The young woman pursed her lips but didn't answer.

He let it hang in the air between them until tension filled the space. Weird. Why wouldn't she answer? Not that it mattered. There were more pressing issues. "Where's Xan?"

Her eyes darted out the doorway before coming back to Athan. "The guy you were traveling with?"

"Yes." He drew the word out for several seconds. Who else would he be asking about? And why was she so nervous?

"He has been detained." Her smile patronized him and offered no comfort. "But I'm sure you'll see him shortly."

Detained? Great. Xan wasn't the best at keeping his temper in check. And after that blast, he was sure to be pissed. "Is Dahlia better? Where is she?"

The girl waived him forward. "Come. Now. Let's not keep our goddess waiting."

Our goddess? Hecate? Not likely. But it wasn't worth arguing. Not yet. "Um, one more thing." Athan pointed at his makeshift skirt. "Can I have my clothes back? I'd like to get dressed. And what did you say your name was?"

The woman flinched. "You'll have clothes momentarily." She indicated that he follow, and she stepped out of the room.

She'd again not answered his questions. Athan rubbed his hand over his face. His options were limited, and they both knew it. He tucked the corner of the blanket at his waist, and hoping it would hold, he followed her out of the cave.

Only to realize they'd been in a cavern of a much larger cave. Athan followed the girl through a series of tunnels. She never once turned to see if he was following, and step-by-step, his resentment and frustration grew. Two left turns and a right. Down a set of stairs, another right, then left, then up two levels . . . She was leading him in a maze.

He debated telling her. After all, she was clearly trying to confuse him by taking him in circles. But she'd withheld information, so he saw no reason to spoil the fun. Fifteen minutes later, they were exactly down the hall from the bedroom he'd woken up in, and his escort led him into a space the size of an Olympic stadium.

"Isn't that Hecate?" He pointed to the goddess reclining on a chaise lounge. Two young men wearing nothing but loincloths stood on either side of her, fanning her with large palm fronds. Their rich mahogany skin was painted in intricate designs of scales and feathers, and their shaved scalps were bare except for one long lock of hair.

She frowned. "Yes. Our goddess is anxious to meet you."

The goddess didn't look anxious.

His skin crawled as unease skirted through him. They crossed the large room, and Athan took inventory. He was dressed in a skirt, barefoot, weaponless, and the only other people, if he could call them that, were girls in dresses, who also appeared weaponless, and two men waving foliage. Nothing that could help him.

Maybe Hecate was one of the good gods. His father had once been close to her—consorts was what the textbooks called it. Lovers, really. But it had ended long ago, like *ancient Greece* long ago.

All Athan could think as he crossed the stone ground was witchcraft and magic.

"Son of Hermes." She sat up. "What are you doing alone in the Underworld?" The goddess waved at the two young men, and they stopped their fanning. Her hair hung loose, the maroon waves framing her in a halo of blood all the way down to her waist. Her flowy chiton was a pale green fabric, almost completely sheer except in a couple of strategic places. Hecate perused him from head to toe and back again. "Or is your father here, too?"

As he swallowed back disgust at her obvious once-over, he considered his options. Lying to Charon hadn't gone over well, but did Hecate have allegiances to Thanatos? "No, he's not. I'm here to collect someone."

"Shame." Her blue eyes gleamed. "Is the person you're *trying* to get alive or dead?"

"Hopefully alive. Are my companions safe?"

She waved away his question. "Does your father know you're here?"

He shrugged. "I didn't tell him I was coming, but he's probably aware of it by now."

She nodded. "Probably."

TWENTY-TWO

HOPE

THEY WERE OUTSIDE a stone house. The double doors were painted a deep burgundy, and vines of emerald leaves climbed the right corner of the building, extending over the arched doorway. The blue shutters were open, revealing curtained windows. The porch was covered with terracotta plant holders, and the geraniums and chrysanthemums sparkled in the light. The home was isolated in a valley surrounded by black hills. The air was sweet, clean, with a hint of earthy undertones that told Hope dirt was nearby.

"Where are we?" Hope whispered. Thanatos had never shown her this part of the Underworld.

"The in-between of Elysium and the Isles of the Blessed. Very few are here, relatively speaking." Lachesis pointed to the door. "Go ahead and knock."

Butterflies took flight in Hope's stomach, and her palms became clammy. "Here?"

All of her travels and risks, and now she was finally here.

"All of your answers won't be here, but it's a good start, young one. Before I go, I must ask, did you by chance bring your *Book of the Fates* with you to the Underworld?"

Hope shook her head.

Lachesis bit the side of her mouth in a very human gesture. "Then let me give you a gift." She held out a thin book, its buttery yellow cover embossed with an intricate diamond pattern. "The *Books* are bound here as we are bound. We cannot add to your book while we are bound. One day you will be able to read it, and it will make sense."

"Whose is it?"

Lachesis shook her head and motioned for Hope to knock.

Hope glanced at the book in her hands. She flipped through the pages, but they appeared blank. Her mind raced. For it to be unreadable could only mean one thing. "Whose—?"

Hope looked up, but Lachesis was gone.

To read a person's *Book of the Fates*, one must have pure intent toward the individual. Athan was able to read hers, and she could read the ones in the Olympian library. Xan initially wasn't able to read hers, which given his history of slaying monsters made sense. So who did Hope hate so much that she wouldn't be able to read their book?

With a deep breath, Hope switched the book into her left hand and knocked on the front door.

A handsome blond man answered. He was several inches taller than Hope, with broad shoulders and a square chin. His muscular arms were bare, and his fitted tank top revealed that his upper torso was just as strong. He raised his brows and asked, "May I help you?"

Everything about him made Hope cringe. Her heart raced with revulsion and fear. His sky-blue eyes confirmed his heritage. She shook her head. Denial, fear, incredulity. "I'm looking for Leto Nicholas."

He smiled, and his entire countenance lit up. "Of course. Come in."

She wouldn't budge. There was no way her mother would let one of them into her home. Her mind reeled with the puzzle, trying to explain to herself why he could be here.

The man disappeared down the hallway, leaving the door open.

Voices drifted out to her, but Hope couldn't focus. She looked down the hall, then to the book in her hands. She turned and looked out at the expanse of lawn, realizing there was actual grass here, which would explain the smell of dirt. How could the grass grow without the sun?

A gasp came from the house and then a squeal. Hope turned to see her mother running at her.

"Hope!" Leto crashed into her daughter, wrapping her arms around her in a smothering embrace. "Good gods. I can't believe you're here. How did you get here?" She patted and kissed and squeezed. "And you're still alive; I can feel your warmth. How? How can this be?"

Hope let her mother ramble, but when Leto tried to pull her into the house, Hope refused.

"What's the matter?"

Hope pointed into the dark hall. "Why is he here?"

Leto's eyes widened. "Luc? I . . . You better come in and sit down, sweetheart."

That wasn't going to happen. Nausea roiled through Hope, and she could feel the crushing weight of a boot on her face. The taste of blood. The smell of ash. Apollo's hand as he caressed her cheek. Hope shook her head, clenching the book in her hands. "No."

Leto sighed and closed the door behind her. "Don't be melodramatic, Hope. I wouldn't let anyone—"

Hope barked out a laugh. They were in the Underworld, Leto was dead, living with a son of Apollo, whose brothers had tried to kill Hope, and she was being melodramatic?

"Let's go sit in the grass," Leto said. Like they had when Hope was younger.

Hope stepped off the porch and into the lawn. She sat, one leg extended in front of her, the other foot on the ground with her knee bent. Her hand was braced with the book against the ground, in case she needed to quickly stand in guard position.

Leto stared at her daughter as if absorbing every detail. "You don't trust me?"

More than anything, Hope wanted to deny it. "Him. I don't trust him."

Leto knelt in front of Hope. "Please, baby, please don't be mad."

"Who is he?" Why was he here? And how could her mother have gone from loving Paul a year ago to loving a son of Apollo?

"Your father."

She absorbed the words as if they were a sucker punch. Her muscles twitched, and her jaw went slack. There were no words. And then just as quickly something akin to relief burst through her. "The curse."

Leto only offered a wan smile. "I promise you'll be safe. Just, please, come inside and let him talk to you."

Holy crap. *Holy crap!* Leto had married a son of Apollo?

Hope moved as if in a daze. Her mother guided her through the door and then into a small parlor off the entryway.

"Stay here and let me get Luc."

Luc? "I thought my dad's name was Symeon."

Her mother turned to face her and gave her a watery smile. "Symeon is his middle name."

Hope studied the room. This wasn't like the homes she'd been used to. The apartments they'd lived in were barren, void of adornment. This room had pictures of Hope at every stage of growth, from infant to . . . was that from last year in Goldendale? A beautiful sunset hung over the mantle of a fireplace that held several logs, as if waiting for a match to bring life to a cheery blaze. The end tables held more frames, and Hope looked at pictures of her mother as a child, and then . . . was that her grandfather and grandmother? Undoubtedly, the women of the family shared a strong resemblance, but their own uniqueness, as well.

Hope was looking at a small figurine of a Sphinx when she heard two sets of footsteps in the hall. She set the small ceramic down and turned to face her mother and father.

Leto reappeared holding the hand of the beautiful Luc Symeon Nicholas.

To his credit, he appeared every bit as shocked as Hope felt. His turquoise eyes were cloudy with emotion, and his hands trembled as he reached out to touch her.

Hope withdrew a pace. The man was a complete stranger, and he wanted to hug her? Hot anger surged through her, and she put up her hands as if to block any further approach. "I don't know you."

"I'm so sorry." He pointed to an upholstered loveseat, indicating that she sit. He then grabbed a chair from the other side of the room. "You're right."

Hope perched on the edge of the small couch, her knees angled toward the doorway, her hands clenched into fists. She had no idea what he would say. What could he say? There was no excuse for his abandonment.

Luc offered the seat to Leto, who looked back and forth between her husband and her daughter.

Hope didn't want to care where her mom sat. But if she sat next to *him* . . . It would be like she was siding with him. The fear that her mother would choose a son of Apollo over Hope made her chest hollow with hurt. The ache lessened when her mom sat down, scooping up Hope's hand and giving her a gentle squeeze.

But then Leto smiled at her husband, as if an apology to Luc. Hope wanted to scream but withdrew her hands from her mom, clenching them so tight nails dug into her palms; a physical release of her emotional tension.

With a deep breath, Luc stood and began pacing the small room. "Growing up with Apollo as a father was tumultuous. He was not patient. He expected his sons to excel and pushed me to pursue my interests in music and art. He also stressed the importance of self-defense and had me train with one of the sons of Ares as well as several other demigods. Eventually, demigods are expected to spend some time in service at one of our conservatories."

Hope gritted her teeth. "I know. I've been there."

Leto gasped, and Luc's eyes widened. "Did you get in?"

"Yes." Hope filled them in on the briefest of details of her time in the conservatory, keeping it to the deception of her mother's identity, the hunt for information in the library, and the supposition that Hades's realm was next. Both were so intent on her words, but she didn't understand why Luc was pretending to care.

"Astonishing," Luc said.

Leto beamed with pride and grabbed Hope's hand again.

This time, Hope let her mom hold it but leveled her gaze at her father. "Go ahead with your story. I've wanted to hear this my whole life."

Luc paused in his pacing and offered her a tight smile. "I understand you're upset. But, I promise, I didn't leave you on purpose."

Hope said nothing. She wouldn't give him the satisfaction of saying it was okay. It was most definitely *not* okay, but she would let him tell his side. She set the bar low, knowing it wouldn't be good.

"I was training to be *psachno,* and I was given a final test to see if I was ready. The goal was to find a demigod and bring him in." Luc sighed and squeezed in next to Leto. "I rented an apartment on Mercer Island."

"And you needed to go to the grocery store," Leto started and then laughed. She reached out and grabbed Symeon's hand, and the demigod scooted closer to his wife. "Do you remember?"

He nodded, his golden hair flopping over his eye, and he brushed the lock out of his face. "Of course I remember, love. It was on a Tuesday—"

"It was a Monday." She laughed again.

Hope stared at the two of them, her face pinching into a scowl. Anger and wonder warred in her heart. How could her mother not be upset? Not only was she not upset, they looked in love. Luc and Leto looked barely older than Hope, and it was the strangest sense of déjà vu, as if talking to Haley and Tristan. Hope could hardly believe . . .

"I know it was a Monday because I went to see Priska at Mr. Davenport's office every Monday afternoon, and that was the only time I went to that store."

Symeon pursed his lips and then nodded again. "Right. On a Monday. I remember it well."

Hope immediately caught the reference to the old movie her mother loved. They'd spent many nights watching the classic musical. Her mother's tears made a little more sense now.

"So . . ." Hope urged the tale to continue.

Luc stared at his wife, adoration in his eyes. "Why don't you tell it, Leto?"

Hope shook her head. She didn't need her mother to tell her how she and Luc had met. She'd heard *that* story dozens of times. "I don't care how you met. I know that. I want to know what happened. Why did you leave? If you loved her so much, why did you take off? Why didn't you come back? How did you end up here?"

Understanding dawned, and Luc's features went from light to dark. "You are here to break the curse."

Spine-tingling chills crawled over her skin despite the warm, humid air, and her anger dissolved into dread.

"Yes," she whispered.

He leaned toward her, and Hope inched forward to meet him.

"He will do everything he can to stop you," he whispered.

Even with her keen hearing, she had to strain to make out the words. But this wasn't anything she didn't already know. Apollo's ruthlessness had been demonstrated when he'd killed his own sons in her bedroom.

"Why are you whispering?" Hope asked. It made no sense. Luc was dead. How could he still fear Apollo, a god from Olympus?

Luc turned to look behind him. "He has eyes everywhere."

Gods, he was paranoid. She started to wonder if her father was not right in the head. Her mom wouldn't have fallen for just a pretty face, right?

"Have you read Phaidra's history, Hope?" Leto asked, still holding Luc's hand.

Hope nodded. She'd spent all those hours in the apartment with Priska, reading her grandmother's history.

"What does Phaidra's story have to do with Symeon?" She waved her hands as her irritation mounted. It was going to take some time to get used to his other name. "I mean Luc." She couldn't bring herself to call him *Dad.*

"Do you remember when she met Khafre?"

Hope ran through the stories in her mind. Khafre, pharaoh of Egypt, responsible for killing his brother Djedefre to ascend the throne. He'd had Phaidra kidnapped and tried to marry her. He'd promised her it would fulfill the curse because . . .

Hope shuddered. She closed her eyes and rubbed them with the palms of her hands. This was insanity. But her anger had dissipated, and she said, "Tell me."

TWENTY-THREE

ATHAN

ATHAN STUDIED THE gems running in veins in the black rock of the Underworld. Red, green, blue, and white streaked the dark walls, glimmering in the light. Something deep within told him to watch his manners, but this was ridiculous. He narrowed his eyes and wondered what Hecate could want with him and his companions. "Where are Xan and Dahlia?"

A crease formed between the goddess's eyes, and she frowned. "How are you feeling? All better?"

Now that she mentioned it, he was feeling better, except for the irritation with her inane questions. The despair he'd swallowed from the river was gone, and the bite on his leg no longer ached. He leaned away from her. Why would she have healed him?

"Do you think your father would like it that you're healed?"

Was this about his father? He scrubbed his hand over his face. Of course it was.

"I'm sure he would be pleased, yes?" She stood. Reaching out, she grabbed the arm of the young man closest to her. With her thumb, she smeared the design covering his bicep. "Savon, Henri, you will stay here." Her gaze landed on the priestess who'd escorted Athan. "Evelyn."

The girl blushed and averted her gaze. Had she been staring at the boys?

"You are dismissed." Hecate shooed the girl away as if swatting a fly. Then the goddess turned her attention back to Athan. "Good help is so hard to come by."

Was she baiting him? He shrugged.

"You smell like death. Were you bathing in the Acheron?" She didn't wait for his answer but continued talking as she led him from the dais. "Those other two that were with you are from War and Chaos, correct? Are they smart? I wouldn't imagine they could be too smart to have followed you here."

They entered a small chamber outside the auditorium.

"You may get dressed there." She pointed to a screen inside the doorway, the same black fabric and gold rods as the cot in the room.

He stepped behind it to find his pack sitting on a stone bench, as well as the clothes he'd been wearing when the Skia attacked. His immortal blades were in their sheaths next to his boots. Everything was clean, as if the fight had never happened. As if the dust, dirt, and grime of their travel had never existed.

As if Hecate hadn't blasted him in the stomach and burned a hole in his shirt. As if.

He stepped out from behind the screen.

The goddess bit the side of her mouth as she studied him. "Thanatos is behind the Skia who attacked you. Both here and in the mortal realm."

His stomach churned. "Why?"

She shrugged, and the strap of her chiton slid off her freckled shoulder. She grabbed the golden clasp and pulled it back up as she led him back to the larger room. "He's a god. You're threatening what he wants."

What would the god of death want with Hope?

Athan followed the goddess of crossroads and magic.

"Get the hell off me!" Xan burst into the room, shirtless, his wrists and ankles in manacles. He stumbled to the floor. With a deep breath, he pulled himself up, flinching as he stood on the uneven ground in bare feet. One of the girls reached for him, but he shifted out of her reach and glared at her. "Don't touch me."

Flanking him were two young women dressed in fitted black clothes, their hair pulled back in sleek braids. Their faces were free of makeup, but their expressions were bold and fearless.

"The son of Ares," one intoned.

These women wore utility belts with bulging pockets, and blades of various lengths were attached. Several more weapons were strapped to their thighs.

Hecate disappeared and reappeared in front of Xan. She clenched his chin and pulled his face down close to hers, her painted nails digging into his skin. "You bring no value to me, so watch your manners."

Xan clenched his teeth.

"What do you want with us?" Athan ground out.

Hecate released Xan's jaw, leaving nail marks on his chin. She faced Athan with a gleam in her eyes. "Not both of you." She sauntered over to Athan and rested her finger on his chest. "Just you."

She walked around Athan, her finger trailing over his chest around to the back and returning to his chest. "Do you have your phone?"

Athan nodded. He knew this was about Hermes as soon as the goddess had asked if his father would be pleased.

"Call him."

He reached into his pocket, wishing his phone would be like most cell phones. Mortal phones wouldn't work in the Underworld. But of course, his screen lit up. He sent a text.

Athan hadn't even exhaled his breath and his father was standing beside him.

Hermes's tousled hair was the exact same shade of bronze as his son's. The two were the same height, with the same runner's build. But Hermes's hazel eyes blazed with anger, and he towered over the goddess. "Hecate."

The redheaded goddess smirked up at the god of travelers. "I'm so glad you came. I wasn't sure you would, really. Do you care for this one?" She tapped Athan on the chest again.

Hermes pulled the goddess's hand away from his son and pushed her back several feet. "Do you care for any of your daughters?"

Hecate's eyes hardened. "It's not the same."

Athan looked around the room. The two girls in black still stood on either side of Xan, their bodies tense, hands on their weapons. The other young women continued to mill around the room in their flowing chitons, oblivious to the tension simmering inside the door.

"No, I suppose not." Hermes blocked Athan from Hecate but also obstructed his view of the goddess. "Do you have anyone here you care for?" The god waved his arms to encompass the room. "Anyone?"

Hecate brushed past them and sauntered back to her dais. She sunk into the cushioned seat and threw her leg over the arm of her chair. The fabric fell away from her pale skin, revealing more golden freckles on her lower extremity.

"I'm willing to bargain with you, Hermes. Since you care for your boy, I'm willing to strike a deal." Her fingers played with the edges of the sheer fabric.

Athan's heart grew heavy in his chest. What had he done?

TWENTY-FOUR

ATHAN

AS IF ANSWERING his question, Hecate turned to him. "You drank from the Acheron. Both you and the girl. You now belong to the Underworld. And I have claimed you."

"Ridiculous," Hermes said with a wave of his hand. "Athan—"

"I threw it all up!" He couldn't contain himself. "Every last drop, every piece of rotten flesh." He spit on the dark stone floor. "None of it stayed in my body."

She would not get him. She would not stop him!

Xan's face was frozen in horror. He shifted as if to step forward, and the guards halted him. "Dahlia," he breathed.

"I will bargain with you, god of travelers, and messenger to the gods. I will make you a deal." The goddess of witchcraft smirked at the other god.

"No—"

"I will speak with my son," Hermes said as he walked from the room.

Athan glared at the goddess and followed his father. As he passed Xan, Athan whispered, "It will be okay."

But Xan's expression made it clear he didn't believe the same.

As soon as Athan was out of the room, Hermes dragged him into the small changing room. In a voice seething with frustration, Hermes asked, "What in the name of Olympus are you doing here?"

Athan opened his mouth to respond, but Hermes didn't give him the chance. "I can't believe the insanity that must be running through your head. Do you owe that son of Ares? Is this a dare? Cronus and Rhea, if you are trying to prove—"

"It's about Hope, Dad." Athan willed his father to understand.

Hermes's furrowed brow relaxed, and then his eyes widened. "The Sphinx?"

Athan hated that his father still refused to acknowledge her as a person. Clenching his teeth, Athan reminded his father, "Her name is Hope."

Hermes broke eye contact. He adjusted his shirt, tugging the fabric away from his skin, and then leaned against the dark rock wall. "What is she doing in the Underworld?"

"I don't know." Athan let out a sigh of frustration. That wasn't completely true. "She wants to break the curse. For some reason, she came here. Myrine told me."

Athan filled his father in on what happened since they'd last spoken. How Athan had searched for Hope, only to find her in the conservatory. He told his father about the Skia attack that had put him in a coma, and how Hope had disappeared by the time he woke up. He told all about the tentative truce with Xan and the difficulty they'd had in navigating the Underworld.

As Athan spoke, Hermes's face hardened into stone. His nostrils flared, and the skin around his eyes tightened. He crossed his arms over his chest and snapped, "You are not meant to be here, son."

"But I must find her." It didn't matter if his father didn't approve. Athan felt the need to help her, an ache deep in his chest, and he wasn't going to give up on her. "She saved my life, and I . . . I love her."

Hermes grunted. "It is not love of which you speak. This infatuation—"

He was done having his father brushing off his feelings. Athan stepped into Hermes's personal space and with a low growl asked, "Have you not been listening to me? How can you even say that?"

"How long have you known her? A month, maybe two?" Hermes waved his arms dismissively.

Athan ground his teeth. His father was such a hypocrite. "How long did you know Mom?"

Hermes straightened, and his eyes hardened. "That was different."

"Mom was only nineteen," Athan whispered. "She said she knew the moment she saw you cross the room."

Pain crossed over the god's features and aged his otherwise youthful appearance. The anger washed away, and his shoulders dropped. "What if it isn't love?"

"A life without risk isn't worth living, right?" But as Athan said the words, something in his soul resonated with them, and he stood tall, accepting the challenge and all that would come with it. "I have to try."

The god acknowledged his words with a small nod. "I can see that you must."

"I didn't drink from the river—"

Hermes waved away the words. "I can see that. So can Hecate. She's trying to get something from me. What about your other companions? Are you here with more than the son of Ares?"

"There is a daughter of Eris, too. She fell in the river." Athan's stomach turned with the memories. "She consumed a lot."

Hermes frowned. "I will not be able to save her."

"But—"

"There are laws, Athan. Hades rules the Underworld in a very organized fashion. I cannot break the law without making recompense." The god of thieves, languages, commerce, and boundaries sat down on the bench, as if the weight of his words pressed him down. "Ares's son is a better fighter, so I would encourage you to take him with you. She drank from the river, so one of you will be bound here. I doubt you will want to trade places with her."

Xan will never forgive me. Nor would Hope. Athan shoved the feeling of betrayal away. In truth, he would likely never forgive himself, but he would save Hope, no matter what the cost.

"Fine," he choked out, but he couldn't bring his eyes to meet his father's.

Hermes put his hand on Athan's shoulder. "It is not selfish to act so. Even if you'd protested, I cannot save Eris's daughter from the Underworld."

Even with his father's statement, guilt pressed on Athan's heart. "Can you do nothing for her?"

"Is she skilled? She is certainly beautiful, but that will not serve her well with Hecate."

His words sounded like a warning.

"Aren't all demigods attractive?" He couldn't help the defensiveness. No one wanted to be judged solely on their appearance. "She's an excellent fighter. Second only to her cousin."

Hermes grimaced. "Is she smart?"

They hadn't taken any classes together, but Xan wouldn't put up with her if she was an idiot. Even if she was family. "She's not dumb."

"Sometimes that's worse." Hermes sighed, and his shoulders sagged with acceptance. "I will do what I can, but she may not thank me for it."

Athan had to believe it would make it better. Better than her just dying.

"No matter what I say, don't protest." Hermes met Athan's eyes with no spark of fun or teasing. "No matter what, okay?"

Athan nodded. He understood what his father wasn't saying. He wasn't going to like the way this went down. Which meant there was a good possibility Xan wouldn't like it either.

Xan stood inside the doorway, still flanked by the two female guards. Hecate rose from her throne as soon as they entered and gracefully glided toward them.

As soon as they crossed into the large cavern, Hermes pushed Athan away from him and toward the goddess. "I can't believe your stupidity. You have not acted in a way befitting your station." The god turned to Hecate. "You may have him."

Athan's stomach hit his toes. His father couldn't be serious. Not after what he'd just said in the hall. This must be part of his plan, but anxiety crawled over Athan nonetheless.

Hermes stepped closer and shoved his son again. "He is remarkably dense for being my son. Probably only good to be one of *those*." He waved at the men standing beside her chaise. "You may as well take both of them. They're nothing more than pretty faces."

Both of them? Hermes words didn't make sense, but Athan pushed away at the doubt crashing into him.

"What?" Xan yelled, stepping forward.

The two priestesses stepped with him, grabbed his arms, and pulled him back to where he'd been standing.

Hecate's face clouded with confusion. "The son of Ares hasn't consumed anything here. He is not bound."

"No?" Hermes pinched his lips. "No matter. I will trade them both for the girl."

Hecate chuckled, but her smirk appeared to pain her. "You favor the daughter of Eris?"

Hermes withdrew a pace as if the words were a physical shock. "Favor her? Absolutely not."

More confusion clouded the goddess's fair face. "But she is quite beautiful."

Xan muttered obscenities under his breath.

"I do not want her for her looks." He indicated behind him where Xan and Athan now stood. "Dip them in the Lethe. They are handsome enough for you, right?" Hermes continued as he stepped up to Hecate. "But I would like the daughter of Eris."

Hecate said nothing as she worried her lip with her teeth.

Athan could almost hear the wheels of her mind clicking through the information. "Is she intelligent? A strong fighter?"

Hermes broke their gaze and stared up at the dark rock. "No, not at all."

The air hung heavy with the lie, and they all knew it.

Hecate narrowed her gaze. "I would look upon the daughter of Eris again." The goddess stepped from the dais. "Come with me."

The guards grabbed Xan and pulled him through the doorway. Athan waited by his father until Hecate swept past.

"What are you doing?" he whispered once the goddess had exited the room.

The resounding crack of Hermes's strike brought tears to Athan's eyes. The initial sting blossomed into an ache that made his head throb.

"Don't speak to me. No son of mine would be so foolish."

For the first time, Athan wondered if his father was really acting. He closed his eyes, willing the tears not to fall. Worse than the physical pain was the doubt. He'd never seen his father so cruel, and there was no reason for it. No explanation. Athan's hesitation cost him any chance of looking into his father's eyes. By the time Athan raised his head, Hermes was gone, and Athan was left to catch up.

There was plenty of noise to direct him down the hall, and as he followed it, he mused that this was close to where he'd woken up. Approaching the door, he realized it was right next door to where he'd been, in fact. He shook his head and entered.

His face still throbbed, but the pain was nothing next to the sight in front of him.

Blood ran down the side of Xan's face, but he knelt, oblivious to the open wound, holding his cousin's hand.

The sheets were twisted around Dahlia's body, and as she thrashed, Athan could see why. Her once vibrant skin was gray and ashen, her lips pale and cracked. Dark bags aged her appearance, and her eyes were sunken deep into her skull. She looked like death.

Athan let his eyes flit over the rest of the room.

The two guards were crumpled in a heap inside the doorway, and it didn't take a genius to see what had happened.

Hermes's face was filled with sorrow, and Athan knew his father was lost in memories of his own loss.

Only Hecate seemed unconcerned with the state of her guests. The Underworld goddess leaned against the black rock, her pale skin and green chiton a striking contrast. Her eyes bore into the demigod daughter of contention and strife.

"You will have to burn through the desperation that has filled her."

Hermes snorted. "It will not be just desperation. Her soul will be filled with anguish and loss." He stared at the goddess until she looked away. "As you well know." He sighed as if put out. "Nevertheless, I'll take her with me."

He approached the bed and nudged Xan.

Xan's head snapped up, and his eyes glinted with fire. He stood; his clenched hands hung by his sides. "What do you want of her, Lord Hermes?"

Hermes stared at Xan. "You have two minutes to say good-bye to her, son. And that's a mercy you don't deserve."

This man was nothing like the father Athan knew. This god was used to getting his way, and humans and demigods were subjects to do his will, nothing more.

Hermes leaned over and picked up a lock of Dahlia's dark hair. He let it drop through his fingers. Athan watched while a mixture of awe and disgust churned through him. Had he not been so focused, he would've missed the pain that skirted through his father's eyes. What was he doing?

Hecate stepped closer, brushing past Athan and coming to a stop in front of Dahlia. The goddess of witchcraft placed her hands hovering just over the demigod's head, then her chest, and finally rested them on Dahlia's navel. With a gleam in her eyes she said, "On second thought, keep your son. Take him and his friend. The girl is mine."

"But we agreed—"

Hecate glared up at Hermes and held up her hand. "There was no agreement."

She turned back to Dahlia and felt her pulse, lifted her eyelids, and then put her hands back on her abdomen. "She will be fine." Violet light pulsed from beneath her palms once, twice, three times into Dahlia's belly.

Dahlia screamed, then rolled to her side to retch over the edge of the bed. Tarry sludge spewed onto Hecate's feet, splattering on the edges of her flowy chiton.

Hecate placed the palm of her hand to Dahlia's forehead and pushed the demigod back to the bed. She then turned to the other occupants. "Get out." Her eyes glowed the same pale purple that had glowed from her palms only moments before. "Right now."

Hermes grabbed Athan and Xan and pulled them from the room.

The door closed as soon as they'd passed the threshold.

Hermes embraced his son but said nothing.

What was going on? "Dad?"

Hermes shook his head.

"When will she be better?" Xan asked.

"Not before you're dead, and maybe not even then."

Xan moved to push past the god, but Hermes blocked him and pushed him back. "The worst thing you could do right now is go back in there. You'd be damning you both to Tartarus, or worse." He shoved him down the corridor and indicated that Athan follow. "Move."

Hermes ducked into the changing room a second time, pulling both the demigods with him.

"Mother Gaia." Hermes released a long breath.

Xan's features were stony, and he glared at Hermes. "Bloody hell."

Athan didn't know what to say. Had his father saved Dahlia or damned her? Athan was afraid to ask, afraid to find out the answer. Something deep within told him he didn't really want to know.

Xan's eyes glistened with unshed tears. He turned toward the door and whispered a farewell to Dahlia. "May you find peace in this realm."

"Why didn't you fight harder for her?" Athan asked.

Xan turned to Hermes. "Would it have done any good? Could I have saved her?"

Hermes glanced down before meeting Xan's eyes. "No."

Xan swallowed hard and glared at Athan. "Don't mistake acceptance for cowardice. She would've never been happy in the mortal realm. Maybe she'll even be able to find Roan."

"Roan is here? In the Underworld?"

Xan flinched. "You aren't the only one who's lost someone because I failed."

Athan knew immediately what Xan was referring to. Xan had spent more than one night, *legless*, as he called it, or rather drowning his sorrows in liquor. He'd been drunk the night he'd taken Isa out. Obviously, he'd made the same mistake years before with Roan. "Did she know?"

Xan shook his head. "I could never find the words."

Gods. He'd never even told his cousin? "*Skata.*"

"Where are you going?" Hermes asked, his body sagging against the wall. Whatever game he'd been playing had made him nervous, too. "Wherever it is, we need to get you out of here before she finds a reason to keep you here. Trust me . . ."

And even though he didn't finish the sentence, the weight of the words was enough to convey the message. They did not want to serve Hecate.

Their best chance at finding Hope was to get the ruler of the Underworld to agree to help them. "We need to get to the palace of Hades."

Hermes ran his hand through his hair again before squaring his shoulders. "I won't be able to help you after this."

Athan nodded.

Hermes placed both hands on Athan's shoulders. "Think before you speak. Don't eat or drink anything. And be very careful what you commit to."

Blinding light exploded, forcing Athan to close his eyes. A deafening boom resonated through his entire body, and his ears began to ring.

TWENTY-FIVE

HOPE

Luc met Hope's eyes and leaned toward her as he started his story. "Leto and I met at the grocery store. I admit I was mesmerized by her beauty, but after an afternoon of chatting about . . . well, everything, I knew I couldn't let her go." He ran his hand over Leto's head in a soft caress. "We dated and, as you know, fell in love and got married."

"If you loved her, why did you leave?" Hope wasn't angry anymore, but she wasn't going to let him off the hook on this either. "People don't abandon those they love, right?"

"You are right." Luc's shoulders slumped. Then, after a deep breath, he continued, "We'd been married for about a month, maybe two, when your mother asked me to sit down. She had something she needed to tell me . . ."

He closed his eyes and took another deep breath. When he opened them, his features smoothed out and he smiled, as if the memories were right there, in front of him.

"I wanted to put the conversation off," he said then turned to Leto. "Remember, I wanted to go on a date."

She swallowed, and her eyes filled with tears. "I remember."

"It was almost like I could feel your fear, and I wanted to make it better. But mostly, I was worried, because I had deceived you. You called me Symeon, and every time it made my heart ache. I hadn't even told you my first name."

Leto waved away his concern. "I love both your names."

Hope wanted to tell them to speed it up already; their mushy declarations of love were weird and made her uncomfortable. Like her parents needed some time alone. "Do you want me to come back another time?"

Leto smacked Hope's leg. "Manners."

Hope blushed from the reprimand. She was being rude. How hard would it be to bite her tongue while he finished his story? Clearly, her mother loved Luc. It was the least Hope could do. "Sorry."

Luc leaned over toward Hope. "It's okay that you're upset. I won't begrudge you that. But I do care, and I think you really do want to know what happened."

He was right, and Hope settled back into the couch to hear his story.

"Your mother refused to go out, saying that what she had to say couldn't wait, not even a few hours. We sat down on the sofa, and . . . I held her hand in mine. I think that was the first inkling I had there was something more about her. Her skin was . . . is the same golden tone as mine."

"She made me promise not to be angry, and I was so surprised. What could she say that would make me angry? I promised. Of course, I promised. Then, she asked me if I believed in the gods." He flinched as if the memory caused him physical pain. "In that moment, my concern shifted to apprehensive unease. Had she already suspected me? Did she know what I was?"

Leto shook her head. "I had no idea."

Luc nodded. "I know, dear." He looked back to Hope. "I tried to be casual and asked her why she wanted to know, but I had no idea what was coming. She told me she wasn't human, whispered it in a pained voice and closed her eyes. She was so afraid of my reaction she refused to look at me, and it made my heart ache. But inside, I was relieved. I thought she'd meant she was a demigod, and I was excited with all that could mean. We could spend eternity together if we were careful. I thought the Fates had smiled on us. I thought it was a divine blessing."

He pursed his lips.

Hope no longer wanted to interrupt him. She clenched her mother's hand and waited for more.

"I tried to reassure her, but she cut me off, telling me there was more she needed to say. Her persistent anxiety was making me nervous, and I wanted to tell her it was okay because we were the same. But she had to tell me something before it was too late. *Too late.* Those were the words that made me close my mouth and just listen."

"She told me that a god had tried to court her grandmother, and my frenzied mind misunderstood. I knew how demigods were formed. But then she said that her grandmother had refused the god and chosen her mortal lover. That's when I knew something wasn't right. That couldn't be right. But it was her next words that made my heart stop. She asked if I believed in curses."

Pulling her hand away from Hope's, Leto wiped at the tears streaming down her face. "I'm so sorry."

Luc knelt in front of his wife. Cupping her face with his hands, he wiped away the rest of the moisture with his thumbs. "You are not to cry for me anymore. I don't mourn my choice. I've never regretted it."

He sat on the floor at his wife's feet and looked up at Hope. "Leto asked me if I believed in monsters. I couldn't believe it at first. It was impossible. Monsters were half-breeds, and your mother was physically human. I knew that was what she was implying, that she was a monster, and for a brief moment, I thought maybe she was insane. But as to my belief? I knew that monsters existed. I'd seen them: centaurs, the Mer, even a griffin. I admitted my knowledge, even as I wondered where the conversation was going."

"She told me that her mother was a monster, and I tried to think of how that could be possible. The only explanation I could conceive was that some of the primordial deities had the ability to appear as monsters as well as human. But your mother assured me her mother wasn't a primordial deity.

Luc sighed. Resting his head on the couch, he closed his eyes as he continued, "My father used to tell me stories. He'd tell me of conquests . . . and curses. I'd heard the story of the Sphinx more than once, but I didn't know she could become human. I don't think anyone did."

"Leto told me that her grandmother refused the advances of the god, and in vengeance, the god had killed her and cursed her newborn baby. The baby, her mother, sought the aid of the Graeae, who reinterpreted the curse, thus allowing the monster to live as human . . . most of the time. She told me that the curse had passed from mother to daughter, and she now carried it. In that second, that very second, I knew."

He straightened and faced his wife and daughter.

Hope's heart seemed to be breaking as she watched the pain wash over her parents.

Looking up into Leto's eyes he continued, "I knew what you were going to say, but I prayed I was wrong. I wanted so much to be wrong in that moment. But then you said the words. As soon as you admitted to being the Sphinx, I felt so much shame. It was my father that cursed you. My own father. I knew he wasn't perfect, far from it. He is emotional, rash, and dismissive. But there is one thing I've seen him totally fanatical about, and it's consistent."

Luc raised his hand and pointed at Hope. "He is fanatical about his ownership of the monster he created. You are the one creature he considers wholly his, and he is determined to possess you. The entire purpose of the curse is to break you to his will. He will stop at nothing . . . absolutely nothing."

He swallowed. "I was too weak, or too naïve, to fully comprehend what that meant. I kissed your mother and offered false platitudes that we would be fine. That it was okay. But my words were in earnest. I never meant to be untrue. And every assurance of my love was sincere and heartfelt. I did, I do, love her." He stared up at Leto with wide eyes. "I love you."

Hope was still trying to reconcile the story her father was telling with what she'd believed her entire life. Not that she didn't believe him, but if he loved Leto so much . . . "So what happened? Why did you leave?"

Luc stood and resumed his pacing. "She told me she was going to change at first light, said I could leave if I wanted to. As if I would abandon her so easily." He pointed at Hope. "Which is probably why you believed me to be so callous. And I'd be lying now if I didn't admit I was scared. There was no way to hide what I'd done, and I didn't want to. But I also knew my father would find out, and I'd need to explain what had happened. At some point I would have to face him. But as I held your mother in my arms, I knew with every fiber of my being, I couldn't let her go. And I would do whatever was necessary to keep her safe, even if it meant defying my father."

Hope had never really understood the term *watching a train wreck happen* until that moment. She knew where this was going, but she couldn't bring herself to say anything to stop it.

TWENTY-SIX

ATHAN

THE AIR SHIFTED, and the faint smell of pomegranates tickled Athan's senses. The murmur of voices grew distinct as the tinnitus from their translocation faded.

"Is not this agreeable, Lord?"

Athan knew that rasping voice. His eyes flew open, and he stared across the throne room, his vision tunneling on the Skia that had killed his girlfriend almost a decade ago.

Darren stood at the bottom of a dais of three steps, his back to Athan. Torches hung in twisted iron holders spaced throughout the cavernous room, casting the space in ominous shadows. Hades occupied an obsidian throne at the top of the platform, and positioned next to him was an intricately carved throne of a deep red crystal, the color of pomegranates.

Hades's features were a study of contrasts. His hair was cropped just shy of chin-length, and the smooth dark locks shone like polished onyx. His goatee was trimmed short, and the depth of color made the pallor of his skin distinct. His angular features and broad shoulders created an imposing picture.

"Do you believe she is here?" the lord of the Underworld asked. "I have heard whisperings of it, but my Skia have not been able to locate her."

"Nay, Lord. The Sphinx is just—"

Athan's movement at the mention of Hope was inadvertent, and Xan grabbed his sleeve too late.

Darren turned even as Hades's gaze shifted to the two demigods that stood in the shadows.

"Demigods?" Hades stood in a fluid movement.

Darren's eyes narrowed and then widened in recognition. He grasped at his beltline. There was no time to think. Athan reached for his blades, but Xan was faster. Athan was thrown to the ground as an inky Skia blade whistled past them. Hades yelled a command that was muffled by Xan's heavy body.

The tension in the room continued to rise, and Athan pushed against Xan's weight. Had Xan been hit? Was Darren still alive?

Xan rolled to his feet, stood, and extended his hand to Athan. He didn't even have to look to see if he'd hit his target. Irritation pulsed through Athan's heart.

"Skata," he muttered as he brushed away Xan's hand and looked across the room.

Darren clutched the hilt of the silver dagger protruding from his chest. A perfect throw, the blade was buried to its rubied hilt. Darren opened his mouth to scream, but blinding sunshine poured from his dark depths. The Skia begged his lord with his eyes, pleaded for intervention. The rays seeped from the edges of his wound.

Hades's jaw tightened, but he said nothing as his servant disappeared, crumbling from within from the exposure to the divine light.

The silver blade clinked on the stone.

Xan gave Athan a once-over. "You all right?"

Athan snorted his disgust. As if he would need to be taken care of.

"My Lord." Athan bowed to the god.

Xan inclined his head. "Lord Hades."

Hades stepped down from the dais. His fluid movements were like a predator stalking his prey.

"Son of Ares." The god of the Underworld pushed Athan away from Xan and continued to circle the demigod. "You do not belong here."

Xan said nothing, keeping his head down. The muscles in his neck tightened and strained against an unseen force of tension.

"And you, Son of Hermes." Hades turned his gaze to Athan. "I have always treated you well as a guest, have I not?"

Athan nodded. It was true. The god had always been gracious when Athan had been in the Underworld with Hermes.

"And yet you bring death to my world?" Hades held up his hand before Athan could protest. "Do you know the sacrifices Skia make? Do you understand the necessity of their service?"

The god tapped on his chin as if contemplating what more to tell them. "You are young and impetuous, demigods. You would benefit from some depth of understanding." He waved his hand in a clear dismissal.

Athan felt the floor yanked out from under him.

Cold, like the blade of a Skia, blistered his skin. Athan shook with the sudden change in temperature. The icy air swirled around him in tortuous ribbons of pain. He needed to see if he could get out of the trajectory of the bitter wind. He stepped back and fell over a large boulder.

The boulder grunted.

Athan blinked, trying to force his eyes to stay opened. In truth, he wanted to curl in on himself to avoid the abuse the air was delivering.

"Shite. Where the Hades are we?"

Oh. The talking boulder was Xan. Athan crouched down next to the other demigod.

"Are you all right?" Athan yelled, but the words were swallowed in the maelstrom.

Xan tilted his head to the side and cracked an eye, gaze settling on Athan, and motioned for him to huddle close.

Athan lifted his shoulder in silent question. What good would it do to coil up here? But even as he thought it, the wind continued buffeting him. It was much like sparring multiple attackers at once, and there was no way to avoid the blows. He strained to find a way to escape, but eventually his natural instinct took over and he curled into the fetal position on the ground.

Tortured screams assailed him, the sounds grating against his sanity. The physical pain intensified, and despair pounded in his heart. They would never escape. They would die here. It had all been a waste. He wasn't strong enough to rescue Hope. He wasn't strong enough to save Dahlia. He wasn't there to keep Isa home. He couldn't save his mom. He was worthless, and now he was going to die in this hell. The worst thing was, he knew he deserved it. Despair filled him, and he wished for death.

"Enough." The feminine voice was soft, barely over a whisper, but the accent of the divine cut through the tumult.

The wind stilled. The overwhelming emotions evaporated, and three young women sat cross-legged on the dark stone.

Athan unwound his body, stretching his stiff muscles.

Xan eyed the women warily, his hand resting on the hilt of his remaining dagger.

They had not changed. The three girls looked nothing like sisters with their different skin tones, hair color, and even facial features. Atropos wore modern clothing befitting a military assassin today, only shears of varying colors and lengths hung from her utility belt, the only weapons she would ever need. Her skin was ebony, and her pointed features matched her purpose. The Fate responsible for cutting the thread of life offered a knowing smirk, and Athan turned away.

Lachesis laughed and almost dropped her measuring instrument. The long rod was covered in markings running the length of it. The goddess who measured the life of man had warm russet skin, the same color as her eyes.

"Don't scare him, Atropos." Her thick auburn curls swayed with her laughter.

The air warmed, and the only sound was the clacking of Clotho's eternal needles.

"He's one of the good guys." Lachesis held up her measuring stick as if to indicate he measured up. "They both are."

Xan snorted.

Had Xan lost his mind? Athan wanted to warn him, but there was no way to do so without the goddess knowing it. Perhaps they would not find him rude.

Atropos laughed, and when she spoke, the bitterness had disappeared from her tone. "Regardless of how good they are, they are all we have to work with."

"You are too eager to cut betimes." Even with the reprimand, Clotho continued her knitting.

Atropos inclined her head. "Perhaps." She regarded Xan with interest. "Perhaps not."

Xan narrowed his eyes. "Are you going to kill us then?" His lip curled in a sneer of disgust. "I think not, or you would've done so already. Are you trying to break us?"

"Enough," Clotho said in the same soft tone. Her head tilted up, and her blue eyes gazed at them as she set her needles aside. "We are not your enemies, Son of Ares."

Xan rolled his eyes. Athan well understood his sentiment. The gods were no one's friends either.

Clotho touched his knee. "The gods have been unjust to her, and this must stop. You must stop it here. Even now . . ." She closed her eyes and pinched the bridge of her dainty nose. "Even now they are working to thwart her."

Xan scrambled up and drew his blade. "Where?"

Athan's focus remained on the youthful-appearing goddess before him. Her golden hair fell in soft waves well past her shoulders, but her worn dress was a testament to how infrequently she took a break from her knitting. Her unlined skin couldn't hide the depth of wisdom in her eyes.

He'd read most of the *Book of the Fates* regarding the Sphinx. He knew they'd intervened to help Phaidra after Apollo's curse.

"Why? Why are you doing this?"

Clotho blinked. "Not all gods are motivated by self-interest. Some have a spark of justice within." She picked up her needles. "You'd better hurry. Your fate is unfolding."

Atropos glared at her sister. "You told them too much."

"Oh, stop. You forget our interest is in their success." The clacking of needles commenced.

Lachesis helped Clotho stand, and Atropos followed.

"You're out of Tartarus now, and when you step from our protection, you'll need to cross Persephone's garden to enter the palace." Lachesis exhaled slowly as her gaze measured them. "Your worth is more than one decision; it is the grand sum."

"Bullocks," Xan muttered.

Athan glared at him. They did not want to offend the Fates.

But Atropos laughed again, and her sharp features softened. "I like you, Son of Ares. You're brash but honest." She pulled a small set of embroidery shears from her waist. The handles were a milky white with silver veins that matched the blades. She handed them to him. "Be very careful how you use them."

The small pair of scissors disappeared in his palm. He raised his brow and tucked the pointed end into his empty sheath. "Aye. Best not nick my finger on them, too, right?"

Atropos smirked. "You're welcome."

TWENTY-SEVEN

HOPE

LUC PACED THE small room, his anxious energy diffusing into the very air. The pain he'd suffered still clung to him, and he grimaced as he relived his story.

These memories were still so fresh in his mind, and Hope felt nothing but pity for the man before her. Her rash statement at the banks of the Lethe seemed ignorant in the face of her father's anguish. She watched him cross, back and forth, while he sorted through the words of his final account.

Luc stopped and faced Hope. "I asked Leto what time she would change, mentally trying to prepare myself for what was coming. But when I looked at her, I saw how scared *she* was. She was curled in a ball on the sofa, and her body language screamed her fear. I needed to do something to make it right. Something to show her how much I loved her."

"I decided to go get all of her favorite things, just a quick trip to the grocery store. If we were going to be stuck inside for two days, we should have an indoor picnic, play board games, and watch movies. I was determined to make her experience of telling me her secret not just good, but great. I didn't want her to feel unsure, but mostly, I wanted to make it right."

"I figured I could stop by the conservatory and talk to my friend, Xan. He was the senior demigod at the time, and while he was brash, he had a good heart. He was older than any other demigod I knew, so I was hoping . . ."

Hope smiled at the mention of her friend, and she felt a new sense of connection to her father.

Luc shook his head. "There was so much I didn't know, and I was hoping he'd have some insight. I needed to tell Leto my secret, and it felt impossible to broach the subject what with the part my father played in her curse. And there was the matter of my father, too." His shoulders sagged with the weight of his burden, but he pressed on. "Anyway, I promised to pick up movies and treats and something for dinner. When I hugged her goodbye, my heart pounded as if it would beat its way from my chest. I was that nervous. But I kissed her and told her how much I loved her. And then I left."

"It was late enough that I went straight to the conservatory. But Xan was gone. There were only two demigods in residence, a mere child and a bitter daughter of Eris. But I was desperate for help. I asked if they would listen, and both were willing, so, keeping it as vague as possible, I told them of my situation. It's funny, I thought the child would hold more prejudice to monsters, but it was the older demigod who dismissed my worry with a wave of her hand. She repeated rhetoric about monsters not being fit to live, words all the demigods said. She stressed that Xan would tell me the same thing, and I feared she might be right."

"But then the little boy spoke. He told me not to listen to her, that she was just sad because her husband had left her. Gods, he was so little but talked just like a grown up. A smart grown up. Dahlia, the other demigod, yelled at him then left, but the boy stared at me with his wide eyes and asked me if I really loved the girl who was a monster. I assured him I did. I'll never forget what he said. *Dads are supposed to take care of their kids.* He was so cute and naïve, but that didn't make what he said less true. Fathers *are* supposed to take care of their kids, and want what's best for them. He said I should talk to my dad. And that love means you make it work, and always tell the truth."

Luc closed his eyes, and Hope wondered what memories were there that he wasn't sharing.

"I dismissed myself and thanked the young demigod for his time. Gods, I hope he's okay. He was such a good boy. I told him to tell Xan that I said to take him under his wing. I'm not sure that was any help, but it was the best I could think of at the time to thank the little guy for his help."

"There was never going to be a good time to confront my father, but as I drove away from the conservatory, I decided that if I approached him that very day, he wouldn't be able to accuse me of hiding anything from him. I drove to a small outdoor temple on the outskirts of the city, a lovely park with lilies, laurels, and hyacinth. I hadn't spoken face-to-face with my father for years. In truth, he only came to me when he wanted me to do something for him, so I wasn't expecting him to answer my petition."

"I made an offering at the shrine, and there was a moment when I worried he might actually appear, but the birds' songs and crickets chirping were the only sounds. I told the shrine how I met Leto, a bit about our brief courtship, and finally the whirlwind wedding. I begged forgiveness for not inviting him to the nuptials. I told him of my wife's kindness and patience, of her soft temperament. I was stalling, but I didn't know how to say it. I begged for forgiveness; I pled my ignorance and unintentional offence. The one thing I would not apologize for was my love for her. I asked for his blessing, and then I climbed the shrine and whispered in his ear her name. I waited for the roof to crash down on me, and when it didn't, I gathered my courage and whispered that Leto was the Sphinx."

"Nothing happened. My panic drained, and with it most of my energy. I told myself that maybe my father wouldn't be angry. Maybe he would give us his blessing. I left and went to the grocery store, the one on Mercer Island where I'd first met Leto. It was on the way home, and I was feeling nostalgic."

"I filled the shopping cart with all of her favorites: movie candy, popcorn, chips, soda, steak and potatoes, and several kinds of ice cream. As I wheeled the cart to the check out, I grabbed a bouquet of flowers, something a little extra to reinforce my words. I thought I'd have two whole days to show Leto how much I loved her, regardless of her form, or more accurately, regardless of Apollo's curse. More than anything, I wanted her to know that I was first and foremost the man who loved her."

"I paid for the groceries and walked out to the parking lot. The sun had just set; I remember the evening sky was tinged with pinks and lavenders like the flowers I'd just bought." Luc swallowed then rubbed at his eyes. After a deep breath, he continued, "I felt his presence before I could see him."

He fixed Hope with a wild, desperate look. "I have never known such panic. I scrambled for words. I was frantic . . . pleading for a miracle. In truth, I couldn't even tell you what I said. I just knew that if I didn't get out of there . . ." Tears streamed down Luc's face. He swiped at them roughly, as if frustrated with the way his emotions were spilling out. When he'd collected himself enough to speak, he merely said, "He's fanatical about his ownership of the Sphinx."

"He killed you." Hope said the words, already knowing of their certainty, and her heart ached for what should've been for Luc and her mother.

Leto reached for her husband, and he pulled her into a hug.

"I'm so sorry," he whispered into her hair. "So, so sorry." He pulled back far enough to see Hope. Luc smiled at his daughter, but his eyes remained filled with haunted pain.

"The next thing I knew I was at the river Acheron. Hermes was at my side, and he made payment to Charon so I could cross. I begged and pleaded, but the gods of the Underworld would not grant my petition. Truly, all I ever wanted was to love your mother."

Hope wanted to speak, but words utterly failed her.

TWENTY-EIGHT

ATHAN

The Moirai were gone, and Athan and Xan now stood just outside a knee-high stone wall. On the other side, a vibrant green lawn extended with lush flower gardens and blossoming fruit trees. If the black rock of the Underworld hadn't still surrounded them, Athan might have thought they were back in the mortal realm.

"Persephone's garden," Xan announced and stepped over the wall.

The ground was soft beneath them, the grass a welcome change. Athan's spirits lifted as the demigods followed a path next to an orchard.

"Don't eat anything." Athan said it just as much to remind himself as they passed trees heavy with peaches.

Xan rolled his eyes. "Don't be an arse. I know better."

The smell of the sweet fruit made Athan's mouth water, and he quickened his pace. Xan seemed to understand and matched step for step.

The palace of onyx rose before them, and Athan tried to formulate what he would say. They needed to get Hope, which meant they needed to find her. Which meant . . .

All thoughts ground to a halt as they turned the corner.

Isabel.

The raven-haired beauty looked the same as she had almost ten years ago. Her gray eyes dilated with surprise, and she squealed as she ran toward him. "Athan!"

Isabel.

The demigod daughter of Aphrodite Xan had found in England. He'd brought her to the conservatory; was it a decade ago? No, more like fifteen years. Athan had been twelve when they'd found her. She was seventeen. Could that be right? It seemed forever ago.

Isabel wrapped him in a hug, and his arms instinctively reciprocated. "Isa," he breathed.

She pulled away from him and cupped his face in her hands. "By the gods, I've missed you."

Her smile was like the dawning sun. Her eyes like the storm clouds over her native country. The words came back to him, the things they'd said to each other. His heart churned with trepidation.

Her lips brushed his, then his cheek, then his ear.

"Have you come to stay? Do you still live in the mortal realm?" she whispered. "It's okay if you do. We'll make it work."

Had he pulled back or had she? He opened his mouth, but nothing came out. The son of Hermes was at a loss for words.

"Isa. Athan." Xan looked at them both, his brow drawn in confusion. Without another word, he turned his back and walked off.

Athan wanted to call out. He wanted Xan to . . . save him? The thought made Athan's stomach clench. This was not right. He should be happy to see her, not wanting to leave.

Isabel unwrapped herself from Athan but tugged on his hand. As she led him down a garden path, she continued to speak. "Are you still angry with him? You shouldn't be. It wasn't his fault. Not really. He tried to fend them off, but there were too many."

Somehow they'd arrived in a park-like area with benches. Pink petals floated on a breeze. The air felt fresh, like right after a spring shower. Life surrounded him in the realm of the dead. And his heart hurt.

"Do you remember when we would spar, six or seven of us against Xan. He would always win, right? He was always the best of us at fighting." She was silent for only a moment before continuing. "There were twelve Skia that night. It was an ambush. I tried to help, but . . . You know I was never very good at fighting."

No. She was never any good at it. But he'd foolishly thought it wouldn't matter. Someone—no not just someone, *he*—would always be there to protect her. Except he wasn't.

"I'm sorry," he whispered. "I should've been there."

Her laughter was carefree, but she stopped when she saw the expression on his face. "Is that what you think? Gods, Athan. I'm so glad you weren't there. They would've killed you, too." She smirked. "Well, maybe that wouldn't have been so bad. We could've been here together, right?"

That was just it. If he'd died, he would've never met Hope, and she was someone he didn't want to live without.

"Don't be sad, love. We're both here now."

Yes, they were. But his heart was not. He didn't know what to say. Didn't know how to say it. But this . . . this needed to be said. "Isa. It's nice to see you." He shook his head. "It's great to see you . . ."

She tilted her head, and her face grew somber. "But?"

Just like a Band-Aid. "I'm not here for you."

Her smile faltered. "You've moved on."

It wasn't a question. He knew that she knew, but she deserved to hear it from him. He would not make the same mistakes he'd made so many times before. He would be honest.

He took her hands in his. Hands that were small and soft. She would always be this girl. The one he'd first fallen in love with. His first real kiss. But she wasn't who his heart ached for now. She wasn't the one he loved anymore. "I never stopped caring about you."

She nodded, but her eyes told him she knew better. "But it's not the same."

He pursed his lips. "It's not the same."

She cupped his face, and her thumb rested on his lips. She took a deep breath and squared her shoulders. "Will you tell me about her?"

So he did. He told her how he'd seen Hope and suspected her immortality. How he'd tried to woo her, and she'd resisted, pushing him away. How he'd finally broken through and then when his feelings shifted. "At first she was only another job, another demigod to get to the conservatory. I had no room in my heart for anyone but you. She has your same innocence and naivety, which is what probably cracked my shell. It just happened . . ."

"That's as it should be." She patted his cheek and then rested her hands in her lap. "Is she dead?"

This was more difficult. What would she think? But even as he thought the question, he realized he didn't care. His decisions would not be determined by what Isa would think. His heart belonged to Hope.

Athan told Isa the rest. He laid it all out. How Hope was considered a monster because of Apollo's curse, her risks in coming to the conservatory, how she'd saved his life, and then coming to the Underworld to try to break Apollo's hold on her. Athan told of how he'd come to the Underworld to help. "Myrine said she was stuck here, and I came to get her back."

Isa listened without interrupting once. Her eyes grew big as she absorbed Hope's story, her risks and bravery. When Athan finished speaking, Isa leaned toward him. "You must love her to risk so much."

The truth of it resonated within him, as well as the truth of what Isa hadn't said. "I do." He reached forward and brushed away a lone tear sliding down her cheek. "I'm sorry."

Isa shook her head and scrubbed away the rest of her tears. She looked him in the eye and said, "We were both very young. I'm not sure either of us really knew what love was."

It was true, but it still stung. "Even so, I'm sorry."

Because he could've done it differently. All those times in the Underworld . . . he could've sought her out.

Isa stood and offered her hands to help him up.

Athan clasped them both and, after standing, wrapped her in a hug. "I hope you find happiness here."

Her smile was just shy of the dawning sun. "I will, Athan. And I hope you find your Hope and save her."

He brushed her cheek with a kiss. "Goodbye, Isa."

"Be safe, Athan."

He could feel her eyes on him as he marched toward the castle, but he refused to look back.

"Athan, wait!"

He closed his eyes. Gods, did she not know how hard it was to walk away? He still cared for her, but . . .

"Please. You will need to get past Cerberus, and I want to help."

He froze. He should've known. "I'm sorry." Was he forever going to be misinterpreting? "I would really appreciate that."

She taught him two hand commands: sit and stay. "But most important will be the words you use."

"Ancient Greek?" He ran through the two words in the old language.

She shook her head. "The divine language."

He swallowed. Of course. The language of the gods. The only language he didn't know.

She taught him the two words. So similar to ancient Greek and yet distinctly different.

"Thank you, Isa. I'm sure you just saved my life."

She nodded. "Yes, but it is a life worth saving."

The wisp of a demigod stood on her tiptoes and kissed his cheek. "Goodbye."

He hugged her close, and a feeling of deep peace settled over him. "Goodbye."

The regret and bitterness he'd carried had been washed away. And he'd never felt so strong.

TWENTY-NINE

HOPE

LETO LEANED INTO Luc and whispered something in his ear, making the obvious pain on his face clear.

"You know what this means, right?" Leto smiled at her daughter, a look of sheer triumph.

She did. But it was so preposterous. "Why wasn't it fulfilled when I was born, or when you got married?"

"The family has to be with Apollo, or his offspring. Apollo killed Luc before you were born. He knew what it would mean, and he tried to prevent it."

"Do you think he knew?" Even as Hope asked, she knew the answer. That was exactly why he killed his son. Hadn't the sun god proven time and again how ruthlessly possessive he was? It was just so bewildering to think . . . "Is it really fulfilled?"

Leto bit the side of her mouth in a familiar gesture of worry. Luc patted her arm and turned to his daughter.

"Apollo will argue that it was not. That all the requirements of the curse were not fulfilled. But technically, they were. The Sphinx's offspring married Apollo's offspring and"—he pointed at Hope—"you are the child of that union."

Hope's mind was racing. If the curse was fulfilled, then why was she still changing? Why was she still a monster?

"He must acknowledge it, and if he will not, then the gods must rule on it. While it was technically fulfilled, Apollo could argue that technically it was not."

A technicality? The almost uncontrollable desire to hit something pulsed through Hope. The fulfillment of the curse was hung up on a technicality? Gods! She really wanted to hit someone. No, she really only wanted to hit one person, and *technically* he wasn't even a person. "So, the curse wasn't fulfilled because he killed you?"

"It would not be the first time filicide was committed by the gods to achieve their ends."

Right. A fact she was all too aware of. If she thought about it, she could still smell the char from Apollo's sons in her room. The memory made her shudder. And then another thought crossed her mind. "He's your dad."

Symeon nodded.

"Which means . . ." The thought of the god caressing her cheek made her whole body shiver. "He's my grandfather."

Neither of her parents seemed shocked by her declaration.

"But he still wants me?" She couldn't help but cringe even as she said the words. That was disgusting to even think about.

"Zeus married his own sister," Leto said.

As if that wasn't revolting. "Well, in my world, that is incest. And it's gross. Moving on, please." Hope couldn't go there. "So then what? What would have to happen to get rid of the curse?"

Both women looked at Luc, who ran his hand through his hair in a gesture very reminiscent of another demigod.

"You will have to go to Olympus. Bring the curse and its fulfillment to the attention of the counsel. If Apollo won't acknowledge it, you must get the gods to rule on it. Themis is probably your best bet. If you can convince her."

Themis. The name sounded strangely familiar. "That's it?"

Luc offered an indulgent smile. "It will be a trial to even get there. But I'm confident you, daughter, will make it happen."

She wanted to ask him if he'd read any Greek mythology at all. But it would probably be rude to point out that, after all the studying she'd done in the conservatory, her odds actually didn't seem particularly great. She looked around the small living room of her parents' home in the Underworld and decided she didn't really care about the odds, or else she would've never come here. Squaring her shoulders, Hope ticked off her next objective. "Go to Olympus and make Apollo acknowledge what a dirtbag he is. Got it."

Leto laughed as she stood and crossed the room. She sat on the loveseat and wrapped her arms around Hope in a hug. "I will miss you, daughter of mine."

"Do I have to leave now?" She'd just gotten there. Just met her father. Just . . . "I don't want to go."

Leto nodded. "I don't want you to either." She ran her hand over Hope's hair and tugged at the ends. "Do you know you've always had a profound sense of justice? You have more courage in your thumb than I have in my whole body. Even when you were little, you would tell me that one day you would break the curse. You have every talent and characteristic you could ever need to fulfill your destiny."

Hope choked back a sob. Tears spilled down her cheeks, and her heart . . . her heart was breaking. "Mom . . ."

"Don't squander all your glory down here. Make things right." Her mom pulled her close again and whispered in her ear, "For all of us."

A thousand hugs would never be enough.

The gate clicked shut, and Hope turned to wave one last time. She held the *Book of the Fates* in one hand, and her other hand came to rest on the necklace her mother and father had given her. A picture of the two of them on their wedding day on one side, and a picture of her mom holding Hope as a baby on the other. It was priceless, not because of the material it was made of, but because of the memories imprinted on the photos held within and the love they represented.

Hope squared her shoulders and walked away from her parents' home, but the vast emotional expenditure had exhausted her. The longer she walked, the harder it was to pick up her feet for that next step. The thin *Book of the Fates* seemed to weigh a ton, and Hope switched it from hand to hand.

The muggy air pushed down on her, and the incessant grating of beetles frayed her already stretched nerves. She was walking in the Underworld, albeit a very nice part of the Underworld judging by the large homes and well decorated yards, and she had no clue how to get back to Thanatos's home.

Where had Asbolus run off to?

She passed several souls as she wandered, and it felt as if they were watching her, talking about her, pointing at her.

She turned to see if she could see her parents' house, but she'd been walking a long time, and it had disappeared.

The sweet scent of peaches wafted on the breeze, and Hope's stomach lurched even as her mouth watered. She knew she couldn't eat any, but the fact that someone was growing fruit . . .

In the distance she saw a rich, vibrant green. Not the varying shades of emeralds that dripped from the jeweled trees. These were *real* trees. She had to be close to Persephone's gardens.

Hope's exhaustion fled in the excitement of knowing where she was. If she could get to the garden, she could get to—

Hope skidded to a stop.

The man walking toward her had a gait she would never forget. His broad shoulders and narrow waist came from hours of exercise. His dark hair was mussed as if he'd showered and run his hands through it far too many times. He was scowling and probably swearing to himself as he crossed the lawn. His countenance changed as soon as their eyes met. His face cleared, and a slow smile spread until both of his dimples popped, and he ran toward her.

It took only a second for Hope to respond. She was running to him, laughing with excitement, and her heart was so full it could burst.

She collided with Xan and buried herself in his chest.

"Hope."

He breathed into her hair and kissed the top of her head, and for the second time that day, she burst into tears. He shushed her and held her, letting her soak the front of his shirt with her tears.

She hiccupped, and they both laughed. "You came."

"Aye." He cupped her face. "Did you really think I wouldn't, lass?"

He smelled so alive, like leather and steel, and so much like Xan. She hugged him again. "I missed you."

He chuckled, a low sound that reverberated through his chest. "I missed you, too. Did you get what you came for?"

Her success bubbled up. "Yes. I did. The curse . . . oh, gods. Yes. I need to go to Olympus next and get justice, but . . . Apollo killed his sons . . . And we can break the curse . . . And I met my mom, and my dad. And they're happy. They're so happy. And I can have that, and be alive. I don't have to be cursed." She was rambling, but it felt so good to say the words, to know the meaning, and with Xan there, she was sure to get out and succeed.

She couldn't help but glance behind him. She wanted to know. "Is Athan okay? Did he—?"

Xan's smile faded, and his gaze darted toward the peach trees. He took one step back but kept his hand on her arm. "Aye. He's fine. Made a full recovery."

Relief ran through her followed by excitement. "Is he here, too?"

Xan's gaze again went to the peach trees. "He's here, but . . ."

Oh no. No. No. No. "He didn't . . . He's still . . ."

Xan closed his eyes and ran his hand through his hair. "Listen. Yes. He's okay. He's fine. It's just that—"

"Where is he?" Her worry and fear cycled, creating a rapidly building cyclone of emotions. "Where?"

Xan shook his head. "He's got something he has to take care of first, Hope. He'll come join us."

Did Xan not understand this was the Underworld? There were still Skia here. Vengeful gods. Hades was allegedly looking for her for his own nefarious plans. They needed to get Athan and get out.

"Where?" She grabbed Xan's shirt. "Please, tell me where."

"In the orchard. I'll take you—"

But she didn't wait for him to finish. She couldn't. She had to see Athan. See that he was okay. Tell him about what she'd found out. She wanted to kiss him and tell him they had a chance.

She could hear Xan behind her yelling for her to stop, and he was sure to catch up with her soon.

Hope jumped over the wall, the smell of ripe peaches hanging in the heavy air. The bubbling of the Lethe was beyond the perimeter wall. She turned the corner and practically tripped over her feet in an attempt to stop.

Athan was kissing someone. He was . . . He held her face in his hands, and he was kissing her. He was hugging her. They were so close.

Hope closed her eyes and turned away, but the image was burned into her brain. Tears stung and seeped through her eyelids.

"Hope," Xan whispered. "Come on."

He guided her away from the orchard, toward the back of the garden. And then his glances at the orchard made sense.

Her eyes flew open, and she glared at him. "You knew."

He shook his head. "I would've never willingly let you see that. That's . . . That be all arseways."

"Who is she?"

Xan raised his eyebrows. "You sure you want to know?"

She nodded but then shook her head. "Does he love her?"

Xan blew out a long breath. "I don't know." His long fingers went through his hair again. "He used to."

The knot in her stomach wouldn't go away until she knew. At least if she knew, she could deal with it. She thought of the bricks that had once protected her heart. Athan had torn the wall down. He'd told her he'd meant all the kisses, all the endearment. She could deal with his past. "Tell me."

"Athan came to the conservatory shortly after his mother died. He was maybe eight or ten." He paused and tilted his head as if he were thinking. With a small shake he said, "Anyway, he was young. He was a nice kid, really sweet. He helped out a lot. Everyone liked him."

Xan took a deep breath and slowly let it out through pursed lips. He cleared his throat.

Hope waited for him to continue, fidgeting on her feet as if on the edge of a precipice she was supposed to jump from. The silence stretched, and she wanted to yell at him to continue, to get it out already, but a part of her wanted to run away from what she feared was coming.

He ran his fingers through his hair and offered Hope a small smile. "I found Isa a few years later. Her father had died, and her mother is Aphrodite. Even when she was young, Isa was something to look at, but there is something almost compellingly attractive about Aphrodite's daughters. They are like a magnet for men, and Isa was no different."

The knot unfurled tentacles of dread in her stomach.

Xan shook his head. "But it was like Athan didn't notice. He was friendly with her, nice to her, but he treated her like a friend. I'm sure that's what attracted her to him. They were friends for a couple of years. They would play board games and pull silly pranks like short-sheet all the beds or put plastic wrap on the toilet seats. Totally immature, but they laughed all the time."

Hope could see it. A young Athan and the beautiful Isa laughing, hugging . . . The scene of them kissing played through her mind, and her stomach churned.

"I was away when their relationship changed. There were reports of a demigod in Ireland, and Dahlia and I went to check it out." He shook his head again, and his fingers threaded through his hair, making the ends stand up. "Skia were popping up everywhere, and we struggled to get to demigods in time. When Dahlia and I weren't out on a search, we were training the demigods in the conservatories to defend themselves. No excuses, but I was really busy. All. The. Time."

She could feel the story unraveling, and she knew the drop was coming.

"Athan was off with his dad when I got to the conservatory. Sometimes the two of them would disappear for weeks at a time. Isa and I were friends. She wanted to go out, but I was piss-drunk. We'd lost another demigod, and he looked a lot like Roan. Dahlia had disappeared, and it was just me and Isa . . ."

Hope felt like she'd been sucker punched. "You slept with Athan's girlfriend?"

"I woke up, and we were in bed together. I was still dressed, but she said . . ." He took a deep breath and squared his shoulders. "She said we did."

It was like grasping at straws as they slid through her fingers. She wanted, somehow, for it not to be true. "But you don't remember?"

He closed his eyes and dropped his head. "I don't remember. She told Athan when he got back a couple weeks later. I wasn't sure what had happened, and I tried to tell him that, but he wouldn't hear it. He forgave her, said I'd taken advantage of their friendship. I tried to tell him . . ." He gritted his teeth. "It would've been better if I'd just left for good, but I didn't want to leave Dahlia. She's funny about Seattle. She was . . ."

His emotion rolled off him, pain for his cousin and all that she'd suffered. Hope reached for him, but he stopped her.

He ran his hand down her arm, and squeezing her hand, he said, "Let me finish, or I'll never get it out."

"Okay." Hope clasped her hands behind her back.

"Isa seemed to thrive on the contention she caused. Remember how Marilyn Monroe was? Aphrodite's daughters all have a similar temperament. I don't even know if Athan was aware of how she was behaving. He was in love with her, and she could do no wrong.

"He told me to stay away from her. And I tried. I stopped drinking at the conservatory. I spent more time with Dahl, Dion, and his brother Demitri. We'd lost several demigods over the years, and the Skia were picking off more and more of our numbers. Demitri and I were good friends. My best friend died shortly after Athan got here. Athan and I were tight . . . and then we weren't. Demitri was cool, not like Athan or Luc—"

"So what happened?"

"Demitri died. Skia got him. I . . . I got slammed. I couldn't deal. Then Athan was gone, off with his dad again. And Isa begged me to take her out. She promised to behave. That she wouldn't hit on me again. She left me alone that night. But there were others she . . ." He shook his head, refusing to detail whatever had happened with Isa. "On the way home, we got ambushed. Skia came at us from all—"

Hope held up her hand. "Stop. Please. That's enough."

She couldn't listen anymore. She'd told Priska she wasn't sure Athan was the one, and maybe he wasn't. But her heart didn't believe what she now knew was a lie. Every single good thing had been taken away. Her mom and dad, Priska, Athan . . . Her heart couldn't take it.

She could hear the river spilling over the rocks below. She just needed to get away for a minute. She stepped back, but he grabbed her wrist.

"Don't run off, Hope."

"Please." She wanted to scream at Xan. That somehow it was his fault he'd let her see the kiss. It was like a movie on constant replay. How Athan cupped the girl's face and bent over her to brush her lips, and to know how much he'd loved her—"I need a minute."

This time she didn't wait for a reply, and it appeared that Xan was smart enough to know she wasn't asking for permission.

"I'll be right here," he yelled after her.

THIRTY

ATHAN

ATHAN'S HEART FALTERED when he saw Hades's guard
dog. Cerberus wasn't the size of a dog. He wasn't even the
size of a horse. The three-headed beast stood as tall as an el-
ephant, his thick heads each looking in a different direction.
Any one of those heads could bite Athan in two.

By the gods, he hoped Isa was right. He whistled and all
three heads turned to survey him. The animal took two steps
before Athan barked out the first command. "Sit."

The ground shook as the huge beast parked its butt.

"Stay." Athan held his hand just as Isabel had shown.

All three heads swiveled to watch him cross the threshold of the lord of the Underworld's castle. Athan held his
breath until he was inside the dark walls.

The air felt different. Charged energy tingled about him.
To the left he could hear a deep voice yelling, but the words

were muffled. As he followed the din, he hoped this time his audience with Hades would prove more fruitful, because he needed the god's help to find Hope.

With a deep breath, Athan pulled open one of the heavy doors to the throne room.

Hades, dressed in black, paced the floor, his frustration pulsing with every move.

On the steps of the dais, watching her husband, sat Persephone. The goddess of spring and handmaid to the lord of the Underworld twisted her hands in worry. Her wheat-colored hair was pulled back in a loose braid that hung over her shoulder almost to her waist. Her peaches-and-cream complexion was marred by the worry twisting her features. The front of her dress was grass-stained and dirty, and by the look of her hands, she'd been interrupted from her gardening.

"But you're sure she is here?" Persephone asked. The words hung in the air as she met Athan's gaze.

Hades turned to see what had caused his wife's shock.

"You. Again?" Hades crossed the room and grabbed Athan by the shirt.

"Stop!" Persephone yelled as she ran toward them. "What's wrong with you?"

She batted her husband's hands away from Athan and smoothed his shirt. "Welcome to the Underworld, Son of Hermes."

"Thank you, Lady." Athan bowed.

Hades stepped back and looked at his wife, his voice flat when he stated, "He killed Darren."

Persephone waved the words away. "I never liked Darren."

Athan's esteem for the goddess went up significantly.

"Why are you here?" Hades demanded with a glare. The air around him sizzled with his power.

Xan burst into the room. "What the hell are you thinking?" he asked, glaring at Athan. Xan froze as all eyes turned to him, and then he dropped to one knee. "Lord Hades, Lady Persephone."

"Both of you are still alive?" Hades no longer seemed angry, but rather impressed as he looked back and forth between the two of them. "I've never had demigods escape Tartarus . . ." His eyes stopped on Xan's belt. "Are those Moirai shears?" He took one step forward. "Where did you get those?"

Xan shifted, his hand covering the white handles. "Atropos gave them to me."

Silence, much like reverence, descended upon the room.

"The Fates are involved," Persephone breathed. Her face lit from within. She turned to Xan. "What do you need, Son of Ares?"

"Ah, I think you might want to send someone out to tend Cerberus. I was in a hurry to get through when I saw Athan. Sorry." Xan pinched his lips.

Hades frowned. "Did you kill my guard-dog?"

"No. Just incapacitated. The wound should heal right up, if it's tended to." Xan shifted his gaze and glared at Athan. "You're an arse."

Athan grimaced. There was a lot of truth behind that statement. "What did I do this time?"

Xan looked around the room as if searching for someone. "Wait. Where's Hope? Haven't you found her yet? She disappeared—"

Athan's heart stopped. "Have you seen her?"

Xan paled. "Aye. Have you *not* seen her yet?"

When Athan shook his head, Xan swore.

"Who's Hope?" Persephone asked.

Xan pointed at Hades. "The Sphinx." Xan pulled the scissors from his belt and pricked his finger. Bright red blood welled on the tip. "Thanatos has been keeping her away from you so you couldn't use her as a tool. At least that's what he told her."

Hades looked like he'd been slapped.

Xan turned to Athan. "I came across her shortly after leaving you and Isa . . . doing whatever." Xan grimaced. "We talked for a bit, but then she demanded to see you." His grimace turned to a glare.

Oh gods. Had Hope seen him kissing Isa? "It wasn't like that—"

"I don't care how it was."

"Stop!" Hades's command was filled with his power. "You will stop, now."

Athan said nothing, but his mind churned with what Xan had told him. Hope had seen Athan and Isa. Together. *Kissing.*

Persephone crossed the room and wiped the blood from Xan's finger with her sleeve. "You knew what you carried?" She indicated the scissors.

"Aye. I'm the son of Ares. I know a bit about all weapons." He raised his eyebrows at the goddess. "Even those of the gods."

She nodded.

Athan had never heard of such a thing. And Xan had deliberately cut himself with the scissors . . . Oh, shears of the Moirai. If pricked by the scissors, god or mortal wouldn't be able to speak false. "I thought you *couldn't* lie in the Underworld?"

Hades regarded Athan a moment before answering. "The dead cannot lie. There is no reason to hide from what is or what was."

But Hermes had lied.

"What happened?" Athan asked.

Xan explained it all. His meeting with Hope, what little she'd said about her parents, something about the curse and going to Olympus, and her excitement to see Athan. She'd all but demanded that Xan take her to Athan. He'd taken as long as he could to get there, wanting to give Athan and Isa time to say goodbye. But they'd shown up just as Athan kissed Isa. Hope ran off, and Xan had followed. Until the god of death appeared. Hope had been standing by the river with Thanatos, one minute there, the next gone. "I was hoping, somehow, that you'd come across her."

Hades's jaw tightened when Xan mentioned the other god of the Underworld, and the king's eyes barely contained the fury boiling within. "You are quite sure it was Thanatos?"

Xan held up the shears. "Do you want me to bleed again to prove it?"

Persephone pushed the hand holding the sharp tool down, and Xan slid the scissors back into the leather sheath.

"Hope called him Thanatos. That's all I know."

Hades narrowed his eyes, and it was as if fire blazed within the dark god.

THIRTY-ONE

HOPE

HOPE SLIPPED THROUGH the open gate. She'd used up all her tears, but her chest felt hollow as she descended the stairs to the river Lethe. The cheerful splashes mocked her, and she looked for a rock to toss into the crystal waters.

How dare Athan? But that wasn't even a fair question. He'd loved Isa once; that much was clear. And was it so wrong to eventually move on? Was that what Hope was, his moving on? The idea made her chest tighten. And was it wrong that she still wanted him? Oh gods, what if he decided to stay in the Underworld with Isa?

Hope had said she'd get over it. She'd told Priska that Athan wasn't anything special, but that wasn't true. There was no one out there quite like him. He'd been so patient, and when they dated, he'd been so courteous. He'd risked his life to fight for her, and even come to the Underworld for her . . . or had that been for Isabel?

"Here you are," Thanatos said with a relieved smile. He stood on the other side of the river, extending his hand toward her. "I was worried for you."

The god of death disappeared and reappeared next to where Hope stood staring out at the water.

"Thanatos." She pushed the palms of her hands into her eyes, as if she could push down her emotions. "Are you going to tell me everything happens for a reason? Or it will all work out for the best?" She looked up at him, and the tears she'd been holding back refused to be dammed.

Thanatos scowled, his pallid skin even more pale in the bright light of the Isles of the Blessed. His dark eyes flashed with a strength held in check. "I wouldn't pretend to patronize you."

She wrapped her arms around her torso as if she would be able to hold together her breaking heart.

"He hurt you very much," the god said, glaring up the hill-side. "Come."

He touched her, and suddenly, while still on the banks of the Lethe, Hope could no longer see the gate that led up to Persephone's gardens.

Not that Hope wanted to go back there now. If she had waited with Xan, maybe she wouldn't have seen that. This hurt so much more than when she found out about Obelia, even more than thinking he was just playing her. Why did she hurt so much? She couldn't even answer. If she opened her mouth, she would start sobbing.

"He's a fool. And definitely doesn't deserve you."

The words should have felt a kindness, but the thoughts they invoked continued to shred her heart. It didn't matter that he didn't want her. She still loved him. She loved him, and it hadn't been enough.

Thanatos pulled her close and wrapped his arms around her. "I hate to see you mourn so. You are pure, dedicated, and so, so determined. Anyone who cannot see your radiance is an idiot."

He whispered soothing words, and his hands rested on her back.

She'd thought she had no more tears, but somehow her eyes found a way to pour out more and more. She soaked through his dark shirt but had to pull away. She'd never been this close to Thanatos before, and he smelled of death.

The rational part of her brain told her of course he did, and it shouldn't matter. But it did. He smelled of overripe decay, antiseptic, the copper scent of blood, and the pus rank of infection. He was the god that ripped the soul from her mother's body.

Thanatos went to the water's edge and scooped up a handful of the crystal liquid. "I hate to see you mourn. Here." He thrust his hand toward her. "Three drops will make you forget what you saw. Three drops and your pain will evaporate."

She shook her head. It would be nice to forget about Athan kissing his previous girlfriend. It would be nice to forget about Priska's death. And Leto's. There were so many memories that hurt, but those were the same memories that had given her purpose. Those were the memories that drove her to break the curse, to defeat Apollo, to seize her own destiny. "No."

He turned his hand upside down, and the water dropped back into the river. "You are stronger than that, yes."

She drew herself up. "Yes, I am."

His lips curled in warm appreciation, and he stepped through the grassy bank. "Mother Gaia. You are incredible."

He continued to draw closer, and the smile, the tenderness, the comfort he'd offered all hit Hope with sudden clarity.

Her mouth dropped open, and her eyes widened in horror.

He glanced behind him and then faced her with an intent gleam. "We are quite alone. No one will interrupt us."

She swallowed. "It's okay. I'm better. Will you take me back?"

Thanatos shook his head, his dark hair curling around his ears. "Not yet. There is something I want to ask you."

Her heart fluttered in her chest like a caged bird. In fact, that was exactly what she felt like. This could not be happening. The sweet smell of peaches became cloying. The bank of the river that only moments before felt like an escape from pain became a trap.

"Do you believe in love at first sight?"

His intensity smothered her, and she shook her head. "No."

Instead of it deterring him, he acknowledged her refusal of the idea with a nod of appreciation. "Me neither. When you came here, I had every intention of using you to blackmail Apollo."

As if that would endear her. Her stomach turned with his admission.

"But you are wicked smart, and you pay attention. You have a hefty spark of divinity within you already. It wouldn't take much . . ."

He advanced again, and once again Hope stepped back. What he was saying was madness. She would not become the consort to a god. It would not end well. It never did.

As if he could read her mind, he said, "The gods of the Underworld are not the same as those of Olympus."

Then what was he saying? Her eyes narrowed, and her mind spun with the possibilities, but it continued to land on only one, and the supposition was ridiculous.

"Will you be my wife, Hope?"

Her mind went blank, and her jaw dropped. Time slowed, and the sound of the river lapping at the banks teased her. Nothing in her life was simple. Nothing. And Thanatos . . . "I don't know what to say."

He laughed, a low chuckle. "Just say you will."

Understanding struck her. He thought she was considering it, but really she was trying to think of how she could refuse without offending him. Had she ever done anything to lead him to believe she loved him? "I cannot, Lord."

But it was clear the god did not see that as refusal. "Apollo's curse will not hold here. He has no power in the Underworld. We can petition Hades. He will see the wisdom in our union."

Hope shook her head. "I . . . I do not love you that way."

The idea of having him close, of kissing him, of lying with him made her shudder. She respected him. She valued his friendship, but marriage was for love. And she didn't know him well enough to say she loved him.

"Love grows with time and trust. I'm confident it will grow."

But shouldn't she be attracted to him? She wasn't attracted to him. She could see that he would be attractive to some, but he wasn't to her. Was that wrong? Was there something wrong with her?

"I can't. I can't make that kind of commitment. You're asking for something I can't give right now." Not ever. Not to him. She wanted freedom from the gods, not to be tied to one. "I'm so sorry."

His face clouded in confusion. "You . . . you are refusing me?"

"I don't love you," she whispered. She hated to repeat it. And she wished there was some other way of refusing him, but accepting his offer was impossible.

His jaw tightened, and his eyes narrowed. "You think your life will be better with someone else? You think anyone else will offer you what I'm offering?"

"No." It wasn't about what anyone could offer her. It was about what she wanted. "Your offer is very generous." She swallowed.

"And yet," he said, "still you refuse me?"

Why was he making her repeat herself? She wanted so much to run away from this. She even glanced at the river and wondered if she could swim across it but quickly dismissed the idea. Hope took a deep breath and told the truth. "I like you, and you've been very kind to me. But I don't want to be here. Not forever. In fact, not at all. And I know, someday I will be, but at that point it won't be a choice."

He worried his lip in a very human gesture. "Are you refusing me or the Underworld?"

She steeled herself. "Both. I don't like it here, but—"

"You don't like me either," he snapped. "You used me. You used me to get what you wanted."

Hope opened her mouth to protest, but he cut her off with a wave of his hand.

"Oh, I know all about your meeting with your parents. Was this all a game to you? Manipulate whoever you needed to get what you want?" He clenched his fists. "You are a very selfish and manipulative girl, Hope Nicholas."

She scrambled back, moving up the riverbank. But he was faster.

Grabbing her shirt, he pulled her close. "You have tried to make a fool of me. You used me, and then . . . you made my offer of marriage a mockery."

His smell . . . Oh gods. It was rotting decay, and her stomach churned. Her eyes watered, and she tried to pull back.

He clenched her arms, and breathing in her face, he growled, "Do you think I don't know what you're thinking?"

She was going to throw up. Hope tried to suppress the bile at the back of her throat.

With both hands, Thanatos shook her. "You think I'm disgusting? You wish this had never happened? I can make that come true!"

Panic exploded in her chest, and she struggled and writhed to free herself from his grip. Her feet tangled with his as she kicked to get away. But it was not enough. She was not strong enough.

The ground disappeared from under her feet, and the world tilted as she fell. The water in the river Lethe was cool and welcomed her with an embrace of acceptance. She immediately pulled herself above the surface and looked to find the shore. Her legs pumped in circles to keep her up, treading water to prevent drinking any of the mystical river that now surrounded her.

There was a splash from behind her, and her breath escaped in a gasp of terror as someone pushed her under.

Memories flashed through her mind as Hope held her breath. Seeing Athan kissing Isabel. Hugging Xan in the orchard. Her mother and father holding hands. Thanatos saving her. Charon refusing her passage. Obelia in the Underworld. Hermes abandoning her.

Her lungs screamed for air, but she could not breathe. She struggled against the force that held her under, clawing at what felt like a solid layer of ice blocking her from the air above. She couldn't see anything holding her down, and her hands moved over the invisible surface trying to find the edge so she could get out.

The dark rock above the water fractured in the rainbow crystals of the river. Her lungs were burning, but she refused to give up. Somehow there had to be a way out. She beat against the barrier to no avail, and she wanted to scream her frustration, but there was no air.

The gasp was involuntary, a reflex panic, and Hope choked on the water as it flooded her lungs. Her tears disappeared in the water, and her acceptance of failure came only as she faded into unconsciousness.

THIRTY-TWO

ATHAN

"**LORD HADES**?" **A** lady's tentative voice called from the open doorway, followed by a knock. A young woman with long, copper curls stood in the entrance to the throne room. She was clad in a plain white dress that was clearly too large for her slight frame. As she pulled up the sleeve falling from her shoulder, she shifted her body weight, supporting something heavy just on the other side of the door.

Hades's jaw ticked, and he sucked in a deep breath. "Yes, Imogen?"

Athan's heart froze as the willowy girl pulled and pushed a very wobbly Hope through the door.

Hope's hair hung in wet clumps down her back. Her gray T-shirt was torn up the seam on the side and flapped open, exposing her golden skin. Her denim shorts were frayed, and rivulets of water ran down her legs, leaving a puddle of moisture at her feet. Her fierceness was gone, and she looked like a drowned kitten, lost and afraid. Her normally vibrant gold eyes were glassy and unfocused and looked right past him.

Athan stood dumbstruck as he stared at her. What could have—?

"Hope!" Xan crossed the room with quick strides. He wrapped her in his arms and kissed her forehead. "Gods, I've been so worried for you."

Athan's heart ached, but still he couldn't move. Perhaps he was wrong to want her so. Perhaps he'd been mistaken in coming after her. Xan's feelings were apparent, and perhaps Hope returned them. Maybe she'd gotten over Athan, just like he'd finally let his feelings for Isabel go.

In retrospect, had Hope really had feelings for him, or had he manipulated her? The crack in his heart opened into a jagged fissure, and something deep within sunk with a sense of hopelessness.

The girl, Imogen, stood inside the doorway, hands at her sides, and her face void of emotion. The material of her dress was wet all down the right side, clinging to her slight figure.

Xan continued to whisper to Hope, words of encouragement, compassion, words of love.

Her eyes softened, and her arms moved to reciprocate the hug from the other demigod.

Athan steeled himself for what he knew was coming.

Hope froze, and Athan could see the moment she came back to herself.

She pulled back from Xan, slowly at first, her face clouded with confusion. She clenched her jaw, ripped his hands from her shoulders, and shoved him away, immediately dropping into a fighting stance.

"Who are you?" she spat, her arms coming up into guard.

Shock burst across Xan's face, and Athan knew his face mirrored it.

When no one approached her, she relaxed her shoulders, but her hands remained outstretched, ready to push them all away.

"The Sphinx?" Hades asked with a growl punctuating the question.

"In the river, Lord," Imogen answered neutrally.

Hades strode to Hope, his footsteps oddly silent on the stone floor. She shrunk back, but he grabbed her arm, preventing further retreat. Something about his presence must have told her the futility of fleeing from the god. He touched her hair, catching a drop of the water still dripping from the ends. He put his fingers to his tongue and shook his head. "The Lethe."

Athan wanted to scream in frustration. He turned to Hades. "Can you burn it out of her? If we make her throw it up, can you . . . can you give her back her memories?"

The Lethe. The river of un-mindfulness, where all who drank experienced complete amnesia. What in the name of all the gods was she doing swimming in the Lethe?

Hope looked like a cornered animal, her eyes flitting over each of them as if measuring where her greatest threat would come from.

"Hope?" Xan held up his hands in surrender. "Hope, luv, it's Xan. Do you remember me?"

Her eyes narrowed. "I don't know you." Her gaze dropped to his weapon, and she squinted as if trying to remember something. "You chased me and my mom . . . Don't you hunt monsters?" she asked, and then sucked in a deep breath. "Are you going to try to kill me?"

Xan kept his hands up. "No, luv. I . . . We came to rescue you." He indicated Athan with a nod.

Hope stared at Athan. She glanced at Xan again, but when he made no movement toward her, she let her attention come back to Athan. "Do I . . . Do I know you?"

She sounded so unsure of herself, so hesitant. And he thought his heart couldn't hurt any more than it already had.

"I met you in Goldendale last year." Everything in him wanted to run to her. To reassure her as Xan had tried.

She nodded. "I don't remember, but you seem . . . familiar."

Her gaze ping-ponged between Athan and Xan. Hope cleared her throat and wiped her palms on her wet shorts. "I don't remember . . ."

She grimaced and closed her eyes.

Athan couldn't even fathom what that would feel like. How much had she lost?

Her eyes opened and she searched the room, looking into the shadow as horror etched upon her features. She stared at Hades and Persephone and released a strangled cry. In a hoarse voice, she whispered, "Oh, gods."

Persephone laughed, the twittering of a nervous giggle, but it stopped abruptly as Hope slumped to the ground.

Athan stepped forward, but Xan beat him there again, swooping Hope up into his arms.

"Where can I take her?" Xan's voice was gruff and soaked with emotion.

Hades and Persephone shared a look, and then Persephone motioned with her hand for Xan to follow. "Imogen, you will come."

The fair-skinned girl bobbed a curtsy. "Lady, I live to serve."

Athan moved to follow after the group.

"Son of Hermes," Hades intoned. "Stay if you would."

"I'd rather not."

The god of the Underworld raised his brows. "No?" With a flick of his wrist, the door closed behind the party. "You'll find there is nothing for you to do, and my wife will kick your friend out as well before she assesses the monster."

Athan ground his teeth together but stayed where he was. It would do no good to argue.

Hades swirled his hand and two leather chairs appeared, a squat stone table between them. On the table there was a crystal bar set with etched tumblers filled with amber liquid. "A drink?"

The son of Hermes snorted. "I'd rather not bind myself here, if you don't mind."

Hades chuckled a rich, dark sound void of mirth. "Of course."

One of the glasses disappeared. Hades threw back his drink and then sighed. "Do you trust him? Your friend?"

Why would he ask? Athan's mind went in several directions at once, but all avenues came to one destination. "Yes. I trust him. He wouldn't lie." In fact, Athan couldn't think of a time when Xan had ever lied. "Why?"

"I've been trying to get the Sphinx here for almost eighteen years."

That made no sense. "You have two dead ones here. Isn't that enough?"

Hades chuckled again. He pushed to the edge of his seat and leaned forward. "I need her alive."

Athan scooted back into the chair, the leather so soft he could curl up in it. He scratched his head and tried to put the pieces together. "You want to use her as a pawn?"

The crystal glass refilled, and the god again drained it. "Are you sure you don't want a drink?" He set the tumbler down, and with a wave it was full. "I'm more than happy to make an exception for you. It appears that you could use some fortitude."

Yes, he wanted a drink, but he had no reason to trust Hades. "So why do you want her?"

"Do you know," he whispered, "if she has the *Book of the Fates*?"

Athan willed his face to betray nothing. Why would Hades be asking about that? "Don't you have them all here?"

The god's pale lips twitched. "I was told we were missing exactly six. Up until last week, five of them were in the Olympian library. But they were delivered, interestingly, by your father." He paused as if waiting for information. When Athan said nothing, Hades continued, "Like everything else associated with the gods of the Underworld, the *Books* had been sealed. Those five were requested by Artemis a few months ago, for some research. I hope she was able to complete it before Hera found out."

Artemis had requested the *Books of the Fates* Hope had searched while in the conservatory. "Hera found out what?"

Hades shrugged, but the intensity in his eyes belied his casual demeanor. "Hera was the one that ordered them returned . . . I was told."

Why would Hera want the *Books* sealed in the Underworld? And why would Artemis get involved? And what was going on with Thanatos? Athan's head hurt from trying to formulate answers to questions. His gaze flitted to the door. Where the Hades was Xan? "Why don't you ask my father what's going on?"

Hades tapped the arm of the chair. "We don't speak of it. He . . . He would not get involved."

Not get involved? It seemed that they were all swimming in it. Whatever *it* was. "What do you want from me?"

"And now we come to the crux of it. You are not of my realm, so I can't compel you to serve me. In fact, I can't even request it. So, I need you to think, young man."

Athan tried to sort through the mess of the last few days. The Skia attack in the hospital, and then again in the Underworld. What had Hecate said?

"Thanatos is making a bid for your power." As soon as he said the words, the truth hovered before them both.

"But that is nothing new," the lord of the Underworld said. "There are squabbles all the time. Nothing that ever amounts to anything. We're all stuck here together."

Athan shook his head. Thanatos had tried to suck Hecate into it as well. "Are you really bound to the Underworld?"

Hades nodded. "And so is everything in my realm that isn't mortal in some fashion. My Skia can leave and come back, but they cannot bring anything but the dead with them. I've had them try without success." He held up his hand. "And before you protest their existence, they are a necessity. They provide balance and justice to the realm."

"Balance?"

"Without Skia, the demigods would be immortal, just like the gods."

It was disturbing how that made sense. "But Hope is a monster."

"And as such is immune to the Skia."

That couldn't be . . . Why would Darren attack her? There was a piece Athan was missing. Something didn't make sense.

The door opened, and Xan strode through. "Bloody hell. What is wrong with Perseph—?" He swallowed whatever he'd been about to say. "Ah, I mean, your wife sure knows how to take charge of a situation, Lord."

Hades smiled, his eyes filled with joy at the mention of his wife. It was the first smile from the god that held any warmth. "That she does."

Athan worried over Hades's words. With a nod to Xan, Athan turned back to the god. "Why would Skia attack Hope?"

Hades frowned as if the idea was ridiculous. "There's no reason for them to attack her. They would've been trying to get her here."

One had attacked her. Multiple times. "But Darren tried to cut her throat. I saw—"

His dark eyes flashed murder, and he stared Athan down. "Are you quite sure it was Darren?"

Athan nodded.

Hades stood and threw the crystal tumbler against the wall with a curse. Crystal fragments ricocheted across the floor.

"Both my first and my second," Hades muttered. With a thunderous yell, he picked up the crystal tray and its contents, and they followed the first glass to oblivion.

THIRTY-THREE

HOPE

HOPE WAS LYING on animal fur, but the ground wasn't particularly soft. By deductive reasoning, the animal was definitely not alive, and somehow that made Hope want to relish the softness and warmth. It would be delightful to take a nap, if only these people would leave her alone.

"You must clear as much water as you can," another voice said. A woman's voice, although she sounded really young.

More pressure, this time from both her back and chest. She wanted to tell them to stop. To let her be. Didn't they know how tired she was?

Her eyes fluttered open, and a strange face with blue eyes looked up at her. Whoa, he looked pissed.

The man swore again, and she tried to wave away his worry. She was fine. Just a little tired.

There was a girl there, too. With copper curls, a tall, willowy apparition of beauty.

They were talking about her, but their voices babbled and broke like the sound of water. And it was too difficult to focus on the words. They sounded worried, and she wanted to tell them whatever it was, it would be okay. But first, she was going to rest her eyes.

It was dark, the air thick as pitch, and she tried to push her way through. There was something there that she needed to get to, and she knew she cared a lot, but every move was just so difficult. Still, she wasn't a quitter.

She was at the park with her mom again, and this time she saw the little girl sitting on the park bench, swinging her legs. She saw her mom scoop her up into her arms and run as a man chased them. Her whole life was hiding. And she'd hated it.

Hope stirred and her senses assaulted her. She wasn't on the fur anymore. It was far too soft, and the air smelled of lavender. Her eyes were too heavy, and try as she might, she couldn't lift them.

"I know he wants her to wake up, but she isn't ready yet . . ."

The voice faded, and Hope snuggled into the comfort of darkness. Her mom would be there when she woke up, like she'd always been. And they would move, her mom's persistent attempt to find safety, like they always had.

THIRTY-FOUR

ATHAN

"MOTHER GAIA!" PERSEPHONE burst into the throne room. Her gaze went from her husband to the two demigods, and finally to the particulate matter that was once a bar service. "Stop this at once." With a wave of her hand, the shards of crystal disappeared.

Athan's heart jumped with anticipation. "Is Hope okay?"

"Is she awake?"

Xan asked his question at the same time, and Athan felt the increasingly familiar anger swell. But it wasn't anger, not really, because anger was always something else at its core. He pushed away the introspective thoughts and focused on the queen of the Underworld.

Persephone shook her head. "She is not awake, nor is she in any way okay. She is sleeping in oblivion, and the longer she stays there, the more she will forget."

"Can you not wake her?" Hades asked.

Everything in Athan hinged on the answer to this, and he willed Persephone to make it so.

"I cannot." She frowned.

Athan wanted to yell, but he clenched his fists and held his frustration inside.

Xan did not. With an obscenity, he turned and punched the black rock behind him. His face was ravaged, and his fist dripped blood.

Persephone grimaced. "I don't need more work."

The tall redhead came through the door. "My Lord and Lady—"

"Imogen, will you take the hothead here and bandage him up, please?" Persephone offered a weak smile as she indicated Xan.

"Of course." The thin girl bowed and waited for Xan to join her.

"Not happening, Ginger. It will heal up fine in a bit." Xan shooed her away.

"But—" Imogen's gaze flitted to Persephone.

Persephone closed her eyes. "Never mind. Thank you, Imogen. That will be all."

Imogen shot Xan a glare, the first real expression Athan had seen from her, but it was gone as she glided from the throne room.

"How do we wake her?" Xan asked.

Persephone looked back and forth between the two young men. "It must be a strong memory. Something with a lot of feeling or emotion. A big success, her first kiss, or her mother's voice, although this may be traumatic as she is dead, correct?"

Xan looked at Athan, and Athan looked at Xan.

"Is her mother dead?" Persephone asked again.

"It wasn't that long ago, right?" Xan asked.

Athan shook his head.

"Were you her first?" Xan choked on the words.

Persephone turned to Athan. "Are you her first kiss?"

Was he? Had she told him that? "I . . . I think so."

"If he kisses her, will it wake her?" Xan clenched his hands, his face stricken with emotion.

It was like out of a fairy tale.

"It might," Persephone acknowledged, "if the memory is strong enough. If there is enough emotion behind it."

"Will she get her memories back?" Athan asked.

"Perhaps. The longer she sleeps, the more she will forget."

Xan grabbed Athan's arm and started for the door. "Right now."

Persephone crossed in front of them and then led the way.

"We're not finished, Son of Hermes," Hades intoned, his deep voice a chilling promise. The god of the Underworld followed them out of the room and down the obsidian hall.

The room was dark, with only a single candelabra lit in the corner. A plush bed occupied the middle of the room with a large fur rug underneath it. Hope lay atop the pale-blue comforter, her eyes closed.

She'd been changed from her wet clothes and wore a loose white nightgown. Her golden hair was almost dry and fanned out on the pillow. Her lips were parted and her breathing slow and deep.

Xan stopped inside the door. "Go," he said and shoved Athan toward the bed.

Athan took two steps and stopped. What if it didn't work? What if she didn't wake up? What if she didn't remember him? What if she didn't love him?

"What are you waiting for?" Xan growled.

Athan pushed down his fear even as it clawed at him. The what-ifs continued to bombard him, and he was paralyzed by the onslaught.

A warm hand rested on his shoulder, and Xan looked him in the eye. "This isn't about you. It's about her. Please, go kiss her."

And in that moment, Athan knew he was right. This wasn't about getting the girl, or getting anything. This was about Hope having a chance at life. A chance to break the curse and choose her own path. This was about Hope's freedom.

The surroundings seemed to fade. His heart pulsed with feeling. This was for Hope. He sat on the edge of the bed and slid his hand behind her head, his fingers threading into her golden hair. He leaned over her, relishing her nearness. The heat of her body, the sweet smell of her skin. He thought of sunshine and freedom, friends and family, and what could be . . . if only.

His lips brushed hers, and the sun burst beneath his eyelids. Warmth blossomed from his heart and spread outward, like melting honey. This. They could grow old together, have kids together. Defeat curses and raise kings. He'd never let himself believe he would find someone he loved more than Isabel, but Hope . . . he wanted her.

"Athan?" she breathed.

And then her arms were around him. Her strength pulling him closer. Her lips moving with him, telling him secrets, giving him strength.

He wanted to cry with joy that she remembered.

He pulled her close and buried his face in her hair. "Gods, Hope, I thought I'd lost you."

Her body relaxed, and her eyes closed. A sigh escaped her lips.

Glowing with his triumph, he turned to Persephone only to see concern still stamped across the goddess's face.

Why was she—?

Hope's body twitched and twitched again. Then it started to shake violently, thrashing as if trying to escape invisible binds. Her mouth opened, and her body heaved. Liquid the color of crystals poured from her mouth, soaking his shirt, pants, and the bedding beneath him.

Hope shivered, sat up, and scooted away from him.

Her eyebrows drew down in a look he recognized with a sinking sensation.

"Who are you?" she whispered, her voice raspy from vomiting. "Where's my mom?" As soon as the question was out, her hand flew to her mouth. She covered one with the other. Her eyes filled with tears and skirted through the room. Her look morphed from confusion, to surprise, to fear. "Where's Priska?"

Athan stared at her, willing her to remember. "I'm Athan. We met in Goldendale after your mom passed away."

She nodded. "I remember moving to Goldendale." She pointed to Xan and then Hades and Persephone. "Who are you guys?"

Persephone stepped forward and introduced herself and her husband. "These young men came to rescue you here in the Underworld."

Hope's lips formed an O. "Am I dead?"

Hades cleared his throat. "No, my dear, you are not."

"And you?" Her chin jutted out in a look of sheer determination as her gaze fell again on Xan.

He swallowed, but he seemed to choke on his words.

"I know you, right?" When he didn't answer, she closed her eyes. "It's like I know you, but I can't remember from where."

"Aye, lass. We met a bit ago, and we're friends. I came to help Athan get you back."

She leaned forward and froze. "No. No, no, no! You!"

Xan stepped away and held his hands up. "I'm not here to hurt you, Hope."

She scrambled back, until she was against the headboard. She continued to regard them warily. "Hades? Am I safe here?"

Athan wondered what made her ask him, the god of the Underworld.

"You are safe in this room, right now and as long as you stay here. I will not, nay, I cannot, promise your safety elsewhere."

She pursed her lips. "Then I want you all out, right now. Is that okay? Can I . . . May I have some time to myself?"

Persephone shooed them out into the hall. "Hades, please wait for me," she said and then shut them out.

THIRTY-FIVE

HOPE

THE LIGHTS WERE dim, and Persephone closed the door after pushing out the unwelcome visitors. The goddess wore a simple white dress that hung to the floor, the only adornment a golden belt that gathered the fabric at her tiny waist. She crossed the dark floor, almost as an apparition.

"Are you starting to remember?" she asked. "Is the Lethe starting to recede?"

Hope eyed Persephone warily, trying to put together pieces that made no sense. Hope had moved to Goldendale after her mother passed away. She remembered that. The boy who had been sitting on her bed, Athan, looked familiar. Something about him even felt familiar, and it was clear from his outburst that they knew each other.

She remembered going to the grocery store in the small town, and there was a butcher she was friends with, but his name escaped her at the moment.

Krista. Hope closed her eyes to hide the fact that she was rolling them. Mean girl number one. She concentrated on the town of Goldendale. Priska had gone to find out who had killed Leto.

Hope scratched her head. It was like knowing the information was there, but she couldn't access it. There was nothing else. And for some reason, she'd come to the Underworld alive. It made no sense.

And why was that other guy there? She remembered him, he'd chased after Hope and her mom when Hope was a child. Leto had believed he would kill them, which meant he was a demigod. So then why was he here to help rescue her?

She shook her head, not so much to clear it, but in an attempt to dislodge the information she wanted. "What happened?"

Persephone sat on the edge of the bed. "There was an accident."

Hope shook her head again. That didn't ring true. At all. "No. I fell. Or did I hit my head?"

"You don't remember?"

Persephone's gaze was intense, and Hope glanced down at her hands fidgeting with the duvet cover. "No."

The goddess stood. "We're looking into it." She tapped the edge of the bed. "I will have Imogen bring you a tray."

As if anticipating Hope's protest, Persephone held up a hand. "It will be sealed and from above ground."

Hope scooted down in the bed. It was nicer than any bed she'd ever been in, and all she wanted to do was snuggle down and go to sleep. "Is it okay for me to sleep?"

Persephone paused at the door. "Yes, but you're going to want to eat and drink, too. I have a feeling you'll be needing your strength."

Hope again struggled against the mental barrier that kept her memories from her, but something she'd learned in school nagged at her. "I thought you hated Hades. That you hated coming to the Underworld. He kidnapped you."

The goddess pinched the bridge of her nose and closed her eyes. After a deep breath, her gaze bored into Hope. "You can't trust what the myths say. Of all people, you should know better."

Hope cringed. Persephone was right. Hope should know better. "I'm sorry. Thank you for your hospitality."

The goddess inclined her head and ducked out of the room, closing the door behind her.

THIRTY-SIX

ATHAN

THE THREE OF them stood out in the hall. Athan wondered how Hope had recognized Xan, and from where, but the other demigod studied the ground as he pulled his hand through his hair.

Hades stared at Hope's door as if he could see through it. Perhaps he could. The god visibly relaxed when Persephone joined them in the hall.

"We will need to have a tray sent to her right away," she said to her husband.

"Of course, dear."

"I'll have Imogen bring it to her." Persephone offered a small smile to the demigods before kissing her husband, bidding him farewell, and disappearing.

Hades pointed down the hall to an open doorway and then led them into a large room. The space had all the makings of a swanky hotel suite with a plush L-shaped couch in front of a widescreen television. There was a small kitchen, an open door to a restroom, and two other doors that Athan hoped led to bedrooms.

Guilt stabbed at him, and he pushed his increasing fatigue away.

"I will leave the two of you here for now. Sleep if you can, or eat, or whatever else you want to do. I have other business I must attend, but I'll return shortly. If you ring this bell"—Hades was suddenly holding a silver bell in his pale, slender fingers— "Imogen will be happy to serve you."

Thinly veiled contempt dripped from the words, and Xan snorted.

"I'm sure we'll be fine," Athan said, shooting Xan a look. The last thing they needed was Xan's temper. "Thank you."

Hades exited the room, and the door clicked shut.

They sat silent for a time. Athan's thoughts swirled around Hope, his emotions vacillating from optimism to despair. "She recognized you."

Xan paled. "Not in a good way. She remembers me chasing her when she was a child." He circled the couch and collapsed into the cushions, draping his arm over his eyes.

Athan sunk into the overstuffed couch. "She doesn't even remember me."

Xan sat up. "No? You do remember her breathing your name after you kissed her, right?"

Wait. "Are you jealous?"

There was no mirth in Xan's dark chuckle. "Of course I'm jealous. But like I said, this isn't about you or me. It's about her."

He was right. "I don't understand why she would go to the Lethe." Xan's gaze was so heavy, Athan squirmed under it. "I don't."

"The last thing she saw before she ran to Thanatos . . ." Xan sat up.

The last thing she'd seen was Athan kissing Isa. Oh, gods, it was his fault.

Xan hopped over the back of the couch and grabbed the bell. "Prepare yourself for something quite dreadful. That Ginger girl is right mad."

He shook the bell and then sprinted to the door.

Seconds later, the willowy girl appeared. Her pink lips were pushed up into a smile, but the skin around her eyes was tight with tension. "Yes, Son of Ares?"

"Was-Thanatos-anywhere-near-the-river-Lethe-when-you-pulled-Hope-out?" His words were rushed, blending together with his heavy brogue and making them incomprehensible.

She looked to Athan as if he could translate. Athan repeated the question slower, enunciating clearly so there was no way the girl could misunderstand.

The girl's pale blue eyes dilated with fear, and she stepped back into the wall. Without saying anything, she scooted along until she got to the door, and then she fled.

Xan pointed at Athan. "I think that be a yes."

Athan nodded. "But why?"

"Shite." Xan picked up the silver bell again. He rang it over and over, and when no one came, he opened the door. Stepping out into the hall, he yelled, "Immy! Genny!"

Had he gone insane? "What are you doing?"

"If Thanatos pushed her in, then it was because Hades had commanded it, right? He wouldn't have done something like that on his own. I mean, he has to answer to someone—"

Athan shook his head. "No."

It wasn't Hades, at least not if the lord of the Underworld was to be believed.

"Imogen!" Xan punctuated his bellow by burying his immortal blade up to its hilt in the black wall.

The pale girl stepped out from a dark doorway, her slight frame trembling. "I will take you to Hades." She didn't wait for a reply as she scurried down the hall.

Poor girl.

"You requested an audience?" Hades stepped out of a room and closed the door behind him. He wrapped a black silk robe around his waist, covering his pale chest and the top of his pajama bottoms. Pointing down the hall, he said, "Let's go to your room."

Imogen transferred her weight from foot to foot, her gaze flitting about the hall nervously.

Hades pursed his lips. "You are dismissed, Imogen. Thank you for your service."

The young woman bobbed a curtsy and then fled.

"Is she immortal?"

Hades scratched his head. "No. Not yet."

They continued walking back to their room.

"So, what's her story?" Athan didn't care, but he needed something to distract him as they walked.

Xan frowned at him, and Athan rolled his eyes. Besides, they couldn't very well talk about treason or mutiny or whatever it was out in the open.

"Imogen has reached Elysium twice. She would like to be reborn again in an attempt to make it to the Isles of the Blessed."

Athan stopped. "The Isles of the Blessed exist?"

Hades smirked. "Of course. Where do you think you are now?"

Isles of the Blessed. Those who make it to Elysium had the opportunity to be reborn, and if they made it back to Elysium three times, they would be able to reside in the realm of the Isles of the Blessed and have unimaginable joy and happiness forever.

"That twiggy girl has made it to Elysium . . . twice?" Xan asked incredulously.

"She is very selfless," Hades answered.

"Even so, you don't like her," Athan said.

Hades smirked as he entered the room. "She is naïve. But I don't think you really wanted to talk about Imogen."

Athan closed the door behind Xan and faced Hades. "Thanatos is trying to overthrow your right to rule."

"You got me out of bed to tell me that?" Hades pushed past Athan and gripped the doorknob. "Tell me something I don't know."

Athan flushed as the god opened the door and stepped into the hall.

"He pushed Hope in the Lethe."

Hades came back into the room and closed the door behind him. His gaze narrowed. "Do you know this?" he asked in a hushed tone. "How do you know?"

Hades's intensity made Athan nervous. "I don't know—"

Hades rolled his eyes, and his face fell.

"Imogen got really nervous when we asked her." Xan hurried the words. "You should ask her. She knows something."

Hades dark eyes hardened to flint. "She would've . . ." He sucked air through his teeth and whirled to face them. "Say nothing. To anyone." He glanced around the room, his face granite. "Don't even speak of it here. I will summon you shortly."

Xan returned to the couch and slumped into it. "Do you feel like we jumped from the frying pan into the fire?"

It was worse than that. The outcome wouldn't just affect them. Not even just Hope. Imogen would be affected, and Thanatos was a god. The gods had infinite memories.

"You better get some rest. I have a feeling tomorrow's going to be in the crap-pot, and you already look like death. Best not tempt Hades to keep ye here."

It would be a miracle if Athan could sleep, but there was wisdom in Xan's counsel. "Right."

Athan walked toward the closed bedroom doors and opened the one to the left. "There's another one here." He confirmed it by pushing the door open. "You're bound to get a better night sleep on a bed than the couch."

Xan waved Athan away. "Who said I'm going to be sleeping? Go to bed, Athan. I need you to be smart. I need to be able to fight. I think tomorrow will be filled with a need for both."

THIRTY-SEVEN

HOPE

THERE WAS A yellow bound book on the stand next to the bed. Hope picked it up and flipped through the pages. It reminded her of her *Book of the Fates*, but in this one the pages were blank. Figured.

The door clicked shut.

Hope startled from sleep and sat up. She glanced around the dark room, the black rock walls, the dark-red bedding. The smell of lavender had dissipated, but the stale air stirred with the new occupant.

A tall, thin girl with auburn hair stood frozen inside the door, holding a serving platter. The smell of beef and gravy drifted from the metal tray.

Hope's stomach growled in appreciation, and she wanted to tackle the girl and pull the food away. She shoved down her instincts and pointed at the dish in the girl's arms. "Is it cursed?"

The young woman shook her head. "No. Hades had Hermes bring it down. It won't bind you here."

Hope studied the girl. Isn't that what they would say if they were trying to bind her? "How do I know you're telling me the truth?"

The girl glared at Hope.

"I never lie." Her voice was closed off and icy, as if Hope had offended her by asking the question. The girl crossed the room, her heavy footsteps at odds with her slender frame. She slammed the tray down on the bedside table and turned to go.

"Wait," Hope called. She was tired of being alone, even if she didn't know how long she'd been alone. She grasped for something to say. "What's your name?"

"Imogen." The girl was clearly still offended, as she didn't even turn to acknowledge Hope.

"Please, Imogen. I'm sorry. I didn't mean to hurt your feelings."

Imogen paused with her hand on the door.

"I'm sorry, too," she whispered and left the room.

Hope lifted a silver dome. There was a frozen meal, still in its package, but the cardboard edge had been turned back. There was a package of crackers with fake cheese and a bottle of water.

Something about the bottle bothered her. She picked it up, turning it over in her hands. The cap was still attached to the thin plastic seal. But there was really no way to know if it had been tampered with. Unease crawled over her.

Something was wrong, but she didn't know what.

The tray was gone in the morning, and Hope was filled with a mixture of relief and frustration. How had she not heard someone enter last night? It didn't bode well for survival if someone could sneak into her room.

She sat up, and her head spun. She was going to have to find something to eat today. She scooted to the edge of the bed. Hope stood and her legs wobbled. Her vision blurred, and there were two choices: she could sit back down or she could fall to the floor. She put her hand behind her and dropped to the bed.

She wore a loose white dress, more sheet than dress really. It reminded her of pictures of toga parties she'd seen online. There was thick twine wrapped around her waist and tied in a knot. Someone had dressed her at some point. Hope rubbed her hand over her face and then through her hair, her frustration mounting.

There was a knock at the door.

"Come in," Hope called.

The door opened, and Persephone came in carrying another tray like the one Imogen had brought the night before.

"I brought you some breakfast," the goddess said, setting the large platter down on the bed next to Hope. "I was surprised when Imogen brought everything back last night. I would've thought you'd be starving." Persephone pulled the lid off the tray to reveal a yogurt, protein bar, and a bottle of milk. "It's not much, but it will get you started."

"How do I know you're not lying? How do I know this won't . . . bind me here?" Hope itched to grab the food, to chug the milk and scarf down the protein bar.

Understanding dawned on the goddess's face. "Is that why you wouldn't eat anything last night?" She took a deep breath. "I swear on the River Styx that nothing on this tray will bind you to the Underworld."

The words brought instant relief. The gods were bound when they swore on the Styx. Hope grabbed the milk and drank deeply.

Persephone sat on the edge of the bed and watched.

Hope ate the protein bar, washing down the dry substance with the rest of the milk. She opened the yogurt but set it down after two bites. "Why am I so tired?"

The queen of the Underworld pursed her lips. "You have been slowly starving since you arrived. Add to that a major trauma . . . It will take some time for your body to heal here."

"But up in the mortal realm—"

"Your curse doesn't follow you here. Not the good or the bad."

Which was why she hadn't changed while she was here. "When can I leave?"

Persephone set the wrapper on the tray. She pulled the spoon from the plastic yogurt cup and wiped it clean with a napkin. Then she met Hope's gaze. "My husband would like to speak with you."

Was he asking permission? The idea of meeting with Hades filled her with dread, but for no reasonable explanation. "Okay. Is he coming here?"

Persephone coughed. "Ah . . . no. He is requesting an audience."

"Which means this is a command."

Why not just say that? Why were gods so obtuse? It was something they seemed to pass on to their offspring, too . . .

Oh. Oh, oh, oh! All at once, a flood of memories came. Meeting Athan at school, finding him reading her *Book of the Fates,* hearing him talking to his father, Hermes. She'd run away from Athan because Hermes had demanded that his son hunt her. She'd met Artemis and gone to the conservatory. Xan. Oh gods, Xan. He was her friend. She remembered them training. And then Apollo's sons. Athan getting attacked by Skia. Apollo killing his sons. It all came back. She'd left the conservatory to come to the Underworld to find a way to break the curse. And Priska . . .

"Is Priska here?"

Persephone's shoulders slumped, and she nodded. "Artemis's daughter. She will be judged after . . . Much has happened in the time you've been here, and we are still sorting things out."

Hope sat up. "What does Hades want to talk about?"

"Do you feel up to going now?" The goddess stood and extended her arm to Hope.

Hope felt as though she were being pushed into a corner. Her instinct was to say no, but she couldn't think of a reason to put it off. Hades must want something from her.

Incidentally, she wanted something from him, too.

THIRTY-EIGHT

HOPE

HOPE SCOOTED TO the edge of the bed and took Persephone's hand. It was cool and dry, and Hope had an odd sense of having been in the same position before with the goddess. As Hope stood, her toes curled into the soft fur rug. She wanted to be strong, despite the unease crawling through her. With a deep breath, she straightened, pulling her shoulders back. But she couldn't stop the trembling in her legs.

Persephone wrapped her arm around Hope's waist. "It's just to talk."

Hope wanted to explain that she wasn't nervous, but she was. She was going to leverage whatever it took to get what she wanted. And she hoped she would come out on top.

The entire Underworld was made of the same dark rock, and Hades's castle, in its entirety, was no exception. The black walls were buffed smooth but with a matte finish.

Not so with the throne room, which was where Persephone led Hope.

The thick double doors were open, but they closed behind her as she entered the spacious room. Hope jumped as she noticed the guards at the door were Skia. These didn't look like the ones in Thanatos's home. These had the telltale leer, but rather than brandishing knives, they each held a black spear, and at their waists were belts with the familiar hilts of the blades that brought immortals to the Underworld.

There were a few parishioners wandering the room, women like the girl, Imogen, wearing pale chitons, likely waiting to be of service. Hope couldn't help the derisive thoughts running through her mind. Stupid sycophants.

Hades sat upon a throne as black as the rest of his world, speaking to a Skia who leaned over the lord of the Underworld. Next to him, an empty seat of jeweled ruby waited for his wife.

Persephone led Hope to the bottom of the dais and then abandoned her to sit next to Hades.

Hope squared her shoulders and waited.

The Skia straightened and inclined his head. "It will be done."

Hope gasped as the Skia descended. She recognized the monster and instinctively reached for daggers she didn't have.

"No," Hades interrupted with a wave of his hand. "I've requested your presence. The Skia will not harm you."

Hope wished there was a way to kill all the Skia.

"And here you are, Sphinx." Hades stood and descended his throne, coming to stand in front of her. "I've been wanting to meet you for a long time."

She should use her best manners, but her gut told her he wanted to use her. "Why?"

"Hmm," he said in a voice so low it was almost a growl. "I can see why Darren disliked you so much."

She put two and two together. "He tried to kill me. I'm guessing on your orders?"

Hades shook his head. "I'd never want you dead. Besides, it's impossible to kill you in the mortal realm because of the curse. I merely asked him to bring you to me."

Right. Which led to the knife against her throat. "And down here?"

He circled her as if measuring her capability or worth. She itched to move but refused to let him see that it was bothering her. She clenched her hands and waited.

He stopped in front of her and, tapping her shoulder, said, "Down here, it wouldn't behoove me even to try. I don't want you dead."

She continued to stare at him, waiting for the other shoe to drop. The air pulsed with want. It was coming; she knew it.

"I'd like you to do me a favor."

The skin on her hands prickled and then got clammy. She wanted to scratch them and wipe them, and she kept telling her heart to stop pounding so hard. She balled her hands into fists so tight her nails dug into her palms. "I'm listening."

"I'd like you to go to Olympus for me. It seems there has been a . . . misunderstanding." He rolled his neck. "All the gods of the Underworld have been sealed here for just over thirty-seven years now."

"What do you want me to do? It's not like the gods are going to listen to me."

Hades cocked his head to the side. "I think you underestimate yourself and your . . . family."

Thirty-seven years. There was a significance, but . . . Why would the Olympians care about her family? "My mom would be thirty-seven years old . . ."

"Bingo." He stepped away from her, offering a tight, unfriendly smile. "I knew you would be smart."

The insincere compliment was irritating, most especially because she *didn't* know why her mom's age would matter to the Olympian gods.

"Do you know what I'm known for?" He turned and walked back toward the dais. Without waiting for her response, he stepped up to his wife and caressed her cheek. Then he sat in his throne and looked down at Hope expectantly.

"Being lord of the Underworld."

He nodded. "And . . ."

"It is said that you bless mortals with wealth."

He waved her words away. "What else?"

"You are more just than the other gods?"

Hades pointed at her. "Precisely so."

It didn't seem that he was particularly just. Darren had tried to abduct her, and there was nothing just about that. Although, looking at Persephone, Hades clearly had a propensity for abduction. Maybe in his mind that was just; he wanted a wife, so he took a wife. Gods did seem to have the most egregious sense of entitlement.

"Do you know what Zeus is known for?"

Hope snorted. "Sleeping around," she muttered to herself before answering, "King of the gods."

Hades raised his eyebrows. "Yes." He paused. "On both counts."

Persephone laughed. "He is awful."

Hades turned to his wife and muttered, "I will never forgive him. Really, someone should castrate him."

The room spun, and Hope swayed on her feet as if the floor had shifted. She stumbled, righted herself, and then stood tall. It would not do well to show weakness now.

"You have maybe five minutes before she collapses, Hades. She is still not well." Persephone seemed to float to Hope's side and wrapped an arm around her waist.

Hope's protest died before it could even get to her lips.

Hades leaned forward on his throne, his eyes gleaming in their intensity. "Do you know what Hera touts above all other virtues? What she has appointed herself the standard-bearer of?"

It was in every text she'd ever seen on the goddess. It was mentioned first in every lesson, on every Internet search, and even on the papers given to her in the conservatory. "Marriage fidelity."

"But you and I know that isn't true, right?" he whispered.

Hope nodded. She'd asked as much and been shut down for it. But what did that have to do with her going to Olympus?

Hades straightened in his seat. "She's a hypocrite, and all this time . . . Hera thought she could get away with it. She slept with that shepherd, gave him the baby, and stayed out of it when Apollo killed her and cursed your grandmother. After Thebes, it was generally believed that the Sphinx had died, but I knew better. *I knew.*" He swept his hand through the air, indicating his throne room. "This is my realm. Of course, I knew. Years passed, decades, centuries, and everyone forgot how the Sphinx came to be, and her divine lineage. When your grandmother finally died, word got out that a Sphinx still existed and Apollo had killed her. Rumors started flying, and there was chaos on Olympus. I wouldn't have said anything if I'd known it would lead to our binding. Not that I like the mortal realm, but the gods of the Underworld suddenly could only leave if we were escorted by one of the Olympians. And I no longer count as such."

It was obvious he was put out by his confinement, but Hope brushed aside his complaint. His purported theory was preposterous. "Are you saying Hera had you bound because she didn't want anyone to know about her and Damon having a baby?"

Hades raised his eyebrows. "You know his name?"

"It's in my *Book.*"

306

Hades licked his lips. "You have it? You have your *Book of the Fates?"*

Hope's heart was beating like she'd run a marathon. "Yes. It's still in . . ." Her intuition stopped her words. He was fishing for information. "Why?"

Persephone squeezed her side. "He wants you to expose Hera and see if you can break the binding. It's probably the Fates that have been affected the most. And their *Books* are all here, except for the one you have, instead of in the Olympian Library like they used to be."

The pieces were coming together. "Hera had all the *Books of the Fates* and gods bound to try and hide the evidence of her infidelity? Does anyone even care?"

She knew the goddess of matrimony was fanatical about faithfulness. Myths of her vengeance were still taught in school.

"You want me to take my Book up there and ask that the binding be loosened?"

He nodded, but the movement brought no reassurance. Hope bit the side of her mouth.

"You would be doing a service for everyone," Hades stated.

She stared at the god as if he'd just declared the entire world free from evil. Hope shook her head. He was getting something out of it, not that she even wanted to know what it was. The less she knew, the better. "Don't try to pretend you're being magnanimous."

He steepled his fingers. "Perhaps there is a service I could do for you."

It was the opening she'd been waiting for. "Indeed. I will consider your request, but I would have you consider mine as well. I want you to let Priska return to the mortal realm."

He leaned forward. "Really? This is your request?"

Persephone cleared her throat, and Hope felt like she was being outmaneuvered in a game where she didn't even know the rules.

"Why don't you both think about it and let Hope get a little more rest, hmm?" Persephone didn't wait for her husband to finish and guided Hope from the room.

As soon as they were out the doors, whatever adrenaline keeping Hope upright drained from her body, and she sagged into Persephone. The goddess said nothing as she helped Hope into her room and into bed.

"Don't forget where you are and how you got here," Persephone warned Hope.

THIRTY-NINE

ATHAN

"**LORD HADES AND** Lady Persephone have requested your presence in the throne room. They also require the son of Hermes to attend."

"We will be there shortly." Xan's voice floated down the hall and into the bedroom.

Athan rolled off the bed as the door clicked shut.

"Hey, Sleeping Beauty," Xan teased, and then he made a face. "You stink. Take a shower before we go."

Stretching his taut muscles, Athan wished for a long, empty stretch of road and a long run to pound the tension away.

"Oh, and our backpacks appeared last night with a change of clothes. Have a bite to eat afore we go; there are bars and bottled water in there, too."

Next to the blue canvas bag was a change of clothes, all the way down to clean boxer briefs. Athan shaved the scruff from his cheeks, eating several protein bars through the process. He showered and brushed his teeth with the bottled water, and then went back to his bedroom to get dressed.

Laying atop his clothes were his jeweled immortal daggers.

"Who did you say brought our stuff?" he yelled over the noise in the bathroom.

"I can't hear you!" Xan yelled back.

It didn't matter. It was here, and Athan wasn't about to turn away anyone's aid. In less than thirty minutes, he slid the daggers into the sheaths in his belt. "I'm ready to go."

His hair still dripping, Xan emerged from the other bedroom, wrapped in a towel and holding his daggers. "Both of mine are here."

Athan nodded. "Who brought the packs?"

Xan furrowed his brow. "That servant girl. Immy. Gen. Imogen. Said she was told to deliver them." He tilted his head. "Do you feel like we're pawns?"

Athan refused to believe it. More than that, he refused to be a pawn. "Let's get Hope and get out of here. She can recover her memory elsewhere."

Xan buttoned his cargo shorts and pulled on a blue T-shirt. "You know it's not going to be that easy, right?" He brushed by Athan and opened a bag of trail mix. "When we get back, you owe me dinner."

The words made Athan smile. It was reminiscent of when they'd been friends and constantly teased each other about who owed whom. "Right."

Xan slung his pack over his shoulder. "Let's go rescue the princess from the evil god of death."

He opened the door, and the willowy Imogen stood in the hall. "Are you ready?"

Xan snorted in disgust. "Are you a lapdog for every god here?"

Her pale skin blanched to almost translucent, and her freckles stood out like spots on a leopard. "You're an ass." As soon as the words left her mouth, she clamped her hands over her lips.

Xan smiled, but Athan laughed out loud.

"Truer words have never been spoken," Xan murmured.

Imogen blushed scarlet and said nothing as she led them down the hall.

Xan jabbed Athan with an elbow, but there was no pain with the ribbing.

The fire reflected off the stone, making the dark walls glitter. The air was heavy as if the very space was weighted with tension.

Imogen said nothing as she pushed open the door to the throne room. She bowed to the monarchs of the Underworld and flinched when Hades called her name.

"I would have you stay," he instructed her.

She shot a wary glance at the two demigods but nodded her assent.

Hades's face was set with grim determination as the door banged open.

"What is the meaning of this, Hades? You have no right to . . ." Thanatos entered the large space flanked by two Skia. He froze as he took in the room.

"Thanatos," Hades warned.

But the god of death would not go quietly. With a flick of his wrist, Skia appeared, their pale skin and dark hair reflective of the gods they served.

Four harbingers of death circled Athan and Xan, black blades drawn.

Xan laughed as he drew his immortal blades. "If this is the best you've got," he sneered, "it's not much more than a game."

He threw his two blades, and the Skia vaporized. Xan stepped forward to retrieve his blades, and two more creatures materialized.

Athan dodged the first blade and charged the Skia that had thrown it. He collided with the solid being and drove his blade deep into the monster's chest. He yanked it out in time to slice the arm of another.

Xan punched one in the groin as he dropped to his knees. He grabbed his blade, sinking it into the Skia's leg and then abdomen.

"Call them off," he yelled as he dodged another blade.

What was the meaning of this? But there was no time to process the mayhem surrounding them as Skia after Skia appeared, only to be dispatched by one of their blades. After killing yet another one of the creatures, Athan realized how easy it was. These monsters were nothing like Darren, or most of the other Skia he had fought in the mortal realm. These were slower, clumsier, untrained.

Why was Hades still sitting on his throne, doing nothing?

Athan dodged another dark knife and sliced his blade across the Skia's chest. "It's a distraction!" But from what?

"Halt!" Hades yelled. He stood, and the room froze. The air pulsed with his power as he surveyed the occupants. "This is beneath you, Thanatos."

Hades threw his arms out, and the Skia dropped. Every single one of them. Their bodies lay on the stone floor, their limbs contorted at odd angles, their obsidian eyes glassy and empty.

Thanatos stood with a blade at Imogen's throat. "If you move, she will die."

Hades locked his gaze on the other god. "That is not your place to decide." The lord of the Underworld pinched his fingers together. "Good luck, Imogen."

She swallowed and then braced as if for a physical blow.

"Do you think I'm stupid? Do you think I would make a move without sufficient support? Do you think I don't know what she is?"

Hades released his fingers, and his power washed over the room and every occupant in it.

Imogen slumped in Thanatos's arms, and then her body was gone and only the slip of her dress remained.

"Your power is what I let it be, God of Death."

Thanatos's eyes bulged, and he struggled against an unseen force.

Hades crossed the room, stepping over the Skias' bodies. As he passed, each body crumbled into a dark dust, blending into the black rock beneath. He stood in front of Thanatos, hand clamping around the god's throat.

"You would defy me, here in my own realm? You know the consequence of insubordination."

Thanatos mouthed his fear, a silent plea.

A piercing scream shattered the silence of the room. The noise built, and then a second scream joined the first.

Athan shuddered.

This was the sound of Tartarus. A third voice, a wail of loss and sorrow, joined the cacophony.

The air swirled around their feet, picking up the dust of the dead Skia, building from a breeze to a dust storm, to a whirlwind.

The force buffeted him, and Athan curled in on himself as he'd done before, covering his ears with his hands to provide a barrier to the noise and tucking his head with his eyes closed. The seconds passed, and his heart pounded with the promise of a painful death. Death singed his exposed skin, like rapid-fire insect bites stinging and burning on his neck, arms, and ears.

"Oh, stop." Persephone's voice was as clear as a bell despite the raging noise.

The air stilled, and silence descended like a blanket.

Athan's ears rang, and he allowed himself to blink to see if the dust had also settled.

His blurred vision made it seem as if three identical women stood by Hades. Athan blinked again, but the multiple images remained.

"Sisters." Persephone stepped off the dais and glided to the three women. Their hair hung in thick waves the color of ash, charcoal, and fire, and it writhed as if the wind still teased through it, almost serpent-like. Their skin was the same pallor as the other gods of the Underworld, but their lips were the color of blood. Their slight frames bordered on emaciated, and their chitons were plain and thick.

It was then Athan realized they were three separate women, although identical in appearance, even in dress.

Persephone embraced each of them, kissing them on the cheek. "Thank you for coming."

Xan had uncurled but continued to squat low to the ground. He had a wary look on his face, and his gaze was glued to the triplets.

Thanatos shook, his mouth working faster to form words that had no sound.

Xan's face flashed with fear, but he schooled his features as if he were staring down death.

"Alecto. Megaera. Tisiphone." Hades nodded to each of the primordial goddesses.

These were the Furies responsible for the torture in Tartarus.

"There they are." One of the goddesses looked at Athan and Xan, and her sisters' gazes followed. "We'd wondered where you'd gone." She turned to Hades. "Did you know Clo and her sisters took them out of Tartarus?"

Hades raised his brows at Athan. "Really?"

"Yes. It seems there is more than one god pushing for change, hmm?"

The voices were different. The second girl had a deeper voice, her tone less nasal.

"Shall we take them again?" The third one lit up with excitement. "We can take them now, if you will."

Athan understood what she was really saying—if you will let us. It was enough to get him to his feet.

"No," Hades said. "The demigods will stay."

The Furies raised their brows in identical question.

"Thanatos will be spending some time with you."

Horror washed over the god of death's face. Thanatos looked around the room as if waiting for aid. As if willing it to happen would make it so. Hecate had told Athan she would not help, and whomever else Thanatos solicited had also abandoned him.

The door opened and the Fates walked through, Atropos guiding Clotho by the elbow.

"You requested an audience, Hades?" Lachesis asked. Her gaze travelled the room, settling on the Lord of the Underworld.

The Fates were not here to help the god of death. There was no one. Defeat settled slowly, and Thanatos's shoulders fell.

The smell of char grew with the proximity of the Furies.

"Sisters." The nasally one greeted the Fates with a small nod. Her eyes gleamed with excitement, and she asked, "Shall we take him now?"

Hades stared at the god of death. "Say hello to my father if you see him, will you?"

Hades nodded to the three Fates, and Lachesis pulled the end of an ashen gray thread from her messenger bag. She measured the length of it on her stick as she pulled several meters out, the strand puddling on the rocky ground. Atropos pulled a pair of shears with dusky crystal handles from her belt and snipped the thread.

Thanatos gasped and brought his hand to his chest.

Atropos took the cut end to Clotho. "Weave and bind."

As Clotho's needles clicked against each other, a black thread joined the gray.

As if on cue, the Furies opened their mouths and intoned, "We are jealous rage, vengeful destruction, and we are endless."

A distant wailing was a portent of what was to come. Bitter wind blew in from the open door, shrieking over the rocky walls as it swirled and thrashed in a buffeting pattern of abuse. Athan closed his eyes and ducked his head in anticipation of the pain. Two blasts battered by him, getting stronger each time, and he braced for more. An ear-splitting cry built into a painful crescendo.

The third pass of air was like the coil of a snake, and he was knocked to his side. The pressure squeezed the air from his lungs, and bright stars burst across the blackness behind his eyelids. He couldn't . . . breathe.

"You really should speak to them about their manners," Persephone said.

His head throbbed, and Athan opened his eyes, grateful for the dim lighting of the Underworld.

"As if they would listen to me," Hades replied.

The thrones were empty, and Hades and Persephone sat on the steps of the dais. Persephone was holding Hades's hand, her fingers tracing the lines on his palms.

"Even so, you could command them and then they'd have to listen." She batted her eyes at him. "I just hate the noise, not to mention the mess they leave."

She waved her arm, and Athan followed the trajectory.

The remaining Skia bodies were all in one corner. The primordial goddesses were gone, as was Thanatos.

Two young women, in gowns much like Imogen had worn, were sweeping the floor.

"Are you both awake?" Persephone asked, her gaze going from Xan to meet Athan's. "Excellent."

Xan was shifting from a fetal position to sitting. He rotated his neck and then twisted his back side to side.

"Remind me to never end up in Tartarus," he said as he stood.

Athan rolled his eyes.

"Can we go see Hope?" he asked. If he could see her, it would remind him of why all of this was okay.

"She should be awake soon, I think," Persephone said, glancing at her husband.

"How is her memory?" Xan asked.

"Improving."

"I think it would improve much better in the mortal realm," Xan muttered.

Athan agreed. The Underworld was no place for the living. Whatever she'd learned, she'd eventually remember, and then they could break the curse. "When can we leave?"

Hades stood. He slowly descended the dais like he was measuring each of his steps. At the bottom of the stairs he waved his hand toward each of the demigods. "You may leave at any time. Neither of you are bound to this realm."

Xan smiled and shifted as if to run out the door, but paused as he caught Athan's frown.

"What about Hope?" Athan asked.

"There are rules. Rules keep order." Hades frowned. "I am not like my siblings."

Xan opened his mouth as if to protest, but the words died on his lips. He stared at Athan as understanding dawned on his shocked features.

"The Lethe," Athan said.

Their victory over Thanatos was completely empty . . . and worthless.

F O R T Y

HOPE

NOISE AWOKE HER, voices arguing and the clanking of metal and stone. It felt as if she'd only been asleep for a few minutes. Her body ached, like she'd worked out with Xan for too long. But she felt more like herself. Her mind wasn't as cloudy, but she felt like there was something she was supposed to remember but couldn't.

"Hope!"

She sat up and rubbed her eyes. A young woman with dark hair sat on her bed. Everything about her was angular and sharp, even her voice.

"You sleep like the dead."

Especially her voice.

She wore a strap of leather across her chest, with several pairs of pinking shears, and a belt with various sizes of scissors. There were some with odd markings, others with jeweled grips. Some with thick long blades, and others with short pointed tips. The girl's dark hair was cut in an angled bob, coming to points at her sharp chin. Dressed in a fitted dark-navy chiton with slits up to her thighs, the goddess leaned toward Hope.

"Do you know who I am?"

Hope swallowed her panic. "I thought you were supposed to appear with your sisters."

Atropos pursed her lips and inclined her head. "I'm only here to deliver a message. You have to go to Olympus next, so don't argue about that. Second, and most important, be sure to include everyone that has sacrificed their immortality to Hades on your behalf when you make your bargain with the Lord of the Underworld, or you'll have bigger regrets than Priska's death."

Just the words made Hope cringe. What did it say that Hope hadn't even considered that others would sacrifice for her? Of course that made sense. Was it a dream, or had she seen Athan here? Her thoughts raced and jumped, and Hope shook her head to clear it. "Are you talking about Athan?"

Atropos jumped and looked at the door. She brought her finger to her lips and then indicated that Hope lie back down.

The lock on the door clicked, and Atropos disappeared.

Hope lay down but tried to keep her eyes barely open. Just enough to see . . .

Persephone entered with another covered tray. She stopped as soon as she'd crossed the threshold of the room, and her eyes narrowed. She took a deep breath and came to the bedside. "You don't have to tell me who was here, but don't pretend you're still asleep. It insults us both."

Hope considered her words, and it seemed ridiculous to pretend anyway, so she sat up. "Sorry."

Persephone waved away Hope's apology. "Don't. You have several gods making requests. You're in a rare position of power."

"I don't feel that powerful," Hope muttered. Her muscles protested every movement, as if trying to remember how to function properly, and she knew she'd lost a chunk of her memory. "But I think I'm ready to know what happened."

Persephone raised her brows. "I think you'd better eat first. You need to talk with Lord Hades before you can bargain with anyone else."

Hope oddly wasn't hungry. Shouldn't her appetite be back by now? She ate one cracker and washed it down with the bottle of water as she mulled over the information she had. Hades wanted her to go to Olympus, face Hera, tell her she was a hypocrite, and get the Olympians to unbind the gods of the Underworld. If she were to believe Atropos, she had to go to Olympus anyway. Gods, she did not want to screw this up. She thought of the goddess of Fate's words.

Hope scooted back to the edge of the bed, her sheet-like toga sliding up to her knees. She pulled down on the fabric so it wouldn't ride any higher. "Can I brush my teeth first?"

Persephone smiled and pointed to the bathroom. "Be my guest."

The chiton was a soft gray, and for some reason the color made Hope uneasy. Regardless, she put it on and made her way out. She was stronger today, if only a little bit so. Still, she wouldn't be able to fight her way out of any situation physically, and she hoped her words would be enough.

"You're better," Persephone seconded. "In another few weeks, you'll be healed and ready to go."

Hope opened her mouth to protest. She couldn't wait a few more weeks. Urgency to get out of the Underworld pulsed with every heartbeat. But it made no sense to argue either; at this point, she couldn't even stand on her own for more than a few minutes. How could she be so tired when she was sleeping so much?

"Patience. You'll get there."

Persephone offered her arm, and Hope accepted it. The walk to the throne room was long.

The hallways were void of parishioners or Skia today, and the quiet made Hope's skin crawl. As if the very structure were awaiting her decision before life moved on.

"Is Athan here?"

The corners of Persephone's eyes tightened. "Why do you ask?"

It was hard to determine what was memory and what was dream, but she was pretty sure that was real. And it seemed like it had happened yesterday. Hope rubbed her forehead. "Didn't he and Xan come into my room? Didn't Athan kiss me?"

Persephone said nothing, and Hope was too tired to really push it. Her head ached, and she concentrated on the roiling of her stomach.

The throne room, like the hallways, was devoid of parishioners, but two Skia stood at the door with weapons in hand. Hope wasn't sure, but they looked familiar.

"Ah!" Hades smiled at her and descended his throne. "Have you had a good rest? Are you ready to discuss our agreement?"

It was déjà vu. The sense that she'd just been in the room compounded the fogginess in her brain.

"You want me to go to Olympus and confront Hera?"

Hades smirked while nodding.

"I can't guarantee that anything will change." There was no way she was going to have what she asked for contingent on his desired outcome.

A dark chuckle escaped before he answered. "Oh, things will definitely change, young one."

She would roll her eyes if it didn't take so much energy. "I'll do it if . . ."

There were certain words she should use. Didn't the cutting goddess say something about specific words? Gods, she was so tired.

Hades raised his eyebrows. "Yes?"

"If everyone that gave their life for me is returned to the mortal realm and allowed to live a long, normal life. Without any influence from your realm until they die a natural death." Was she forgetting anything?

"Not everyone," Hades said, holding up his hand. "I will not override the effect on anyone the other gods have taken."

"Fine." She had no idea what he was referring to, but she trusted in the words of Atropos.

"If this is about your guardian, why not just ask for her back?" The god of the Underworld cocked his head to the side and studied her.

But Hope refused to answer and just stared at Hades, waiting.

"Done."

The tightness in her chest loosened a little. "Swear on the Styx."

A slow smile spread across his face.

It resembled the leer the Skia wore. Suddenly, she wondered if that was where it came from. Her heart skipped a beat.

"I swear on the Styx," he sneered.

Hope shook her head. "I want to hear you say the words exactly like I did."

Hades repeated the words she'd spoken, along with his oath to abide by his word. He then asked that Hope do the same.

The words rolled off her tongue. She would have to fulfill her oath or she would spend eternity burning in the hatred of the River Styx. But confronting Hera was the least of her worries. Hope swayed on her feet. "Are we done? May I return to my bed?"

Hades waved her off. "Yes, yes. You need your beauty sleep before we send you to Olympus."

Hope was too tired to correct him. She had no intention of going straight to Olympus. She needed to see Priska settled and check in with her friends. She missed Haley, Xan, Dahlia, and especially Athan. She missed Mr. Stanley, and wondered if everyone was okay now that Apollo's sons were ash.

Persephone led her to the door. "Your room is the fifth door on the left. Do you think you can make it?"

Hope looked down the hall. It wasn't that far. She nodded and stepped into the hallway. Only seconds later she was at the room. It was right there. Had they come some circuitous route on the way to the throne room? Was she losing her mind?

Hope opened the door and went straight to the bed. She lay down but hadn't even shut her eyes when there was a knock at the door. "Come in."

Persephone entered. Her hair was no longer up, and it cascaded down her back in honeyed waves. Her blue eyes were rimmed in red.

"I'm so sorry," she whispered. "Here is a sleep aid for you."

She held out a vial of silver liquid.

Hope shook her head. She was so tired she could sleep for a week. "I don't want to take anything that will bind me here."

Persephone offered a small smile. "It will not bind you here. It is a gift, from me. It is manufactured in the mortal realm, so it's safe."

"I appreciate your kindness, but I don't want to take anything. If you let me sleep until I wake up, just one good sleep, then I'll leave."

The goddess of the Underworld crossed the room and sat on the bed. She leaned over Hope, and Hope scooted up in bed so she was sitting against the headboard.

"Either you can drink it . . . willingly, or I can call in help. It is a restorative tonic"— she held up her hand—"not that kind of restoration. It is for the body, not the mind. Hades would have you healthy before you leave us."

Hope ground her teeth. "I have no choice?"

Persephone shook her head. "None. But I swear on the Styx it will not harm you, nor will it bind you here."

The liquid was cool and sweet, like drinking the juice of a peach, and Hope had a fleeting thought of a peach orchard before darkness blanketed her.

FORTY-ONE

ATHAN

"**BUT IT IS** Thanatos's fault!" Xan protested, the vein in his neck pulsing. He faced the lord of the Underworld and with deadly calm followed up with, "That is not right."

"I agree with you, Son of Ares."

Hades's acknowledgement did nothing to calm Athan. The god had not said he would release her and, in fact, had prefaced his declaration with a statement about rules.

Rules be damned!

"What will it take?" Athan gritted his teeth, waiting to hear how, and even if, the god of the Underworld would negotiate.

"What do you mean?"

"What will it take for you to let her go?"

"Before you demand it, whatever the cost, listen to me. If she stays here, she will be protected from the gods of Olympus. She will remain here, safely, forever."

It was the forever part that made Athan sick to his stomach. He was tired of having the gods meddle. Tired of feeling impotent to change things.

"If she stays, she will not have the one thing she wants most of all," Xan challenged.

"Oh? You know her well enough to speak for her?" Hades raised his brow and circled the demigod. "What is it she wants most of all?"

"Her freedom."

Xan's face looked as weary as Athan felt.

"Why won't you fix this? You're a god. The ruler of the Underworld. I refuse to believe you can't." Athan glared at him. "You *won't*."

"If I make this exception, it will not only affect you. And you." Hades pointed at Athan then Xan. "And her. It will be an exception that my entire realm will know about. If you want me to do this, you must come up with a way to make it not only compassionate but just. After that fiasco with Orpheus and Eurydice, it was centuries before we had order from the chaos. I will not make that same error again."

Error. Of compassion. But even as Athan wanted to complain about the words, there was sense in them. Reason even. Which was all the more frustrating.

"The way I see it, Lord Hades," Xan began, his jaw set in determination, "you owe us for our service to you. Thanatos was getting ready to lead a rebellion, and we helped stop it."

Hades chuckled. "Do you think this is the first, or will even be the last, time my reign of the Underworld is threatened? Unlike Olympus, ruling here is a responsibility. I would think you both could understand it."

Damn if that didn't make complete sense. Athan struggled to come up with a plan. Something that would get Hope out of the Underworld, something that would give her the opportunity to break the curse.

"But you did do me a favor, Son of Ares," Hades conceded.

Both of the demigods stared at him in anticipation.

"I will reward you with a favor." When Athan's face lit up, Hades added, "A *reasonable* favor, just for you."

"Meaning not Hope," Xan grumbled.

"Let's go to her. Now." Hades led them from the room.

Athan couldn't help but feel like he was getting played. It was like being caught in the middle of a game and not knowing any of the rules, let alone who all the key players were. But it didn't matter. He wanted this more than anything, and he muttered to himself, "Yes, let's go see her."

Xan shot Athan a look that spoke volumes of distrust. At least they were on the same page as far as that was concerned.

Xan brushed by him and whispered, "He wants something."

It was very likely the case. But what?

The room was dark and smelled of lavender and mint. A single candle at the bedside cast a warm glow over Hope's still frame. Her chest rose and fell in a rhythm of slumber.

Next to the bed sat Persephone. Her gaze traveled over each of them before settling on her husband.

"She will wake up?" Athan whispered.

Hades nodded. "This is restorative sleep. A gift from my wife." He pointed at Persephone. "You can both be given a tonic that will aid in your recovery if you'd like. As a gift, it will not bind you here."

Xan snorted, but Athan didn't even dignify it with a response. "Do we know how much of the Lethe she drank?"

"No."

She could have forgotten her entire life if she drank enough. There were stories of this, of those who died with memories so painful they chose to drink from the Lethe.

"How much will she remember? Will she know who we are? Will she remember how to break the curse?"

"You wish to know how much she'll remember?" Hades went to the bedside. His hand brushed over Hope's eyes and rested on her temple. He looked up at Athan with an unspoken apology. "She will not remember anything of her time here."

"Nothing?" She'd been here for weeks. "And this? Will you do anything to fix this?"

Hades's eyes narrowed.

Persephone stood and took his hand.

"Is there anything that *can* be done?" Xan's weary voice cut through the mounting tension.

Hades's gaze bounced between the three of them. His lips thinned, and then he nodded. "Do either of you know of any of her memories here? I can give her a tonic that will help recall her memories, but you will have to be able to tell her of her time, something true, and her . . . soul will push the memory back into her consciousness. It is all I have to offer."

Xan nodded. "How long will we have to restore her memory?"

"A few minutes, ten at the most. The more of the solution I give, the more malleable her memory will be."

"You mean—?"

"You would be able to plant false memories, and she would never know the difference."

Athan stared at the ground. The rug was actually some type of animal hide, the short hair of the beast a soft barrier to the hard rock beneath. He dragged his foot through the fur. What was the sense in recovering her memory if she couldn't leave the Underworld? And if he could get her out, would she still be able to break the curse with what little information they could give her? If she remembered him kissing Isabel, could he explain? Would Hope ever forgive him? Was there any way to make it right?

"If . . . If I trade my immortal life for hers"—Athan stumbled through the words but pushed ahead before his courage failed him—"would that meet the demands of your justice? Would you let her go?"

The air seemed to still. Xan looked like he was going to be sick.

Hades's gaze pierced Athan, but he refused to look away from the god. If this was what it took, he would do it.

"Yes," Hades finally answered. "That would be a fair exchange." He glanced at his wife and then held his arms out wide. "You see I am not without compassion."

Athan nodded. It was not what he wanted, but then . . . It did give Hope the opportunity she needed. "You'll watch after her, Xan?"

"Aye," Xan whispered, his voice thick with emotion. "Are ye sure?"

No. Not at all. But he'd meant what he said to his father. He squared his shoulders. "Give her the tonic. She needs to get out of here."

Hades held his hand out, and a dark opaque vial appeared. He popped off the top and let three inky drops touch Hope's lips. As if on instinct, her tongue slid over the fluid, absorbing the darkness and the opportunity it would give her.

And then she sat up. Confusion lined her golden features, and her gaze traveled from Hades to Xan and then to Athan. "You're here!" Her eyes lit with joy, only to be replaced with confusion. "What happened?"

"You drank from the Lethe."

Hope nodded slowly, as if trying to process the words.

"Do you remember anything else?" Athan's heart beat with hope. He wanted her to remember what she'd learned. How to break the curse? That was why they were all there.

"I . . . I came . . . here. To the Underworld. Priska died, and . . . I came here." Her eyes filled with tears. "Priska's dead."

He wanted to go to her, somehow comfort her, but knew her every second counted. "What else, Hope? This is really important. What else do you remember?"

Her forehead furrowed as she strained with concentration. "Hades and I talked, but before that . . ." She chewed on her lip. "I don't remember."

"You came to find out how to break the curse." Xan stood against the wall, his face now hidden in the shadows.

"Yes." She nodded, her head bobbing up and down. Tears still streaked her wet cheeks. "Yes. That's why I'm here. I need to break the curse."

Gods, she sounded drunk. No, worse. Time was ticking . . .

"Did you find out how?" With every hope in him, he wanted it to be true. He willed her to remember. To answer his question and smile with confidence.

She grimaced, and her body tensed.

"That is not how it works, Athan." Xan pushed himself off the wall and crossed the room. Pushing into Athan's space, Xan continued in a low voice, "Quit making this harder than it is. Tell her; don't ask her."

Hope looked back and forth between the two. Her eyes widened, and she worried the edge of the bedspread. "Why don't you like each other?"

Xan snorted and backed away.

"We're fine." There was no way Athan was going to tell her all the reasons they didn't like each other. Or, that they hadn't liked each other. Because over the last few days, even in spite of himself, Athan had grown . . . at least respectful of the other demigod.

Xan rolled his eyes at Athan as if to contradict his statement then turned back to Hope.

"You saw your mum," Xan said. "And your father was with her."

He was telling her the things she'd told him when Athan had been with Isa.

Hope's eyes lit up. "My mom?"

Silence fell as they waited. Mere seconds later, Hope gasped. "I remember! I remember my mom . . . and I met my dad." Her brow furrowed. "What did they say? Are they okay?"

Athan glanced at Xan, who nodded. "She's fine. They're happy, even."

Relief washed over her face and then peaceful acceptance. "I remember. She is happy, and she's with my dad. I came about the curse." She turned to Athan and asked, "What did I learn?"

Athan looked to Xan, but this time he shook his head.

Hope followed Athan's gaze, and her smile brightened. "Xan, I'm so glad you're here."

He sat on the edge of her bed. He reached forward and grabbed a lock of her hair, twisting it around his fingers. "You remember me now, lass?"

She laughed. "Of course. How's Dahlia? Did she come, too?"

Xan stopped. "She's not here, luv. But she sends her well wishes."

Hades stepped between them all. "Your time is almost up. Better make it quick."

Hope's gaze fell on the gods, and her jaw tightened.

Xan took a deep breath. "You need to go to Olympus. You found out something about the curse while you were here, and you need to confront Apollo. And make sure you get justice, or have justice with you, when you confront him."

Hope drew back from the onslaught of information, and Athan wanted to hit Xan for the rapid dump.

Grimacing, she closed her eyes and rubbed her temples. "What does that mean? Justice? Gods, my head hurts."

Xan shrugged helplessly. "That's what you told me."

It was too much, all at once. Athan had no idea why Hope wasn't screaming at them all to leave. It was almost like the tonic had a sedative in it or something, something that was blunting her emotions.

Hope bit her lip, her forehead furrowing in concentration. When she looked up, her eyes were full of tears. "It's like I know it's right there"—she pointed at her head—"but I don't remember." Her gaze went to Hades. "Why don't I remember? What trauma did I have? You never told me."

"You drank from the Lethe," Hades answered.

Her expression morphed into horror. "Why would I do that?" She looked at Athan then Xan. Both shook their heads, Xan obviously taking his cue from Athan. She looked up to Hades, again, expectantly.

He stared down at her, his jaw set.

Athan knew he should answer. Was it wrong that he didn't want to tell her?

"If it was bad enough that you drank from the Lethe, do you really want to remember what it was?" Xan walked over to her and extended his hand. "Even if he knew, Hope"—Xan indicated Hades—"would you really want him to tell you?"

Hope sucked in her breath. "You knew. All this time . . . You knew I drank from the Lethe, and you didn't tell me."

Xan ran his hand through his hair then turned to Hades. "All this time? It's been what"—he checked his watch—"twelve hours since they brought her in?"

Hope glared at the god, and then her eyes dilated. "But . . ." Her jaw dropped. "If I . . . if I drank from the Lethe . . . am I bound to the Underworld?"

Athan hadn't planned to tell her. Not yet.

"No," Hades said.

Athan's vision tunneled. He'd given his heart, and now his life, for her. And she deserved to hear it from him. "I . . . can't go with you."

FORTY-TWO

HOPE

HOPE'S HEART STOPPED. Surely he couldn't mean— "You can't go with me where?"

Athan pursed his lips and held up a finger indicating that she wait a minute. She glanced at Xan, but he refused to meet her eyes and instead studied the dark comforter. Hades met her gaze, and his lips curved into a smile. But he, too, obviously was going to let Athan explain.

Athan blew out a slow breath. "You drank the Lethe . . . and it was my fault. I saw Isabel here. She . . . She was my girlfriend when I was younger. I gave her a hug."

He cleared his throat, as if the words were somehow stuck there, and breaking eye contact with her, he dropped his chin to his chest.

It was preposterous to think that would drive her to jump in the Lethe. She shook her head. Nothing about that made sense.

In a voice filled with shame, he whispered, "And I kissed her goodbye."

She wrinkled her brow. He kissed his dead girlfriend goodbye? That she could believe, although it sounded weird, really. And if she had seen it . . .

And she remembered. She had gone to the Lethe. She was upset about Athan. But she'd decided not to drink.

"That wasn't your fault. I mean, it was your fault that you kissed Isabel, but . . ." It wasn't like she owned him or that they had some kind of boyfriend-girlfriend exclusivity. She waved her hand. "It wasn't your fault I fell in."

Xan stood with a huff. "Shite. Do you hear yourselves? It was Thanatos that pushed her in. Let it go already. Both of you quit torturing yourselves."

Flashes of the thin god of death ran through her mind. "Where is he now?"

"Tartarus," Hades answered. "He committed treason and will spend some time with the Furies."

More and more of her memory fell into place with the mention of Thanatos, and she wished it were possible to purge those memories. She'd trusted him, and he'd betrayed her. But he'd also warned her about . . .

Hope sat up in bed. "Why am I not bound then? Why is Athan?"

"I traded my immortality for yours," Athan said with a shrug. As if it weren't the biggest sacrifice one could give.

"You are bound?"

He nodded. "At least this way you can go to Olympus and break the curse."

Hope couldn't believe it. Her thoughts raced with the implications and meanings, and rage filled her. Hades had bound her to go to Olympus when he'd known all along that she was already bound to the Underworld. He'd anticipated Athan's sacrifice. He'd played them all.

"How dare you?" she spit out through clenched teeth. Oh gods! She thought of her fatigue, her overwhelming exhaustion, and how her sleep had never been enough. Xan said it had only been twelve hours. "You made it seem that I was . . ." She turned to Persephone. "You kept waking me up."

At least the goddess had the decency to look away.

After nearly drowning, they had deprived her of sleep. No wonder her mind had felt so sluggish. Gods! If Atropos hadn't come, she would've promised anything.

Realization settled slowly like warm honey pouring over her mind, her chest, and then her heart. She smiled and it morphed into a smirk. She turned to the lord of the Underworld. "What did you hope to gain?"

He pursed his lips, and his eyes narrowed. Leaning toward them, and with a wide smile he said, "Do you mean what *did* I gain?"

Unease crept down her spine. There was still too much she couldn't remember. Had she promised him more?

As if he couldn't contain the news, Hades chuckled. "A psychopomp demigod in my realm, and in my control."

Her mind stuttered over the words, as if collectively they made no sense. She looked to Athan, waiting for him to refute it.

"Not in your control," Athan said with a shake of his head.

Hope pushed to the side of the bed and leaned toward the god. "No. I don't think you get anything. You swore on the Styx . . ."

Hades's face blanched. "He did not die for you."

Indignation flared. Did he think this was a joke? "He gave his life. That was the deal."

"We were talking about your guardian."

Hope's heart galloped and jumped in her chest. Her stomach clenched. This could not be happening! She looked around the room in a panic for help, but not one person, or god here, could make Hades keep his word. Her gaze landed on the bedside table on a familiar-looking yellow tome.

She reached for the book. "What about Priska? How will you return her to the mortal realm?"

Hades shrugged. "The Fates," he said with an indication of the book she now held, "will remove her immortal thread. They will find a way to make her strong enough to live without it."

As if on cue, the air shimmered and the three youthful-appearing goddesses stood in the room. They were each dressed in traditional chitons of vibrant red, the long flowing skirts puddled on the ground. Clotho was bent over her knitting needles, and Atropos held her elbow. Lachesis wore a leather messenger bag across her chest and held her measuring rod as if a walking stick.

The primordial goddess offered Hope a smile. "You still have Luc's book."

Hope nodded, but she had no idea who Luc was. She took a deep breath and pointed at Hades.

"He and I had an agreement." She filled them in on the details, then asked, "Does he actually change the life of a person, or do you?"

Silence descended upon the room.

"We change it," Clotho said, clenching both needles in one hand. She glared at the lord of the Underworld. "I shall have to weave Priska's thread with that of another's. It will bind her life there in the mortal realm."

"You bind her to another person?"

Clotho went to the messenger bag and pulled out several feet of a thread the color of midnight. She held up the frayed end, and it was clear there were several threads all connected together. The goddess pulled at a thread from the center, and the rest of the pieces frayed, tangled, or broke. "Her life would not be strong enough on its own to survive."

The goddess pulled another thread out, this one a pale silvery white. She knit the two of them together into a sliver of the night sky while she said, "They will do very well together. Her immortality will be gone, but she won't be quite human. Immortality is not an easy thread to remove." She finished and put the thread back in the messenger bag. "There now, all done."

With her heart in her throat, Hope asked, "What about Athan?"

Clotho tilted her head.

Lachesis frowned.

Atropos winked at Hope with a small smile.

"I traded my life in exchange for Hope's freedom. So she wouldn't be bound here," Athan said.

Hades narrowed his eyes.

Xan chuckled as he studied the Lord of the Underworld. "Damn."

"Were those your exact words?" Lachesis asked.

Athan's face clouded over as if he were trying to remember.

"He traded his life in the mortal realm. He didn't die. He just agreed to stay here in the Underworld and serve me."

"No." Athan's eyes dilated at Hades's words. "I never said I would serve you."

Lachesis straightened, and the light danced across her skin. Her young face aged, and then she had no face, only a decaying skull with markings similar to what was on her rod. The light faded, and the woman asked, "What were the words?"

Hades clenched his teeth and said, "He said he would trade his immortality for hers."

Clotho grabbed at the air, and a thin book with leather the color of moss appeared in her hands. She opened the tome and read, *"If I trade my immortal life for hers, would that meet the demands of your justice?"* She snapped the book closed, and it disappeared. "If he gave up his immortality, the demands of his oath and your justice will be served, Lord Hades."

"That was not the understanding," Hades said, seething. "It was a trade, not a sacrifice."

Clotho pursed her lips.

"Perhaps we should call our sisters to judge betwixt thee?" Lachesis's lilting speech was laced with bite.

Their sisters were the Furies. Hope cringed to think of them joining the throng in her now cramped room.

Athan and Xan both blanched with the threat.

Hades stepped up to the goddesses, pushing into their space with his dark presence. "This is my realm. You would do well to remember that."

The muscles in the god's neck tightened. His glare made Hope shrink back but did nothing to intimidate the Fates.

Atropos drew a pair of dusky crystal shears, the light refracted in their cut surface scattering dark rainbows around the room. With an arched brow and a deadly gleam, she volleyed back, "We do not serve thee, Lord Hades. We never have. And even the lives here will be affected by our shears, as you well know." She put her arms around her sisters. "You would do well to remember that."

Hope held her breath.

"Fine," Hades said and stepped back from the three sisters. "He will no longer be immortal though."

Clotho inclined her blond head. "As you had agreed."

The pale goddess went again to the messenger bag. She replaced the dark thread and extracted one the color of buttery jade. She pulled another thread, the color of wheat in the afternoon sun, and deftly wove the two together. It took only seconds but felt like an eternity.

Hope let her breath out slowly through pursed lips as the weaver of life put the combined thread back into the messenger bag.

"It is done."

Hades pointed at Hope. "This does not change anything between us. You are still to deliver as promised."

"I will." But if she'd learned anything in her time in the Underworld, it was the power of words, and the exactness of their interpretation.

FORTY-THREE

ATHAN

HOPE TURNED TO Athan. Emotions flashed across her face: confusion, horror, pain. "You saved me."

He wouldn't agree to that. He'd done nothing more than what was necessary. And after the pain he'd caused, it was the least he could do. A small token of recompense. "With a lot of help, you will save yourself." He nodded to Xan.

Tears filled her eyes. "I . . . I don't think I deserved that."

"It doesn't matter if you deserved it. It's what I wanted." The sacrifice had felt right.

"It's a strange thing, love. It can be so selfish and selfless all at the same time." Hades twisted a pale gold band on his finger. He glanced at his wife.

Xan extended his hand to Athan.

Surprise flitted across Athan's face, but he accepted the outstretched hand, and Xan pulled him in for a brief one-armed hug. Xan then extended his hand and waved Hope toward them. "Let's get out of here."

Athan couldn't agree more.

Xan winked at Hope and Athan then turned to Hades. "I'd like to thank you for your hospitality, and I wish I could say it was a pleasure, but . . ." Xan held his hands up. "I can't."

Hades's demeanor morphed in an instant and surprised them all. His chuckle was deep and long. His frustration seemed to evaporate. "Demigod of war, you are nothing and everything like your father. I wish you the best of luck in your next adventure. And when it is your time to come here to the Underworld, I will be very glad to have you."

Xan backed away from the lord of the Underworld. "Right. I still hope that's not for a very long time."

Hades inclined his head. "That's understandable."

Athan watched the discussion unfold with awe. It was like the god was possessed with multiple personalities or something.

Hope seemed to share all of his thoughts but none of his reserve when she asked, "Are you always like this? All over the board with your . . ." She waved her hands.

Hades turned his dark eyes on her. "No, Hope." He drew in a breath before he continued. "I'm much more tolerable, and tolerant, when I have my wife with me. And I calm much more quickly."

He turned to Athan. "Your sacrifice speaks volumes about the depth of your feelings." He looked again at Persephone. "I understand that, and I will give you a promise: no Skia will harm you, ever. As soon as you cross the threshold to the mortal world, your immortality will be gone. Do you understand?"

Athan nodded. He had known the cost, and looking at Hope, he would do it again. Even with Hades's gift, part of his soul ached with his loss. But, this wasn't the end. "I understand."

"There is nothing else here for you," Hades addressed them all. "You may leave. My guards will see to your safety until you return to the portal."

They acknowledged his command and prepared to go. Athan and Xan left to get their backpacks. When they returned to Hope's room, she was alone, dressed in regular clothes with her hair pulled up in a ponytail, and slipping on a pair of shoes.

"Well, that's it then?" Xan asked. He crossed the room but stopped in front of Hope. "Are you ready to go?"

She nodded, her gaze flitting to Athan.

He'd hoped she would forgive him. Trust him. That she'd be able to—

Hope crashed into him, wrapping her arms around him. "Thank you," she whispered. "I'm so sorry you had to give up your immortality."

He wanted to tell her it was okay. That it didn't matter. But the words would've been false. He wrapped his arms around her and pulled her close. Her body molded to his perfectly, and the hole in his chest, the emptiness that had ached ever since he'd woken up, filled with a warmth he'd never felt before.

"Let's go home," he whispered into her hair. He punctuated the words by brushing his lips over her head.

As they stepped from the room, two Skia flanked them, guiding them out of Hades's home.

Hermes met them outside the palace. His hazel eyes were rimmed in red, and worry lined his features and hung heavy from his shoulders. He said nothing as he pulled Athan close and wrapped him in a hug.

His father's sorrow hit him like an anvil. "I'm sorry, Dad." Athan wasn't even sure what he was apologizing for. He wouldn't change it. Hope's freedom was more important than his immortality. But somewhere deep inside, he felt like he'd let his father down.

"Nothing for you to be sorry about." Hermes's voice was thick with emotion. "No matter what, I will always be your father, and I will always love you. If you need anything . . . anything at all, I'll always be here for you."

"Thanks." And despite the loss, Athan was at peace with it. "I saw Isabel while I was here."

"Really?" Expectation flashed across Hermes's features. "How is she?"

Athan chuckled. "Dead. But seeing her made me realize . . . I've moved on. Not that I didn't care for her." To say that would've been a lie. "But my feelings for Hope run much deeper. I've healed from the pain of losing Isabel, and I'm at peace with it. But more importantly, Hope's made it possible for me to have a real chance at love . . . with her."

Hermes's face darkened as Athan spoke. Rather than congratulating him or wishing him well, Hermes said he needed to have a word with Hope. He probably realized he would have to express his gratitude for saving Athan's life, and Hermes, like all gods, didn't like to swallow the bitter pill of humility.

FORTY-FOUR

HOPE

HERMES'S REUNION WITH Athan made Hope's eyes sting and fill with tears. She'd had that briefly with her mom—that memory was solidly back in place.

She watched the father-and-son reunion with a sense of deep satisfaction and gratitude. Atropos had thrown her a bone and then backed her up. Perhaps not all the gods were selfish.

"I would have a word with her," Hermes said, and then he stepped next to her. "May I?"

He led them away from Athan and Xan, just far enough that they were out of earshot.

Hope's heart skipped and tripped in anticipation. Unease crawled over her skin, and she remembered when he'd dumped her in the Underworld as he took Priska to the Acheron for crossing.

"My son has become quite attached to you," he said flatly. The god swallowed, and his gaze darted to Athan before returning to her. His eyes narrowed. "An attachment that appears to threaten his very existence."

Hope wanted to protest. To tell him she'd actually saved his son. But there was truth in his words. Athan wouldn't have ever been in danger if it weren't for her. With slow, dawning horror, understanding washed over her. Every person she was close to suffered or died . . . because of her.

"I'm sorry," she whispered. But the words were an empty shell. She couldn't erase what had happened to Athan, and it would affect the rest of his now-mortal existence.

"Meaningless." He waved away her apology and leaned toward her. "I want you to understand one thing, Sphinx."

She waited for the threat she knew was coming.

"His infatuation will pass, and I can't wait until it does. But in the meantime, I will not help you. You know how much I hate Apollo, but that is nothing compared to how I feel about you. You have taken my one remaining joy, risked it for your gain, and returned it broken and fragile."

She opened her mouth to protest. She'd never asked Athan and Xan to come. She'd never wanted anyone to risk their life for her.

"Out of respect for my son, I won't thwart your quest. And out of courtesy to him, I'm telling you: Don't come to me for aid. If our paths cross, you'd better turn and run the other way." He bent over her and stared into her eyes. "Am I clear?"

She stepped back. Pain, disappointment, and hurt buffeted her. Emotion burned her heart, and her eyes spilled the tears she couldn't contain.

"I understand," she choked.

"Good." He patted her head. "Now be a good girl, and wipe away those tears. We both can agree he deserves better. You don't need to give him anything else to worry about, right?" There was threat and condemnation in his words and tone, and then he sealed it with her own guilt.

She wiped her eyes and nodded. "Right."

FORTY-FIVE

ATHAN

ATHAN STOOD STARING at his father. Staring, but not really seeing. His mind stuttered and stumbled over the fact that he was no longer immortal, but his body didn't really *feel* different. Was he supposed to feel different? Would he feel different once he was out of the Underworld?

Shocking realization washed over him. He'd no longer be *psachno*. He'd no longer live at the conservatory. He'd no longer have to fight Skia. What would he do? His gaze went from his father to Hope, and he pushed away the questions and uncertainty. He would deal with whatever his new life would mean after Hope was back from Olympus. Until then, he would do whatever he could to support her.

Xan tapped Athan's shoulder with a fist. "Bloody hell."

Athan's focus snapped to the other demigod, and he pasted on a smile. "Can you believe it? We're getting out of here. We made it out."

Xan cleared his throat. "Aye. I'm surprised you're so happy."

Happy? Hardly. But there was a point, actually a couple of moments, there in the Underworld, when he'd thought none of them would make it out. Awkwardness gnawed at Athan, and he knew the only way to deal with it was to say it. "I'm so sorry about Dahlia. Have you told Hope?"

"No. And I won't tell her until she's recovered, right?" Xan grabbed Athan and pulled him closer. "She doesn't need to be slapped with one more burden. Let her get her feet under her again."

There was wisdom in letting her get a solid night's sleep. She looked haggard, and it made Athan want to curse Hades for playing with Hope's mind like he had.

"What will you do now?" Xan asked.

It wasn't like there was even an option. "Help Hope get to Olympus. That's what this is all about, right?" He'd help her, but how? They both knew he could climb the mountain, but that was as far as he could go. Mortals were not allowed within the city. "Will you . . . Will you go with her?"

Xan clenched his fist, and his jaw tightened. "I know you love her, but do you know if she feels the same about you?"

The pain couldn't have been much worse if Xan had punched him. "We haven't really talked about it."

Xan leaned back as if absorbing his response. "Do that. Before we leave. Talk it over with her. If you're together, I'll respect that. But if not, I'm going to be upfront with you right now. I mean to make her love me."

Athan flinched. That was worse. "At least I know where you stand."

"As if there had been any question."

Would asking her put undue pressure on her? Was she even thinking about who to date right now? The question sounded insane. If she was, she shouldn't be. Athan shook his head. "Don't be an ass. You're asking her to pick? She needs to focus on breaking the curse. I won't go there with her now. And you shouldn't either. If she makes it back, I'll fight you over the girl, but you're being a complete tool right now."

Xan snorted then laughed. "Fine. You're right. Of course I'll take her to Olympus."

If there were anyone else that would fight for Hope, Athan would ask them to accompany her instead. But Xan gave her the best chance. And more than anything, Athan wanted her to be free from Apollo's curse.

They looked back at Hope and Hermes. Hermes put his arm around Hope as if they were friends, but the incredulity painted across her face told Athan it wasn't appreciated. She pulled his arm off and hissed something at the god, who in turn glared at her.

"Gods, you better go help."

Athan frowned. "He wouldn't hurt her."

But something in his father's eyes made him doubt the statement as soon as he'd said it. Why would his father be mad at Hope? She'd just saved Athan. Hermes should be grateful.

Xan snorted. "I wasn't worried about Hope."

FORTY-SIX

HOPE

"**You have a** natural ability to piss the gods off," Xan said with a smirk. But the tightness around his eyes betrayed his concern. "All of them, it seems. It's practically a talent." He bit the side of his mouth before continuing. "We'll have to be more careful on Olympus."

Hope shook her head. "I'm going alone. I can't . . . I can't lose any more people I love to this."

Xan snorted. "Did you fall on your head, too?"

"No," she grumbled. "Why would you say that?"

He let out a low breath and pointed to Hermes and Athan. "I don't know what he said, but I can imagine. Here's the thing—you didn't do anything wrong, and despite what Hermes said, Athan made his own choices that brought him here. You are responsible for your decisions only, and yes, they affect others, but me, Dahlia, and Athan are all adults.

And the consequences of our decisions are ours." He rubbed his forehead. "Come on," he extended his arm.

It was a welcome invitation, but she hesitated. It wasn't going to get easier to say . . . ever. But it needed to be said. She wouldn't have him help with false expectations, and she cared too much to have him misunderstand. "You know I like you. Lots, in fact. You're my best friend. But"—she took a deep breath and ripped the Band-Aid off—"but I don't like you like I like him. You and I are just friends. That's all I can offer."

He didn't look surprised. And he didn't drop his arm. "All right." He waved her forward. "Now come here and give your best friend a hug."

She looked back at Athan talking with his father, and then she faced Xan again. With a huge smile, his dimple teased her, refusing to let her feel bad for what she'd done. She closed the distance and hugged him tight. "I'm glad you're my friend."

The demigod radiated warmth and strength. The enormity of her task suddenly didn't feel so impossible.

"Aye, lass. Me, too." He then shouted over his shoulder for directions.

Hermes passed them, grumbling under his breath.

Athan stepped up to Hope and took her hand. "Come on. Let's go home."

THE AIR WAS sweet like fresh apples. It tasted of pine, rain, and a faint hint of exhaust that hadn't yet been washed away. It was fresh, and it felt so good.

Hope stared up at the gray sky and had to close her eyes as the misty rain hit her again and again. It was the best feeling.

"As soon as you're done, I think we should get Athan's things," Xan said beside her.

A warm calloused hand gripped hers, and Hope entwined her fingers with Athan's. "I'm sorry to keep you waiting."

He smiled at her, and his hazel gaze soaked her in. "I'm not in any rush."

"Do you think your things will still be there?" Hope wasn't sure how long they'd been gone, but if it had been more than a few months, would the other demigods clean out his room?

"Of course." But he sounded nervous; the lilt of his voice going up at the end of his sentence, almost as if he were asking a question. He smiled, but his eyes shifted away from her before his smile could reach them.

Definitely nervous.

"Come on. They won't keep you out."

Hope crossed the driveway, noting the change in landscape. The last time she'd been at the conservatory, the walk had been lined with azaleas. Now, bright-orange day lilies were in full bloom, and the long grass swayed in the breeze. The tall pine trees seemed . . . taller. But that was probably just memory problems, maybe leftover from the Lethe.

Xan pulled his keychain from his pocket and slid the key into the lock. But it wouldn't turn.

"They changed the locks?" Hope asked.

Athan said nothing, but his frown spoke volumes.

"They never change the locks," Xan replied. "Never." Curling his hand into a fist, he pounded on the heavy door. With each consecutive knock, his scowl deepened.

Athan shifted his weight from foot to foot.

"Why are you nervous?" Hope whispered. "You don't think they'll let you in? How could they refuse you? It's not like you're asking to live there."

They had talked about it on the way to the conservatory, but Athan had refused to let Hope live alone. He said it would be pointless to have him and Xan at the conservatory. They'd have to find an apartment big enough for the three of them. Hope wasn't sure such a thing existed, although they seemed to be getting along fine right now. The door opened, followed by a gasp.

"Oh. My. Gods!" Thenia's voice built into a crescendo. "Kaia!"

She pulled Xan into a hug. "I thought you were . . ."

She didn't finish the sentence, but she didn't need to. Everyone understood her meaning.

"Nope," Xan said with a chuckle.

"Xan? Athan?" Kaia came running down the hall but skidded to a stop when she saw Hope. Kaia's eyes widened, and her jaw dropped.

"Hi, Kaia." Hope gave the daughter of Demeter a small smile and waved with her free hand. Hope had always liked the somewhat spacey girl.

The demigod narrowed her gaze. "I can't believe you would even show your face here again."

The words stung worse than a physical slap, and Hope swallowed the pain. She probably deserved it.

"Kaia!" Thenia stared at the other demigod as if she could communicate with just her gaze. Maybe she could.

"Fine," Kaia snapped. "Whatever. But don't ask me to be excited." She offered Xan and Athan a nod. "I'm glad you guys are back safe. The last couple of years here have been enough to drive me crazy. Maybe we can start going out again. Even if it's just to go shopping."

Wait. Did she say *years?* Hope looked to Athan and then Xan, but both of them looked equally as confused.

"Oh, come on. As if you didn't know. Where have you been? Under a rock?" Kaia snickered as she rolled her eyes.

Hope was having whiplash from the girl's mood. Kaia had always been pleasant, easygoing, and nice. This person was anything but.

"We went to the Underworld," Xan told her in a flat tone.

Kaia's face blanched, and even Thenia looked pale.

"The Underworld?" Thenia swallowed. "It's true? All of it? Oh, gods . . ."

Xan narrowed his eyes. "How long have we been gone?"

"Sixty-four months," Thenia said.

Hope wanted to pinch herself. Five years? How could that even be?

"Shite," Xan muttered.

Athan dropped Hope's hand. "I need to get my stuff."

He stepped up onto the porch, but Kaia moved to block his entrance. "If all that's true . . . you're not allowed in anymore. They told us. And it's your fault Obelia died. You . . ."

Athan stopped, mid-step, and then slowly put his foot down. He crossed his arms over his chest as he drew himself up to his full height. "Excuse me?"

Kaia looked at Thenia, then to Xan, before her gaze hardened. Glaring at Athan, Kaia screamed, "You left. You left us to go after *her*." She pointed at Hope. "Obelia ran off and died. And now you're not a demigod anymore. You did this. It's your fault. It's all your fault!"

"Kaia, stop!" Thenia put her hand on Kaia's shoulder and leaned into her as she whispered, "You need to stop."

Kaia's eyes filled with tears, and without another word, she turned and fled down the hall.

Thenia took a deep breath and faced them. "She took your disappearance hard. It's been a rough . . . couple of years. Athena advised us to stay inside. All. The. Freaking. Time." She took another deep breath. "Olympus is . . . The gods are going crazy." Her gaze settled on Hope. "You need to be very careful."

Athan cleared his throat. "I need to get my stuff."

Thenia bit her lip and shook her head. "Athena said you're not a demigod anymore."

Xan snorted. "I don't think you can change that. Hermes is still his father."

Every single word made sense, but the sentences didn't. How could this be happening? How could the demigods be turning on each other?

Athan stepped toe-to-toe with Thenia and, looking down on her, said, "It's my stuff in there. And I have every intention of getting it. You can either—"

Thenia pressed a silver blade to Athan's neck. "This conversation is over. You aren't immortal. I'm just doing my job, and right now that means telling you to leave. Take Hope and leave, Athan. You're not welcome here anymore."

In the time it took Hope to clench her fists, Xan had pushed Athan away from Thenia, disarmed the daughter of Athena, and drawn his own immortal weapons. Brandishing a knife in each hand, he said, "Don't start something you can't finish."

Thenia dropped her arm to her side, but Xan didn't relax. "Are you going to let him in?"

She shook her head. "I can't. She'll kill me if I do."

Hope gasped, and Athan sucked in a breath next to her.

"Athena?" Xan asked.

Her own mother would kill her if she let Athan in? What was wrong with the gods?

"Yes. So please don't ask me again."

Xan dropped his arms and put away his blades. "Fine. Am I allowed in still?"

"You're still immortal, right?" When Xan nodded, she continued, "Then yes. No one said you couldn't come in."

Xan turned to Hope and Athan. "Tell me what you want, and I'll go get it."

Athan gave him a small list: a few pictures and an old journal. He waved away questions about clothes, shoes, and other normal things.

As he spoke, Hope tried to figure out why the gods would bar him entrance to the conservatory. Why would it matter if he got his pictures?

Xan brushed by Thenia, who continued standing in the doorway.

"Come on," Hope said, and she pulled Athan toward the driveway. "Let's wait in the car."

She climbed into the back seat with him.

"I'm sorry." It seemed so inadequate, but she still felt compelled to tell him. "You've done so much—"

He shook his head. "No. Please. You make it sound bad."

Was it bad? Was he mad at her? Did he regret his choice to save her? Did he finally see the monster she was?

Athan cupped her face in his hands. "I can tell what you're thinking, and you're wrong. You're amazing, Hope. And I'd do it again. All of it again, if I had to. I was so worried that when we came back up here I'd feel different. And I do."

Her heart skipped a beat. She'd been so anxious about this, and he'd said nothing. But of course he felt different. He was mortal now, and she couldn't help but feel like his new weakness was her fault. Her emotion expanded in her chest, a lump forming at the back of her throat, and she choked out, "I'm so, so sorry."

"Stop. Please." He brushed his lips over hers and then spoke without pulling away. "Do you remember, back in Goldendale, when I said you were barely alive when I found you?"

His lips were warm and grazed hers with every word, making it difficult to focus on what he was actually saying.

It was the first time they'd been alone in as long as she could remember. The air around him pulsed with his energy, and she wanted to climb onto his lap. He was beautiful and sad. He'd lost everything and somehow made her feel as though he owned the world. He could've had anything, and he'd chosen her.

His words finally registered. She remembered. They'd been fighting; he'd thought she was a demigod, and she was trying to run before he could find out what she really was. He'd said her life was nothing more than a shallow existence, and he'd been right.

She nodded, and Athan pulled her close. His hands threaded into her hair, and tilting her head to the side, he trailed kisses from her lips to her ear, leaving a path of fire on her skin.

Hope gasped. She didn't want him to stop. Ever. He was like sunshine and warmth and joy. He made her so happy. So, so happy.

He nipped at her ear and then kissed where he'd bit. Burying his face in her neck, he said, "I . . . I was barely alive. I'm so sorry." He pulled back and again cupped her face. "I had nothing to live for. *No one* to live for. And I won't be so dramatic as to claim you are my all." He chuckled before continuing. "But you gave me purpose and the first taste of happiness I can remember since my mother died. I cared for Isa, but . . . you make me want to be better. To be more. To give of myself."

Her heart felt as if it would burst.

"I love you, Hope," Athan said, punctuating his words with a kiss. When he pulled away, he looked her in the eyes. "Somehow, we'll get through this. We'll break the curse, and you'll be free. And when we do, I hope you'll let me win your heart."

Words failed her. She couldn't speak, so she just nodded. But what she wanted to say, the words that were there in her mind but her lips just couldn't pronounce . . . was that he already had.

FORTY-SEVEN

HOPE

PRISKA OPENED THE door, screamed, and then burst into tears.

Hope stood on the brick doorstep with the paper-wrapped bouquet of daisies, staring at her aunt's rounded belly. Hope had left Athan and Xan at the hotel they'd just rented, knowing this visit had to happen before she could go to Olympus.

The smell of banana bread wafted out the door and teased Hope with the sense of hominess. Her aunt's tears nearly undid Hope, and she swallowed the lump in her throat. After an eternity that was no more than a heartbeat, she closed the distance and hugged her very pregnant aunt.

Priska wrapped her arms around Hope, pulling her close, and sobbed into her shoulder. Hope stepped into the house and walked them into the two-story foyer, kicking the door shut.

"Darling, what's the matter . . ." Charlie Davenport rounded the corner and stopped.

Hope looked at the man, her lawyer, her aunt's boyfriend, or was it husband? He was dressed in a pair of jeans and a soft gray sweater. His head was cleanly shaven, as was his face. He was handsome, for an older man. And he was wearing an apron. He was everything her aunt deserved. "Hi, Charlie."

A slow smile spread across his face. "Hope, sweetheart. I'm so glad you made it back to us."

Priska kept one arm around Hope as she wiped her tears and led them both into the living room. "You got out."

"You, too."

"Holy Hades, you both had me scared." Charlie hugged them both.

He smelled of expensive cologne and almond extract. The fact that he'd been in the kitchen baking made Hope smile even bigger.

Priska led Hope to the couch, and the two of them sat. The oven beeped, and Charlie excused himself to pull out the bread.

"How long have you been back?" Hope asked, pointing to her aunt's belly.

Priska coughed then cleared her throat. "Almost two years." She shook her head. "I was gone for three, and you've been gone for five. Charlie almost put your trust into probate, but I had this feeling . . ."

It had been quite a shock to Hope as well when they'd gone to the conservatory to get Athan's things. But five years was not enough to take away the repugnance of Hope being a monster or the rules of *demigods only.*

"Is it different?"

Priska practically glowed with happiness. "Yes, but not altogether. I don't feel that different, unless I get sick. And it seems that whatever you did, and I want to hear every single detail, made it so that both Charlie and I age slower. I'm told I look like I'm in my thirties, and I swear he hasn't aged a day since I've been back."

Hope skimmed over most of her time in the Underworld, just the few details that Xan and Athan had helped her piece together of her memory, and the bargain she had made to confront Hera in return for Priska's life. "It was the best I could think of."

"The Fates?" Priska nodded. "My life force would be tied to Charlie's now. But my immortal blood wouldn't be fully changed." Priska rested her hand on Hope's knee. "It is the best it could be. The idea of losing Charlie . . . like I lost Eryx."

There was a myth associated with that name, the story of a king killed by Heracles over immortal cattle. Surely, she couldn't mean . . .

"I don't want to have to go through that again. So thank you." Priska leaned forward and kissed Hope on the cheek. "And now what?"

Hope let out a slow breath. "We are to go to Olympus. I need to confront Hera with her lie and, more importantly, Apollo about the curse."

Although she was less sure about the last part. She knew it needed to happen, but not exactly what to say. She knew it had something to do with that yellow *Book of the Fates* she'd brought back. And something to do with her father. She still couldn't believe that her mother and father were happy. Together. Every time she thought of how her father had abandoned them, her anger flared and she wanted to hit someone.

"Oh!" Priska jumped up and waddled down the hall. She returned carrying a familiar red leather tome. "This is yours."

Hope cradled her *Book of the Fates* to her chest. "How did you get it?"

They'd left it in the hotel when they went to Pike Place. It seemed like forever ago and more like a dream than reality as Priska sat back down in front of Hope.

Priska waved her hand at the question. "Charlie got it." Her face glowed. "He tracked us down and got all of our stuff. He's . . ."

"Amazing," Hope finished for Priska.

The older woman nodded, her eyes filled with unshed tears. "So you're going to Olympus. Do you have a guide?"

Charlie came into the living room with a plate of banana bread and two glasses of milk on a tray. "A little snack?"

Priska patted the ottoman as she gazed at her husband adoringly. As soon as the plate was in front of her, she reached for a slice.

Hope thought of Xan and Athan. Guides? She'd spent the better part of two days crying over Dahlia when Xan told of her binding to the goddess Hecate. While Dahlia wasn't dead, she was bound in the Underworld, and from what Xan said, she may as well be dead. Both Xan and Athan had been there. So, no they weren't guides. But, they would help, and they'd made it out of the Underworld. Something that was nearly impossible. "I have help."

"Then let's enjoy our time, okay?" Priska broke off a piece of the warm bread and popped it into her mouth.

"Yes," Hope said as she reached for the bread.

Priska curled up on the couch, the picture of marital and family contentment. "When do you leave?"

The bread caught in Hope's throat. She coughed, reaching for the glass of milk. While she drank, she gave herself a pep talk. This was it. And Priska deserved to know.

"Tomorrow."

ACKNOWLEDGEMENTS

The longer I write, the more I understand just how many people it takes to make a good story, and a good book.

First, I have to acknowledge my family: Jason, Jacob, Seth, and Anna. Words are inadequate for how much you mean to me. I love you. Thank you for putting up with me just finishing "one more thing" on the computer.

Nathan. I'm sure there are equal parts love and obligation in our working relationship. I'm still so glad you don't throw your arms up at me. I'm always in awe at your fabulous skills!

To my Beta-Babes: Kate Roberts, Brittianii Jayy, Janelle Dudley, and Sara Meadows. Thank you heaps for sleuthing out the flaws and making the story better, cleaner, and tighter.

Dawn Yacovetta, you caught over twenty-five errors! I'm going to call you my "Final find!" I *might* need to put you on the payroll!

And my mother, Anita . . . I love that you have the enthusiasm to read an ARC, tell me what I need to fix, and still remind me that it's my story to tell. You are equal parts cheerleader and mother, and all-around the best!

To my bestie pals: Alli, Cassy, Katie, Kathy, and Annie. You help me find joy and laughter in the mundane and difficult. Thank you for bringing your light into my life!

Sara Meadows: You are the yin to my author yang! Thank you for your time, energy, talents, persistence, and friendship! I feel so, so blessed to have you as my second!

To Kelly Hashway: You fix problems I can't even see, and the story flows so much better after your edits. Heaps and heaps of thanks!

And Krystal Wade: What does it say that I want your eyes to be the last set on my MS before it goes to formatting? You give the polish that makes me proud of the final piece.

Jo Michaels: I think you have formatting super-powers! I love that you can make my story pretty-looking and easy to read.

To my Renegades!! I never knew having a fan group could be so incredible and fun. Thanks for playing along with my shenanigans, for your encouragement and all your enthusiasm!

And my Mythic Muses!! Best. Launch team. Ever.

And a special thank you to Shannon Dean, Kaley Stephenson, Dana Gray, Tracy Thomas, John Cintron, and Michelle R. Smith from the Renegades for helping with characters and descriptions when I needed a *little* help!

And you . . . the reader of my words. I hope you find power in the stories you read, and pleasure as you read them. Thank you for spending your time with me.

INDEX OF CHARACTERS AND MYTHOLOGY FIGURES

Hope: the Sphinx

Leto: Hope's mother; also a Sphinx

Priska: Hope's "aunt," tasked with protecting Leto and Hope, demigod daughter of Artemis

Charlie Davenport: Priska's employer

Athan: demigod son of Hermes

Haley: Hope's friend from school

Mr. Stanley: a butcher who is kind to Hope; Haley's father

Xan: demigod son of Ares

Dahlia: daughter of Eris, Xan's cousin, friend of Hope

Ares: god of war, bloodshed, and violence; father of Xan

Aphrodite: goddess of love, beauty, desire, and pleasure

Athena: goddess of wisdom, courage, justice, skill, warfare, battle strategy, and handicrafts

Apollo: god of music, truth, and prophecy; twin brother to Artemis. Fell in love with Phoibe and cursed her daughter, Phaidra, when she refused his advances. Hunts Hope and Hope's mother, Leto.

Artemis: virgin goddess of the hunt, twin sister to Apollo. Mother to Priska.

Boreas: god of winter and the north wind

Demeter: goddess of grain, agriculture and the harvest, growth, and nourishment

Dionysus: god of wine, parties and festivals, madness, chaos, drunkenness, ecstasy, and drugs

Eris: goddess of strife and discord, mother of Dahlia

Eros: god of love and desire

Charon: the ferryman who carries souls across the rivers Styx and Acheron

The Fates: three incarnations of destiny, primordial deities who are even more powerful than the Olympians; Atropos (the cutter of life's thread), Lachesis (the measurer), and Clotho (the spinner) are destiny personified. Collectively known as Moirai.

The Furies: primordial goddesses of vengeance: Tisiphone (avenger or murder), Megaera (the jealous) and Alecto (constant anger). Daughters of Nyx, sisters to the Fates. Collectively known as the Erinyes.

The Graeae: three ancient sea spirits who personified the white foam of the sea; they shared one eye and one tooth among them. By name: Deino, Enyo, and Pemphredo.

Hades: ruler of the Underworld; god of the Earth's hidden wealth, both agricultural produce and precious metals; married to Persephone.

Hephaestus: god of fire, metalworking, and crafts; father to Mr. Stanley

Hera: queen of the heavens and goddess of marriage and fidelity, childbirth, heirs, kings, and empires.

Hermes: god of commerce, boundaries, travel, thievery, trickery, language, writing, diplomacy, athletics, and animal husbandry; father of Athan

Hestia: goddess of the home, hearth, and chastity; mother of Obelia

Hypnos: god of sleep

Leto: Titan goddess of Motherhood

Persephone: wife of Hades; queen of the Underworld; daughter of Zeus; goddess of spring growth.

Poseidon: god of the sea, rivers, floods, droughts, earthquakes, and the creator of horses.

Skia: immortal creatures from the Underworld

Thanatos: the personification of death, twin brother to Hypnos.

Zeus: king of the gods, ruler of Mount Olympus, and god of the sky, lightning, thunder, weather, law, order, and fate.

About Raye

Raye Wagner grew up in Seattle, the second of eight children, and learned to escape chaos through the pages of fiction. As a youth, she read the likes of David Eddings, Leon Uris, and Jane Austen. Inspired by a fictional character, Raye pursued a career in nursing, and still practices part-time. She enjoys baking, puzzles, Tae Kwon Do, and the sound of waves lapping at the sand. She lives with her husband and three children in Middle Tennessee.

Facebook:
https://www.facebook.com/Raye-Wagner-173068689524889
Twitter: @RayeWagner
Instagram: rayewagnerauthor
Website: RayeWagner.com

Made in the USA
Middletown, DE
01 May 2017